A
Mutual
Destiny

Anna Renne

A Mutual Destiny

ISBN: 979-8-218-77819-4

Edited by Salvatore Pecorella

Cover designed by Erika Plum

DEDICATION

For anyone who had to go through relationship hell before they found true, everlasting love.

For Dianna and Nala, women's best friends.

For Anthony, may our love story live on forever.

1 Corinthians 1 3:4-8
Philippians 4:6-7

A Mutual Destiny

TRIGGER WARNING

Events in this book are loosely based on my real life. I have tried to take extreme caution with how the topics are dealt with in the story while also conveying the emotions and thought processes that come with them. Those topics include:

- Domestic Violence

- Alcohol and substance abuse, including Ambien and steroids

- Mention of suicide

- Mention of cancer

- Therapy, including PTSD

- Fade to black sexual scenes

If you or someone you know is struggling with mental health or thoughts of suicide, please call or visit the 988 suicide hotline.

If you or someone you know is experiencing domestic violence, please call 800.799.SAFE (7233).

A Mutual Destiny

PLAYLIST

Chapter 1- Gunpowder and Lead by Miranda Lambert
Chapter 2- The Climb by Miley Cyrus
Chapter 3- Courtesy of the Red, White, and Blue by Toby Keith
Chapter 4- Start of Something New by High School Musical
Chapter 5- Flowers by Miley Cyrus
Chapter 6- Remember This by Jonas Brothers
Chapter 7- Lovebug by Jonas Brothers
Chapter 8- Waffle House by Jonas Brothers
Chapter 9- Post Malone (Feat. RANI) by Sam Feldt, RANI
Chapter 10- Location by Khalid
Chapter 11- Thank You, Next by Ariana Grande
Chapter 12- Dibs by Kelsey Ballerini
Chapter 13- Trumpets by Jason Derulo
Chapter 14- What a Man Gotta Do by Jonas Brothers
Chapter 15- This Is It by Scotty McCreery
Chapter 16- My Little Girl by Tim McGraw
Chapter 17- This Is Me by The Greatest Showman
Chapter 18- Rollercoaster by Jonas Brothers
Chapter 19- When You Look Me in the Eyes by Jonas Brothers
Chapter 20- Half of My Hometown by Kelsey Ballerini
Chapter 21- Someone's Watching Over Me by Hilary Duff
Chapter 22- Friends in Low Places by Garth Brooks
Chapter 23- Hesitate by Jonas Brothers
Chapter 24- Take My Name by Parmalee
Chapter 25- Flashlight by Hailee Steinfeld
Chapter 26- Big, Big Plans by Chris Lane
Chapter 27- Best Day of My Life by American Authors
Chapter 28- Simple Man by Lynard Skynyrd
Chapter 29- Invincible by David Archuleta
Chapter 30- A Thousand Years by Christina Perri
Chapter 31- You Make Me Feel So Young by Frank Sinatra
Epilogue- Carolina to Me by Scotty McCreery

CHAPTER 1

ARIA

JANUARY

"Aria! Where are my keys?" Adonis growls. "Aria Jade!"

A 2,100 newly purchased square foot home, and I can hear him projecting as if he is right next to me.

I am sitting in the far back corner of my office, willing my body to melt into the lavender-painted walls. Part of me wants to laugh at the irony. I painted the walls of this room lavender because it is supposed to help one be peaceful. This situation is anything but quiet. Since childhood, I've always been keen to find something humorous in the most chaotic situations. It's part of what kept me in trouble. Smirking when being lectured by your parents is not necessarily respectful.

My already inherited tachycardic heart is bursting at the seams. My back is stiff against the white bookshelf-lined side of the room. What I would do to escape into one of my childhood fantasies now.

My breath catches in my chest as Adonis's six-foot body fills the white frame of my sanctuary. Venom fills my thoughts as I think of him being in the one place of escape I have in this home. A wave of alcohol stench hits me in waves as he edges closer.

"Where are my keys, Aria?" His face is mere inches from mine, staring daggers into me.

I glance blankly down at my toes, digging into the cream-colored carpet, trying to look anywhere but his eyes. I have learned that looking him in the eye only sets him off more.

"Give them to me. *Right. Now.*" His teeth are clenching together, making his jawline more defined.

His fists are clamped at his sides. The veins in his arms bulge underneath his arms, and he has full-sleeved tattoos. His signature black muscle tee and ripped blue jeans emphasize that he is full of steroids, ready to take on the world. The olive color of his skin is sticky with sweat.

"I'm not giving you the keys." I grit out through my chattering teeth. My breath is struggling to keep up with my ever-increasing heartbeat. "You're drunk. I also think you took way more of your VA-prescribed sleeping medication than you should've."

I think back to the empty container I found on the counter when I came home. He just got a new bottle three days ago. There were thirty pills in it at the time.

I brace myself for whatever the outcome is of my stubbornness. I try to keep my eyes from glancing at the small black trash can beside my desk, where I hid the keys. I don't even pray.

Truth is, I couldn't care less if he goes and hurts himself at this point. But I refuse to let his reckless actions injure or kill someone else who is undeserving on the road. If I get taken out in the process, so be it. At this point, I feel like all my life's decisions have brought me to this pivotal moment.

It's my fault I am here. Right?

Rage fills his blue-green eyes. He grabs me by my ankles, pulling me across the carpet. My green UNC Charlotte alumni T-shirt slides up my stomach, making the carpet burn as I slide away from the safety of the corner. I am barely away from the wall when he lifts me into the air like I weigh no more than a sack of flour. My mind flashes to the shotgun he keeps loaded in the corner of our master bedroom on the other side of the wall. He lifts me over his shoulder. With one gym-styled man grunt, he slams me on my back, knocking the breath from my lungs.

CHAPTER 2

ARIA

FEBRUARY

I awaken with a sudden jolt upright. My heart is racing, my breathing is erratic, and my light brown hair surrounds my face, making me feel claustrophobic.

I would love to tell myself this was a nightmare, but it is much more. It's a nightmare of a memory. A memory from only a month prior.

As I attempt to brush the matted hair out of my face, I try to rid my mind of my ex-fiancé's mental image from that night. I don't know where he is now and do *not* intend to find out.

What I do intend to do today is find a dog and a good therapist. Even with as bad as things turned out with my ex, I still felt safer moving out on my own for the first time with a huge Army vet sleeping in the house at night. That is, until I realized how dangerous the inside of my home was, too.

The house is silent as I walk from the rock-hard California king bed to my office. Adonis had insisted on a firm mattress due to injuries he supposedly acquired while in service. I came to find out that those injuries were lies, too, just like everything else that ever came out of his mouth.

Come on, Aria, focus. I think to myself as I turn on my district-provided laptop. One perk of being an elementary school teacher is a free laptop.

I quickly searched for the Charlotte-Mecklenburg Police Animal Control. I pore through pages and pages of dogs looking for loving homes. I try not to cry as I think about all the dogs that need families. Everything seems to make me cry these days.

I see a dog, and the world stops for a second. On the screen is a black and white pit bull mix. Her name is Dianna. She is a year and a half old.

Like the little queen I'll be sure to treat her as.

I peek at the price. My mouth hangs open. She is only ten dollars. The payment covers her city license. It says she is considered VIP. I have no clue what that means, so I will have to ask about that.

I waste no time as I jog back to my walk-in closet. It is cold in Charlotte, North Carolina, on this Saturday morning. February weather can be both spring and winter in one day. I grab a pair of jeans and a blue plaid button-down. I apply my usual, barely there, amount of makeup. I straighten my hair and look at myself in the bathroom mirror. My family has always said never leave the house looking unpresentable. Who knows who you will run into?

***

"Are you sure you don't want to look at any other dogs? A volunteer asks as we walk past cages of dogs, all looking for their second chance.

"I'm certain."

It is hard to walk past so many found or surrendered dogs and not want to break them out. I know what I want, though. I've always been that way. The fact is that pit bulls get a bad rap. Especially, black pit bulls. I'm determined to be her second chance.

The volunteer is tall. Couldn't be more than seventeen years old. She leads me out to a small fenced-in yard.

"I'm going to go get her. Here are some treats for her when she comes out." She slides three bacon treats into my hand. "Little secret, I'm glad you want to see her. She's a favorite around here with the staff." Her black curls bounce as she heads back inside.

I can see her grab a purple lead through the door window. She walks around the corner and disappears.

There she is! Purple. How fitting? The color of royalty.

As the volunteer comes back, I can spot Dianna. Her excitement is palpable. Dianna's tail is wagging so hard her whole body shakes. It looks like her tail might pop clean off.

As the girl opens the door, Dianna comes barreling at full speed. I brace myself with my best football-style stance. All the time playing catch with dad or games of touch football with my older brother and his friends will pay off. I grew up wearing a jersey complete with a pearl necklace. I was a tomboy but knew how to make the sport look good.

Dianna reaches me, jumping up while wrapping her arms around my waist. She rests her head on the curve of my hips. It's the best hug I've ever received.

"I think she likes you." The volunteer laughs, letting go of Dianna's leash.

"I'd say so." I reposition my body to continue holding up Dianna's weight.

"She does have a case of kennel cough and a skin condition called demodex. That is why her skin and hair look patchy. When she is sick or stressed, her skin condition flares. She's on antibiotics for the illness for a few more days."

"Is that why she's VIP?" I look into her big brown eyes, slipping her the treats.

"Yes. Unfortunately, people can't look past that, and that she's part pit. The VIP status is because she has been here for over a year."

"I'll take her." Dianna hops down to lie at my feet. She chews on a small toy bone left outside.

"Awesome. If you want, we do spay dogs for free. The only thing is you wouldn't be able to pick her up today. It would probably be Monday before you could pick her up."

"That's ok. It gives me time to go get everything she needs. "Let's plan on that!"

***

"That's all the paperwork we need. Looks like you can pick her up on Monday!" The volunteer, whom I now know as Claire, staples my papers together.

"Well, Dianna, looks like you're my Valentine this year." Dianna nudges my hand.

I scratch behind her ears before Claire leads her back to her cage. One last weekend for her without a loving owner. Time to enter my "I don't need a man" era.

CHAPTER 3

ANTONIO

"Corporal Ranaldi," I hear a private yell. "You have a call coming in."

"Thank you, private," I put down the hose I held to wash the fleet vehicles. I jog over while wiping my hands on my cammies. Knowing exactly who it was, I answered with a smile. "Hey, Mom."

"How did you know?"
"Lucky guess." She always seems to call around this time to check in.

"How's the motor T world treating you?"
"Oh, you know what they say, living the dream." You can practically hear my eye roll.

Three years in, there were multiple pre-deployment trainings in the brutal Twenty-Nine Palms, and still no actual time overseas.

"Well, I won't keep you. I just wanted to see if you've given any more thought to my idea."

I took a deep breath, wiping the sweat off my shaved head. Choosing a bald haircut is the easiest haircut to have. Keeps me nice and cool in the heat, and I don't have to worry about keeping it cut short for inspections. This is the second time my mom, Tiffany, has called to ask me about her "idea." She wants me to leave my base in Beaufort, South Carolina, for a weekend. She wants me to visit my childhood friend Chris in North Carolina. She thinks his elementary teacher wife, Scarlett, can help me overcome my cheating ex by introducing me to a fellow teacher friend.

"Tif, you do remember my last relationship ended when I found out she cheated, right? Let's not forget her nice surprise for me, too." I roll my eyes thinking about the additional "surprise" my ex sprung on me because of her cheating. My mom never cared if I called her by her first name. Most of the time, she laughed about it.

"I never liked her anyway."

"Ok. You know what. I will call Chris today. I give in. A change of scenery will be good. This doesn't mean I will jump back into the dating pool again. Out of the question."

"Yeah, yeah, yeah. Sir, yes, sir."

"Finally, some respect around here," I smirk into the phone. "Love you."

"Love you too, Ant."

I have always loved the relationship I have with my parents. My dad was older when they had me, so I've always admired his life experiences. My mom has always been my rock. She knows when to butt in and when to bow out. At the end of the day, she is always a presence in my life.

Maybe I really should take a quick trip. Just get away for a few days.

I waste no more time debating it. If I do, I'll change my mind. I called Chris and waited for him to answer.

"Hey, Chris. What do you guys have going on the next few weekends? Care for a visit from your favorite Marine?"

"Aw, honey." Chris coos.

That's us. Ever the sarcastic friendship.

"I thought you'd never ask."

CHAPTER 4

ANTONIO

MARCH

"Tell your dog I said thanks for the warm greeting last night." I joke as Chris lazily walks into the kitchen from his master bedroom for coffee. "I mean for real, man. Is she even a dog?" I sit at the kitchen island, pumping up the height on the barstool.

As if on cue, Harley, a black lab built like my Ram truck, comes barreling in from their room looking for food.

Last night I got in past midnight. Scarlett and Chris left a key for me under their front door mat. They were fast asleep when I entered. I thought my life flashed before my eyes. Harley stood in the entryway growling. Being a black dog in a dark house, all I could see was the whites of her eyes and teeth glistening with drool. I made myself as small as possible, calling her name, sinking to the floor. She slowly edged her way toward me, sniffing rigorously. I put my hand out in submission so she could smell my scent. As if someone hit a light switch, she instantly jumped on me, knocking me over with licks. Eighty pounds of pure muscle. Not the puppy I was used to seeing on my last visit.

"Good morning to you, too. Oorah Marine." Chris weakly bumps the air as he reaches for his coffee pot, filling it with water.

"For the love of all that is holy, never say that again."

"Whatever you say, dear."

"So, what's the plan for today?"

"Well, it's Saint Patrick's Day weekend, my friend. There is only one logical way to honor the homeland." Chris stroked his auburn beard with a horrific Irish accent.

"Not doing much to honor it with that lame attempt at an accent."

Chris fills Harley's bowl, but it's gone just as quickly.

What is going on with this mutant dog?

"Don't be jealous. What do your people have? Pasta?" Chris smirks, holding his hands up in surrender.

"Don't mess with the Italians, Chris. They have the mafia." Scarlett states matter-of-factly, rushing out of the master bedroom, pulling me into a hug.

Chris rolls his eyes, grabs the coffee pot, and pours himself the largest cup I have ever seen.

"Still out of the loop here, guys. Where are we going?" I ask, simultaneously pulling a piece of Scarlett's hair out of my mouth.

Scarlett's hair is something of a myth and a fairy tale. She is a real-life version of a tall, powerful, ginger-positive Rapunzel.

"Green River Revival. It takes place at the White-Water Center, which is in Charlotte. Every year, they dye the water green. People get to kayak, paddle board, or raft down its various streams." Scarlett kisses Chris on the cheek, then pours herself an equally ridiculous amount of coffee.

"The real reason to go is to watch the people who fall of course." Chris sits on the barstool beside me, rubbing his freshly shaven head.

That's the thing about "friends that are more like family." When he heard I had to shave my head upon joining the Marine Corps, Chris wasted no time shaving his own. My hair used to be a shaggy, reddish-blonde mess. Knowing how much I loved my hair, he joined me in baldness. Thankfully, his wife was in full support of the idea. His auburn hair was already short anyway.

"I'm going to call Aria. She *needs* to get out of the house." Scarlett pulls out her cellphone, excusing herself from the room.

"Who?" I grab a bowl of milk and cereal.

"A teacher friend of Scarlett's. You think you've had it rough, my friend. You have *no* idea." Chris takes a long sip of his coffee, shaking his head.

"What do you mean?" I mumble with a mouth full of cereal.

Is that my mom laughing I hear?

I can picture her now with a face-splitting grin, laughing at the fact that I came like she said, and might be introduced to a teacher friend of Scarlett's.

"She was with this Army guy for like a year. They bought a house and were engaged. Moved in. The following month, all hell broke loose. Next thing you know, it's her alone in that house." Chris pours himself a bowl of cereal and sits back down.

My curiosity runs wild as I imagine what could be worse than being cheated on. What could have possibly gone down in one night that's not finding out you have been cheated on?

She probably thinks all military guys are class A jerks now, so much for a pleasant introduction.

"Oh, she did rescue a dog, though, so I guess she isn't completely alone."

"Ok, she's coming. It took some *serious* convincing. Dianna has been quite the handful, but she wants to bring her to help her get socialized. Hope you don't mind, Ant, but I said I have a friend who can help. It was the only way I could convince her to leave the house." Scarlett is giddy, gliding back into the room with Harley trotting by her side. She anxiously bites her bottom lip, waiting for my reaction.

"Great. Protect and serve never ends, I guess." Sarcasm drips from every word.

I came for a good time to get my mind off Danielle, my ex. Now, I'm going to babysit a dog for a woman who will probably knee me in the groin once she learns I am a Marine.

"Guess I'm going to get ready." I reach down for my rucksack that I failed to bring into the guest room last night when I was fighting for my life.

"Don't forget to wear green!" Chris shouts down the hallway as I walk away.

CHAPTER 5

ARIA

The past month has turned into a vicious cycle of teaching my second graders, cleaning the house, walking the dog, hanging with my family on the weekends, and church on Sundays. Come Monday, just lather, rinse, repeat. Getting dressed to be out in public, not formal work clothes or athletic wear, is an abstract thought.

I did end up finding a good therapist for myself, Dr. Shots. We have determined that I have PTSD, post-traumatic stress disorder, from my experiences with my ex. When he first said it, I was scared. You always hear about the most severe cases, where they are usually former military members who go insane and do something crazy. I have quickly learned that it is not always the case. I have turned to overthinking as a response to trying to keep myself out of harm's way. I tend to over-plan so I can control outcomes and predictability to avoid anxiety or stressors. It is a means to protect myself. I am sure you can probably find a cheesy photo of me giving a thumbs up in a crewneck sweater that reads: undiagnosed, untreated, still vertical. His suggestion is to start trying to live in the moment more.

Great.

Fast forward to this moment. I am staring back and forth at Dianna on her pink, fluffy dog bed and my walk-in closet, trying to mentally organize an outfit. I settle on a camo green crop top with dark-washed jeggings. I curl my hair and grab a pair of brown ankle boots.

Nerves begin to build while I slip on Dianna's purple harness and leash. It's not that I can't leave the house, but part of me is always afraid I'll run into my ex again. Charlotte may be a large city, but it sometimes feels like the world's smallest town. Everyone always seems to know the people you know through someone else. You always run into those whom you wanted to forget. It never fails. Here I am, already mentally preparing for the worst-case scenario, like I bump into Adonis, he grabs me, and throws me into the cold, concrete-lined rapids, splitting my head in two.

Dianna nudges my hand, sensing my unease.
"You are right. We can't think like that. Let's go, girl."

We quickly go outside and get into my blue Chevy Cruise. Positive thinking requires upbeat music. Miley Cyrus's *Flowers* is it.

***

"Dianna, girl. Chill out."

Dianna is plowing down the gravel hill, pulling me behind her like she is the real owner in this relationship. I glance up long enough to see Chris and Scarlett's towering six-foot frames waving at me in the distance. I wave back, trying to coax Dianna in their general direction.

The White-Water Center has always been one of my favorite places. It is miles of bike trails, walking paths, rafting, paddleboarding, kayaking, and rope courses. I may live in the city, but my heart belongs to the outdoors. Thrashing waves sparkle in the light of the high-sitting sun. The grassy areas are filled to the brim with people and dogs. Bluegrass music floats in the air, mingled with laughter and the slapping of rafting paddles against the concrete side of the channels.

Growing up, I was always outside with the guys in the neighborhood or my older brother's friends. We played flag football, basketball, street hockey, and baseball. You name it, and we did it. We lived by the 'home when the streetlights come on' rule.

My co-workers on my team always make fun of me because being outdoorsy and sports-loving is not precisely the stereotype that guys in this city crave. Guys around here want to wine and dine you. Nothing wrong with that, but ask them to do something outdoors, and you would think you slapped them in the face. They want women who practically model on the side and know less about sports than they do. The farthest outdoors they typically go around here is an outdoor brewery with cornhole.

"Here, let me give you a hand." Chris interrupts my constant line of thoughts when he comes jogging over with an extended hand for Dianna's leash.

"Thank you. For a forty-pound dog, she pulls like an entire sled of huskies."

"I can see that." Chris laughs, walking back towards Scarlett. He holds her leash tight against his green Irish shirt.

We walk down the sidewalk that skirts the side of the rapids. The first course you walk into is the one Olympians come to train on from all over the country. It has a huge drop where so many rafts flip over. Green River Revival is always one of their busiest times of the year, so we are shoulder to shoulder with a crowd trying to find places to watch the festivities. Dianna is sniffing everyone and everything the whole way. Bluegrass music blares from a stage in a large grassy yard.

As we slowly approach Scarlett, I see she isn't alone. She sits on a black camp chair with a large picnic blanket. Next to her stands a man with his back facing us. I look him over head to toe, trying to place who he may be. It's clearly the friend she mentioned. He is wearing a black beanie, hoodie, blue jeans, and standard-issued combat boots. He is of average height, and he has a runner's body quality to him.

We are a few feet away when Scarlett stands up, waving enthusiastically. The man turns around, and I am floored. A brilliant set of bright blue eyes locks onto me. He smiles, and small dimples appear from the corners of his mouth. That's when I realize his beanie says Marines.

Scarlett rushes over, pulling me into the world's tightest hug. Her hair is pulled into a messy bun on the top of her head. She is wearing a hunter green A-line dress with tan sandals.

"You made it!" Scarlett gushes. "This is Chris's childhood best friend, Antonio."

"Hey, Aria, right?" Antonio extends a beautifully olive-tanned hand in my direction.

Aria? Is that my name? Why am I outside and unable to tell if there is any oxygen? A hand. What do I do? Pull it together, Aria.

"That's me." My mind starts to work correctly again.

I slowly reach out and shake his hand. Our eyes lock, but the jolt of warmth that runs through me at the interaction has my heart thumping in my chest.

I definitely shake his hand longer than I should. Let go, Aria. LET GO!

"This must be Princess Dianna." Antonio bends down, holding his hand out for her to sniff.

There is a slight hesitation in his reaching down. Dianna wastes no time showing her approval. She jumps up, locking his hips into the hug she gave me when we first met.

Dang traitor.

"Queen is more like it." I huff, tying her to the extra pink camping chair they brought me.

We have the best spot for today. We are in a small grassy area right by the significant drop. It is a gorgeous Carolina blue sky day. The sun is pouring out warmth and bouncing off the waves crashing over the concrete eddies.

"Now that you are here, we will go grab a round. You ladies want anything?" Chris asks.

Antonio looks at me. His gaze slides up and down my frame, taking me in. Every time his eyes reach a new point, I feel a pull. Like any part he sees, it wants to touch him in return. When his eyes meet mine, I quickly look at the water, pinching my lips together to keep from grinning like a little schoolgirl.

"I will take a chardon-yay kind sir." I spout out with my best English accent towards Chris.

"Say what now?" Antonio laughs.

"Don't ask," Chris says while I hold out my credit card for him to take.

"Do... Don't worry about it. I got it." Antonio stammers, grabbing my card and handing it back.

Scarlett and Chris look at each other with a knowing smirk. I can't even say anything back. My words are caught in my throat.

Why would someone who doesn't even know me offer to pay for my drinks?

As they walk away towards the pavilion, I feel my face heat. I shift awkwardly in my seat, feeling Scarlett's eyes boring into my face. Antonio looks back over his shoulder and smiles at me.

Can he stop with the dimples? It's illegal. It has to be. Citizen's arrest? I'll put handcuffs on that any day. Wait, what am I thinking?

"So, what do you think?" Scarlett bounces on her chair like it is ice cream day at school.

"About?"

"Oh, come on. Antonio."

"I mean, he is gorgeous. However, I am beyond comfortable in my 'you come near me, and I will taser you' era."

I think. Maybe. Who knows.

"Aw, come on. You were over Adonis' *way* before that night happened. It's been plenty of time in the grand scheme of things."

She isn't wrong. I was over our relationship *months* before it ended. Yet, this is a misconception. I was over wanting to be with him, but the physical altercations between us left a lasting impression that will never fully escape me. After we got engaged about a year in, the abuse started. Verbal, physical, and psychological. I spent the next six months trying to escape while realizing I could end up being one of the cases where the partner doesn't make it out alive. When I bought my house and refused to add Adonis to the title, it did nothing but pour fuel on the flames. I went from living at home post-college to buying what I felt like was my own prison. I am truly alone for the first time in my life.

"You aren't wrong. I guess I'm just hesitant to trust anyone right now. I hate dating. People fake so much of themselves at the beginning. Dating takes too long. I believe you know early on if it is forever or not."

Scarlett looks at me sympathetically.

"So, he is a Marine?" I ask, thinking back to his beanie.

"Yes, but don't let it discourage you. He is coming up on the decision to re-enlist. He may not be after this next year."

"You do remember who my father is, right?" I look over at her, knowing he is impossible to forget.

My dad is a towering six-foot, New York Italian born in Brooklyn. Think, an older replica of Sylvester Stallone with jet black hair and richly tanned skin. Practically all muscles. He was the wing chief commander of the NC Air National Guard Base. He did special forces in the Air Force before I was born. He was a para-weatherman. He parachuted behind enemy lines to relay weather conditions to the front lines. With thirty-plus years of service and me attending many of his events, I can't say all service members are the same based on one bad experience.

"Who can forget him?" Scarlett laughs.

"Forget who?" Antonio asks, handing me a clear cup of my wine.

Our fingers glide over each other's, and electric energy surges through me, causing a shiver.

"My dad. He was in the Air National Guard. He was the wing chief commander." I take a sip of my wine and wait for his response.

"Ah. Amazing accomplishment, but let's be for real. It's still the chair force of America. You know, for their specialty in 'hurry up and sit.'" Antonio's lips quirk up, taking a quick sip of his beer.

"Oh, the crayon eater has jokes. How original." I say without thinking.

Chris snorts. He attempts to cover his nose and mouth, but beer shoots out. Scarlett looks on in disgust.

"My nose. It burns." Chris shrieks in agony.

"I'll let that one off with a warning." Antonio winks in my direction.

Did I just black out? I feel like I just blacked out and came back. His winks are even lethal.

Never has a wink been so knee-weakening in my entire life. I feel like I am a pool of mush on the ground.

"He served for over thirty years. I went with him to teach diversity of temperament classes at the joint forces base. I've been to military balls and spent holidays with him deployed immediately after 9/11. I earned my jokes." I beam with pride.

"I guess you have. You have my respect." Antonio reaches over and cheers me.

"Guys, it's starting!" Scarlett squeals, leaning forward in her chair until she might topple into the current.

We all look up to see bright green water slowly creep down the big drop. Kayakers paddle, spraying green mist with every stroke in a mad frenzy. The White Water Center's Green River Revival has officially begun.

"First raft! Here we go! Whose got bets? Think they will flip over the drop?" Chris wiggles his eyebrows at us.

"Oh, I will take that bet all day. What's the stakes?" Antonio asks with his arm casually draped over the back of his chair.

"I say they'll stay in. The guides are highly trained. Loser buys next round?" I coyly suggest.

"You are on!" Chris says.

Antonio agrees with him.

Scarlett joins me on my side of the bet.

The raft rounds the curve prepared for the drop. The guide calls for all sides to row as fast as they can. Ores clip the side of the concrete walls as they dip into the crashing waves. Usually, as they approach the drop, the rafters are all told to get down between the inflated bench seats with their ores facing the sky. This raft guide loves all the green water hype because he just shouts for them to "dig, dig, dig." The raft pivots, coming down the drop at an angle. The raft flies over the drop, landing with tremendous power. The whole raft flips as if in slow motion, sending everyone sprawling. Arms and legs are thrashing in the waves. Guides on the upper ledges rush over with long yellow ropes, yelling, "swimmer." They throw the ropes as the ejected passengers grab on, pulling themselves up the concrete-sloped embankment.

Chris and Antonio turn towards me, grinning from ear to ear.

"Oh, bartenders! Another round, if you'll please." Chris clasps both hands behind his head, leaning back in the chair.

"Yeah, yeah. What will it be, boys?" Scarlett rolls her eyes and stands up.

As I pull back out my credit card, a hand lands on mine. I look up and brilliant blue stares back at me. Antonio is leaning in my direction, our noses inches from each other. The wind blows. A strong mahogany and teakwood scent wafts past me.

"What kind of gentleman would I be if I let you buy my drink?"

Gentleman? Do those still exist?

"What a pushover." Chris scoffs, crossing his arms.

Antonio stands up and elbows Chris on the shoulder. Chris rolls his eyes but stands up anyway. Once Chris is up, Antonio puts a hand on Chris's shoulder, and the two walk away singing *We Are the Champions* horribly off-key and as loud as possible. People look at them, smiling and pointing.

Who is this guy?

CHAPTER 6

ANTONIO

"Ok, dude, clue me in. You're telling me someone mistreated that gorgeous, funny woman and didn't return groveling for a second chance."

I glance back to ensure we are out of earshot of Aria and Scarlett. I literally stumbled over my words at some point while talking to her. Twenty-three years of living, and it's never happened. I do *not* get nervous talking to girls. It isn't that I am some ladies' man or something. I have just always been comfortable being able to make small talk. I've had the best girl friends, and I was able to turn them into long-term girlfriends. Girls and nerves are not a thing for me, but here I am with sweaty palms and losing my breath every time our eyes lock.

"I don't know, man. I never liked him. He was full of himself and had some serious…issues. Scarlett hated him from the moment we met." Chris shakes his head at the memory.

Scarlett not liking someone is a big deal. She likes and gets along with just about anyone. She deals with me and Chris constantly, acting like we are the real ones in a serious relationship. I smile at my internal joke, but stop when Chris sees me like I've lost my mind.

"She doesn't strike me as someone who would go for that."

Her head is thrown back, laughing, when I look back at her again. Dianna lies at her feet with her head on a swivel, watching everyone who passes.

What I would do to be the one making her smile like that. That smile needs to be studied. It is infectious.

"Guess that is for you to find out." Chris gives me a wink.

We order our victory drinks and start heading back. My mind is spinning with all this new information. Suddenly, I realize I haven't thought about Danielle once today. Instead, my body is pulsing with an overwhelming sense of protectiveness and curiosity over Aria. I want her to tell me about her life, letting me in.

In more ways than one.

I can't seem to look away from her. Her crop top stops right under her rib cage. Just a small bit of warm ivory skin emphasizes her flat abdomen. Her tight leggings hug every part of her the right way. Her hips curve out, begging me to grab them and pull them flush against me. When she stands up to stretch, my eyes leap to her backside. I always heard the phrase, "the eyes are the nipples of the face." Hers are piercing. A starburst of greenish-blue blends into a sea of ocean blue. I've never seen anything like it. I could look into them all day if she would let me. Her lips look so soft that I suddenly want to touch them.

"What do you ladies say about us finishing our winnings, then heading back to our place for food and games?" Chris offers.

I didn't even realize we had already made it back.

I need to snap out of it.

"Only if you prefer losing," Scarlett says, bumping into Aria's shoulder.

"I may be mistaken, but we already won one bet today." I give Dianna a pat on the head. I run my eyes up and down her body. I notice how she stiffens and shifts in her chair.

I make her nervous. Good.

I don't know what everyone is talking about. This dog is exactly what I would want. She is protective of Aria and has just relaxed on the blanket the whole time we have been here.

"You haven't played games until you've played against us." Aria grins at Scarlett, who winks back.

Aria flips her long, shimmering hair over her shoulder. A wave of honey and lavender passes by me.

Great. She even smells good.

Need to be closer rushes through me. Good call on Chris's behalf, making this day go a bit longer by offering her to return to the house.

We spend the rest of the time laughing about the rafters. Aria has rafted out here with her dad every summer since it opened. It is a family affair for her. Her older brother, whom I now know as Giovanni, Gio for short, is a runner. He runs all the 5ks out here. Her mom, Tula, loves to watch and take photos of everyone.

Before long, it is time to head back to the cars. I offer to walk Dianna for her. She looks hesitant. She is trying to figure out if she wants to give up even a small piece of her independence. However, as soon as Dianna starts buckling the system, she huffs, handing over the leash.

I spend the walk back trying to show her maneuvers I've seen the dog handlers do on base. I have a vast desire to make her life easier and more comfortable. She listens intently, giving me small smiles. Whenever she looks me in the eye, I feel like my knees will buckle, and I have to grip the leash tighter, so I don't drop it to grab her. We part ways at the car. Hers is parked next to Chris's red Ram truck. She pulls out with the windows down, blasting Jonas Brothers *Remember This* at full volume.

Interesting. This is a day to remember for sure.

"I knew it. I knew you would like her. Am I a matchmaker or what? I am basically the female Will Smith version of Hitch." Scarlett is giddy getting into the front passenger seat.

"Ok, Scarlett, calm down. We just met." I say clipping into the back seat.

"Oh, Antonio. We have known you for over a decade. You couldn't stop staring at her."

I tell them about my mom's suggestion before coming up to see them.

"See, it's meant to be." Scarlett squeals while Chris starts driving home.

"Scarlett, honey, let the man be." Chris laughs.

"Fine. But I will see what she thinks about him at some point."

We ride the rest of the way back singing songs off-key and ordering food. My fingers anxiously tap against my legs. We just left Aria, and I want to return to her presence.

***

"She's here!" Scarlett calls out, walking Harley back in from a quick walk.

"Heck yeah, I am. What is the game plan? Literally." Aria plops down on the tan sofa beside me.

My heart stutters and then picks up one thousand percent.

Her effect on people is insane. Submit her to clinical trials. Her presence can probably cure rare forms of cancer or something.

"Oh, come on. You know what we're going to play." Chris

enters the living room carrying a box of cheese pizza and napkins.

"Oh my gosh, yes. I am starving!" Aria quickly grabs a slice of pizza.

A city woman who isn't afraid of a few carbs. Add that to the growing list of attractive qualities.

"Someone explain this game." I quizzically look at the box Scarlett puts on the coffee table before us.

I eye the mouthpieces.

What are we playing, dentist? I'll play some kind of doctor-patient game with Aria. Wait, stop. Be the gentleman she needs right now.

"You wear these mouthpieces. You pull a card and read as many as possible before the sand timer runs out. Your teammate tries to repeat it back correctly. The team with the most read back correctly wins." Aria explains.

"Sounds…interesting. Can we eat first? I'm about to kill this pizza." I take a bite.

"Of course, you are, Marine. Are those MRE meal kits just not cutting it anymore?" Chris mocks.

"Nothing like meals with you, sugar." I joke back as Scarlett rolls her eyes, grabbing her own slice. I try to shake the mental image of the pre-packaged "food" they give us at pre-deployment training.

"How long have you been in?" Aria asks.

"Three years. I'm on a four-year contract. My current plan is not to re-enlist."

"Really? What's your plan then?"

Chris and Scarlett excuse themselves to the kitchen to grab drinks and dessert.

"I want to hike the Appalachian Trail back to New York."

I have never seen a person deflate like that before. I pierced the balloon at any hint of seeing her again.

"Where in New York are you from?"

"Cleveland. It's north of Syracuse. My parents live on Oneida Lake."

"Wow. I bet it is gorgeous."

"It is. What about you? How long have you been teaching?"

"This is year three for me. I should get my full license after this year. I'm teaching second grade."

"Congrats on three years. I don't know how you and Scarlett do it. Or anyone, for that matter. I've heard Scarlett's stories. What made you want to teach?"

Aria pauses like she did when debating on handing over

Dianna's leash. It's almost like she is assessing if I am worthy of the answer. When she looks at me, her decision weighs in her facial expression. It morphs into a soft smile that warms me from the inside out.

"Well, my reason is vastly different than most people I know. I had great teachers, don't get me wrong, but I decided to be one after a truly horrific experience. I had a third-grade teacher who picked on me relentlessly. You always hear about kids being bullies, but adults can be too. She would tell me I was wrong with my answers even if I was right. Compared me to my older brother, Gio. Put the other students up against me constantly. One day, I decided I didn't want that to ever happen again to another student. I wanted my classroom to be where every student felt treated fairly, safe, respected, and valued for their uniqueness." Aria shifts on the seat and takes more bites of her pizza.

My whole being is overcome with emotion. Thoughts slam one behind the other in my mind.

Who is this resilient woman?

Red-hot rage fills every inch of protective instinct. Here is yet another person in Aria's life who mistreated her. Then, pride. Her willingness to be different and make a better place for others is unmatched. I involuntarily edge closer to her on the couch. I lean back and place my arm around her seat on the sofa. Her body stiffens at the motion, but she doesn't move away. I quickly put my arm back down, not wanting to make her uncomfortable.

"Ok, enough chit-chat, you two. It's time for war. Girls versus boys. Losers clean up dinner." Scarlett and Chris come back into the room with a plate of brownies. They hand each of us a bottle of water.

"Ladies first." Chris places the stack of cards and the timer in the middle of the table.

Aria puts in the mouthpiece while Scarlett grabs the timer. We all laugh as Aria tries to smile with the mouthpiece in.

Not even a mouthpiece can make this woman unattractive.

"We have one minute. Ready? Go?" Scarlett flips the timer over.

"Quacking. Ducks. Fly. Madly." Aria clips out, holding her hand under her chin to avoid drooling with the ridiculous mouthpiece.

"Quacking ducks fly madly!" Scarlett shouts immediately, shoving another card Aria's way.

What in the world? How did she understand any of that?

Chris looks at me, shrugging his shoulders. He takes a sip of his water.

Aria goes through ten more cards. Every time, Scarlett repeats it right back without missing a beat.

"What just happened?" I ask, stunned at what I just witnessed.

"Every time, man. It is some type of teacher-to-teacher telepathy." Chris looks at his wife with proud admiration.

"This is rigged."

"You could give up and be the good little housewives we know you guys are. Just go ahead and agree to clean the kitchen now." Aria chirps.

"You're marrying us off together already, huh? Aria, we've just met." I nudge her on the couch, giving her a wink.

Aria's face reddens, and she looks away, biting her bottom lip. Her legs cross, squeezing together. I stare at her lips, wishing I were the one biting them.

"Excuse me. Antonio and I have been best friends since childhood. Grew up down the road from each other. Watch and learn, peasants. If anyone is married here, it is us." Chris scoffs while Scarlett raises an eyebrow at him.

Chris plants a kiss on her forehead. I grab a mouthpiece, shoving it in. My jaw aches. I already regret my back talk. This is going to be more complicated than I thought. The mouthpiece digs uncomfortably at the corners of my mouth. This must be the most unattractive thing I have ever done.

"Go!" Chris yells.

"Who. Doesn't. Love. A. Good. Wedgie?" I attempt to hold the bottom of the mouthpiece.

Aria puts her hand to her mouth as she and Scarlett try suppressing their laughs.

"What? English, man, come on." Chris throws up his hands. Aria and Scarlett can't hold it in anymore. They laugh hysterically, clutching their stomachs. I repeat myself several more times with no success. I throw the card down and grab another one. Clearly, he isn't going to get that one.

"Thank. You. For. Sweeping. The. Floor." I make a sweeping motion with my hands.

Chris pauses and repeats it back perfectly right as the timer ends.

"That's cheating!" Aria yells.

"Aria, they got one. I think it's ok." Scarlett pats Aria on the shoulder, leaning across the table from her chair on the other side.

"It's called strategy, honey. All Marines have one."

Did I just call her honey?

Aria stares at me. Evidently, I did say honey out loud.

Surprisingly, she doesn't look upset. She looks like a woman trying to figure out a man's intentions. I'm trying to figure that out too.

"Got that right. Plus, after your guys' performance. We deserve a handicap." Chris throws me a high five.

"Fine, hand signals are allowed. But it's on boys." Aria says, not taking her eyes off me.

Fine by me. She can look at me all she wants because I will be staring right back. Always.

We play round after round between food and refills. The girls won. Every time. Aria and Scarlett are doubled over in laughter every time it is our turn. At one point, Aria grips my arms, laughing so hard, and I miss my whole turn trying to make sure I didn't just simultaneously catch fire to her touch. I take my hoodie off just to cool down. I grab the collar of my red Marine Corps logo shirt, shaking it to get some airflow. Every laugh out of her fills me with awe. I'm obsessed with being the one causing her to smile. It's like a drug. I'm already addicted. A woman who has been through hell, from the sounds of it, yet she is full of joy.

Meanwhile, the most complex parts of my life stem from joining the Marines and being cheated on. It's already made me angry most of the time. Today, though, I can't remember the last time I was this happy.

"Boys, give it up. I am tired, and you haven't won once." Scarlett slumps back in her chair, yawning.

"You're right. I'm tired too." Chris repeats.

"Yeah. I should head back to Dianna." Aria stands up.

Involuntarily, my legs stand up underneath me. Scarlett looks up at me, amused.

"It was nice meeting you. And Dianna, of course." I reach out a hand for her to shake.

"Nice meeting you too. Good luck with your backpacking trip." Aria shakes my hand.

Oh, right, I told her that. How stupid can I get? It is my plan, though. Isn't it?

Aria gives Scarlett and Chris a hug. A wave of jealousy hits me like a ton of bricks.

What I would give to curl her into my arms. Feel the warmth of her surrounding me.

She heads to the door and closes it softly behind her.

As soon as she is out of the door, Scarlett looks at me with a wide grin, creeping across her features.

"Not one word." I grab some plates and head back to the kitchen.

Time for our punishment.

"Oh, boys, thank you for sweeping." Scarlett laughs, referring to the one card Chris got right all night.

"Yep. That's my wife." Chris says behind me, grabbing the broom.

CHAPTER 7

ARIA

"Aria, can you go grab my purse from the car? I left it in there when we got home from church." My mom, Tula, asks about while preparing our weekly Sunday family dinner table.

"Sure, Mom."

My mom and I have a call anytime, day or night, style relationship. I have called her on the best of days and the worst. Living at home for so long, she has met everyone I have dated. They have all told us how much we look alike. Her hair is darker brown than mine. It is lush and flows with voluminous waves. Her eyes differ too. They are a rich chocolate brown. We joke that it is where our chocolate obsession stems from. We are the same exact height and nearly the same weight.

I stand up from the dining room table, smoothing my pink floral maxi dress. As I walk out to the driveway, the neighbors wave, their kids pedal on bikes up the steep hill of their neighborhood. My phone buzzes in my hand. I glance down at the screen. My classroom of twenty-five students smiles back at me on my lock screen with a notification of a photo tag. I click to open it. My heart swells when I see the photo of me, Scarlett, Chris, and *him*. We are all tagged. Antonio is trying his best to smile with the mouthpiece in his mouth, practically drooling. Scarlett and I laugh, and Chris's arms are extended with the world's cheesiest grin, snapping the selfie. I don't know how long I stood there with my parents' red Ford F-150 car door swung open, staring at the screen. My mom leaned out the door long enough to ask if I needed help finding the purse.

"Got it!" I yell back, holding up the small brown purse as

evidence.

I look back at the photo again and open the tagged accounts. A big, blue add friend button is beaming in my face beside Antonio's name. I hear it say, "click me, click me."

Dr. Shots did say I should live in the moment? It is the next day, though. Will I seem desperate? Oh my gosh, Aria just hit the button. It's social media. It's not like I will message him or even see him again.

I waste no more time. I hit the add button and head back into the house. I was stuck in my mental block for a bit because my parents already had the dinner table set.

"Did you get lost out there?" My brother, Giovanni, asks as he pulls the chair out for his wife, Carly.

"Ha. Original." I pat my nephew, Cam, on the back as I sit beside him in his booster.

Giovanni and Carly have been married for almost a decade. They have given me the most perfect godson, Cameron. He is two. I swear the kid tans better than I. His wavy blond locks are to die for.

Carly is the dark brown-haired version of Ariel. Her brown hair flows down to her waist. Her brown eyes and fair skin practically shimmer like a female Edward Cullen. Carly is my sister from another mister in my mind. When her family moved to Texas, she was already head over heels for my brother. I was in high school, and they were in college. The next thing I knew, she had moved in. I gained what I felt like was an older sister for life. Her ability to build, cook, or craft anything someone wants is uncanny. She can make anything. She is my favorite coffee buddy. Every time we talk, I know there will be a "story time" and endless laughs.

My brother's hair is lighter brown than mine and short. Like Antonio, he too has a runner's build. He must have gotten more half-Italian genes than I because his olive tan never fades. It could be the never-ending miles he runs outdoors. He will run no matter the weather conditions. Gio is my role model. His outlook on life and the way he lives is priceless. He travels all over the country with his little family. Nothing is too out of reach for him. He wants to write a book; he has written three children's books. He wants to be involved with the Carolina Panthers; he plays the bass drum for them. He is unstoppable. Gio knows we have one life to live and makes the absolute most of it. Hence, I always seek his advice.

When they moved out after college, they moved within ten minutes of my parents in the opposite direction. When I moved out, I moved ten minutes in the other direction. Together, our houses make a triangle on the outskirts of the city.

"How was your weekend?" My dad, Gigi, asks, carrying a serving plate of steaks.

"Good. I went to the White-Water Center with Scarlett, Chris, and their friend."

"Nice. Who's the friend?" Dad asks, setting the plate down and sitting at the head of the table.

Leave it to my dad to ask the follow-up question. My dad is also named Giovanni. His dad, you got it, Giovanni. Gigi for short. Leave it to the Italians. Neither my brother nor I got his gigantic genes. He looks like the definition of your typical Brooklyn-born Italian mobster. Growing up, he was comparable to a stone in terms of emotional capacity, but the moment he held my nephew, Cam, he became mushy. He is still tremendously protective but will cry over anything slightly family-related. My parents attended every marching band performance. My dad was the one recording or taking photos of everything we did. He is the memory keeper for the family. I'm his little girl, forever and always.

"Just a guy. His name is Antonio. He's also from New York. He's a Marine stationed in Beaufort, South Carolina."

Mom sits down at the opposite end from Dad at the head of the table. I form the pictorial representation of, 'I got it from my momma.' Think Reese Witherspoon and her daughter. Nearly identical. God got tired and said, 'Copy, paste, but the twenty-five-year-old version,' when he made me.

I can already see the concern on her face as she looks across at Dad. If they had it their way, they would have me become a nun and never date again.

"Marine, huh. Interesting. Kind of sounds like a double date."

"This is the guy?" Gio holds up his phone, shoving the picture I was tagged in smack into Dad's face.

I shoot daggers across the table with my eyes. Carly shakes her head and mouths 'sorry.' Gio coyly smirks at me while Dad grabs his phone.

"You just met the guy and tried to operate on his teeth?" Dad asks, confused, about the mouth gear.

"Gigi, honestly. It is obviously some kind of game." Mom says to Dad, taking the phone from him.

"Are you going to see him again?" Dad asks, stabbing a steak and cutting it vigorously.

"Gigi." Looking at him, Mom grips her fork so tightly that she just might bend it in half.

"Fine enough questions. Let's eat."

I am so glad that conversation is over before it could really start. I don't know if I will ever see him again. He plans to be nowhere near this state once his contract is up. Now, I regret even adding him to the app.

We spent the rest of dinner talking about our plans for the week. I update them about how well my students are doing and tell them how Dianna did on our outing. Before long, it is time to clean up and head back home.

***

My alarm blares in my ear at exactly five the next morning. It continues to vibrate and blink as I get more notifications. When I picked up the phone, I saw I had a text message from Scarlett.

Scarlett

How do we feel about this past weekend's festivities?

Aria

It was fun. You know I love the Green River Revival.

Scarlett

Is that all you love about this weekend?

Aria

Scarlett, just ask what I know you want to ask.

Scarlett

Ugh fine. What do you think about Antonio?!

Aria

Very nice, funny, drop-dead gorgeous hunk of a man, but…

Scarlett

No. There is no but to be had here.

Aria

Scarlett, be for real. He lives hours away, he is a Marine, and I doubt he will give up his plan of hiking the Appalachian Trail for a woman he just met. I can't even move if I wanted to, either. I would take a significant tax hit. I just bought my house a few months ago.

Scarlett

Why don't you just wait and see? He may surprise you. You are also way jumping the gun. That would be about twenty steps ahead. He is only set on that plan because he has no one else. I have to prepare for work, so keep an open mind.

Aria

Ok, Mrs. Cupid. I have to get ready for work too. See you at the
morning staff meeting!

***

The workday goes off without a hitch, except I accidentally
called one of my students Antonio. He asked me who Antonio was,
and I think I died on the spot. Turns out my brain can't stop fantasizing
about him.

When I returned home from work, I sent a quick text to my
therapist that I needed an extra session this week. He texts back
immediately and tells me to hop on a video session. His client
cancelled, so he has extra time. I walk to my home office and open my
laptop, signing on.

"So, what's going on?" Dr. Shot asks, sitting up straighter in
his black office chair.

Dr. Shots is in his early thirties. He has curly, nearly black hair, fair
skin, and rich, dark eyes. He always dresses super casually, which only
helps to make me feel more comfortable.

I proceed to tell him about Saturday. I even mention trying to 'live
in the moment' by adding Antonio on social media.

"Oh, I see. You liked him?" Dr. Shots says." Writing
something down.

"Did you write that down? Wait, I can't like him, like him. I…I
don't even know him." I panic.

"Ok, but he piqued your interest, correct?"

"I mean…kind of. It's dumb, though. He is like a three-to-four-
hour drive away and going to New York when he gets out."

"Got it. So, we aren't living in the moment then." The corner
of his mouth quirks up.

"What does that mean?" I groan.

"You already think you know the future because that's his
plan. Plans change. What if meeting you changes his mind?"

"Ok, doc. This isn't a Hallmark movie. Calm down."

"I am just saying, Aria. Stop holding yourself back from things and
chalking things up to losses before they even have a chance. Remember
what we talked about with trauma responses. This may be an occasion
where your fight or flight is kicking in. Right now, the flight is winning.
You are already finding reasons to avoid and letting something go
because you perceive it as a threat. Something that can hurt you or
cause you stress in the future."

I ponder what he is saying. My phone vibrates in my pocket. "No way," I say in shock, looking at the new message.

"What?" He asks, alarmed.

"He sent me a message on the app."

"Well, what do you know? Evidently, I am a therapist and a miracle worker. Happy messaging. Talk to you later."

"Wait! I need your help knowing what to say."

"Aria, you are fine. You are an adult. You don't need a therapist to help you write a message to a crush. I know you are more than capable. Tell me about it in our next session." He smiles and ends the video session.

With that, the session ends, and I am left alone. Just me, Dianna at my feet, and a message from my apparent 'crush.'

CHAPTER 8

ANTONIO

"The usual for you?"

Waffle House. If one can't find me playing video games in my barracks room, they can generally find me here, eating my weight in questionable breakfast food and filling my body with oily coffee. It's early Tuesday morning. I sent Aria a message last night and am ready to discuss it with someone.

"Yes, the All-Star Special, please, Ruth," I say with absolute certainty.

"And you, dear?" Ruth looks at my friend Lee, ready to jot down our order.

"Same. Thank you."

Ruth takes our menus and quickly comes back with two coffees.

Lee is in the Corps with me. He is about six feet of blonde hair and pure muscle. My motor transport unit is attached to his fuel unit. He is a sergeant. Besides Chris, he is one of my best friends. When I got back on Sunday, I told him all about Aria. He thought I needed to ask Scarlett for her number immediately. I am glad I waited. It gave us time to be tagged in that picture. I was astounded when she added me first. I didn't get to tell him I messaged her the next day.

"Ok. So, are you going to message her?" Lee asks

"I already did." I take a bite of my pancakes that Ruth brought over.

"You didn't tell me that! Let me see." Lee leans across the table, nearly knocking my coffee over, and snatches my phone.

Antonio

Hey Aria. I had a great time this past weekend. I plan on coming back up this weekend. I thought we could all hang out again.

"Dude, are you asking her on a date or not with that intro text?" Lee criticizes.

"She is a twenty-five-year-old woman with a less-than-desirable-sounding past, her own self-purchased home, all the way down to her own dog. I'm not going to go overboard and freak her out."

"Pull up her photo again."

"Why?"

"I just want to see how insane you are if you let this opportunity pass you."

I roll my eyes and flip to her profile picture. Honestly, the idea of someone else having the privilege of checking her out makes my blood boil, but I will never turn down the opportunity to see her beautiful smile or stunning eyes. I open the picture. Her hair is half up and half down in loose curls. Her eyes pierce and captivate my very soul. Her lips have the slightest touch of pink gloss. Her cheeks are rosy. She is wearing a red, white, and blue flannel shirt. The white tank top she has underneath leaves out just enough cleavage to make you want more.

"Yep. I knew it. You should have come out of that gate much stronger."

"Just read the rest of the thread, please." I groan.

Aria
Hi Antonio. I had a great time too. I would like that. What did you have in mind?

Antonio
Glad to hear it. How about we all go to dinner?

Aria
Perfect. Have a place or time in mind?

Antonio
I will talk to Chris and Scarlett and let you know.

Aria
I'll be waiting.

"That's it, really?" Lee hands me back the phone and begins to eat his food.

"What? She said, 'I'll be waiting.' See, she is excited. I set up a follow-up date."

"No, you asked her to hang out with many friends. If that's a date, you and I have been going steady for a long time. I'm offended I don't have a ring yet. Where did you say she is from again?"

I have to really ponder this. I spent half of that day nervously thinking about what I would say next to her, and the other half lost in a fantasy of her body on mine. Paying attention one hundred percent of the time was impossible.

"I think she said ice something."

"Iceland! No way!" Lee leans across the table again, but punches me in the shoulder this time. "You found yourself a foreign chick. She have a sister?" Lee wiggles his eyebrows.

"What? No, an older brother." I grind through my teeth, massaging my sore shoulder. "Can we just eat, please?"

"Fine. But this weekend, you need to make it clear you want a date. Just you and her." Lee takes a bite of his meal.

During the rest of the work week, I throw myself into every task and physical training to keep my mind from bombarding her with messages. I do not want to overwhelm her. I am so thankful Chris and Scarlett are willing to let me crash at their house again two weekends in a row. Although Scarlett is living for this moment. With all the romance novels and reality dating she watches, she feels like this is her shining opportunity.

By the time I am done on Friday, there is no walking to my truck, only running. Three and a half hours in the car feels more like thirty. Every mile closer to Aria makes my blood warmer and my heartbeat faster. It turns out that she has a wedding she has to be at on Saturday, when I planned to have dinner, but she is going to come to Chris and Scarlett's afterwards. She is leaving Dianna with her parents, so she doesn't have to stop home first. The idea of her being at a wedding without me has made me anxious. She could meet someone there and dance the night away, forgetting all about me. When I get to Chris and Scarlett's place, my overactive imagination has Aria whisked away by a guy who makes his intentions clear and is probably decked out in sculpted muscle. He probably doesn't live over three hours away.

This time, when I walk in their door, Harley doesn't act like she wants to eat me. Instead, she runs at me, almost knocking me to the floor and showering me in licks.

"Harley," Chris shouts, running over and grabbing her collar to pull her back. "Let him breathe, girl."

"Hey, man." I give Chris a high five and bring him in for a hug.

"She totally likes you." Scarlett comes running from the hallway, stopping before us, bouncing on her tiptoes.

"Really, Scarlett? You couldn't even let him get in the door."

My brain feels like it is short-circuiting.

That meant she had to ask Aria what she thought, right?

"What makes you say that?" I ask, trying to be casual, but it looks awkward.

I place my rucksack by their front door and sit on their living room couch.

"I messaged her, duh. I talked to her at work, too. She finds you attractive. Funny. Nice." Scarlett takes a seat across from me. Her whole body is exuding confidence.

I don't know what to do or how to process this new information.

"Well, that's good. I feel the same way."
"I knew it. Oh my gosh. When you get married, I have to be there." Scarlett leans forward, propping her chin on his elbows.

"Scarlett, geez, take it down like twenty notches." Chris sits down holding a charcuterie board of meats and cheeses, which he grabbed from the kitchen.

"What? I'm just excited. Two of my favorite people could become an item, and I introduced them. Although he almost ruined it with his backpacking talk." Scarlett lifts an eyebrow at me, grabbing a slice of prosciutto.

"Yeah. I had a feeling that wasn't the best thing to say." I lean back into the couch, defeated by my own mouth.

"It's fine. Me and her therapist have both told her to stop acting like she knows the future."

I don't know why, but hearing she is in therapy fills me with pride. So many people avoid getting help. If they do go to treatment, many wouldn't tell a soul. I hope I can one day be someone she can feel comfortable talking to like that.

"Listen, she should be here in about thirty minutes. Why don't you go freshen up?" Scarlett plugs her nose.

"You trying to say I stink?"
"You said it, bro, we just smelled it," Chris says, reaching to grab a slice of cheese.

Before he can grab it, I snatch it and pop it in my mouth. Scarlett covers her mouth, trying not to laugh as I approach the guest bathroom. I turn the heat up on the shower, ready to let the water wash my nerves away.

About twenty minutes later, I am clean, freshly shaved, and have given myself quite the pep talk. I suddenly realized I had forgotten to bring my bag and clothes into the bathroom. I wrap the towel around my hips and lean out the door.

"Chris, Scarlett? Can one of you bring me my bag?" I call from the hallway.

"Sure thing," Chris calls back.

I hear footsteps and wait by the bathroom door. Steam billows out behind me into the hallway. Around the corner, I see a pair of black heels peeking out. I follow them up to a pair of slender, warm ivory legs. A bright red mini dress hugs this goddess's every curve. The round shape of her hips is accented with the swoop of the dress's skirt. The corseted top lies flat over her abdomen, and her breasts are hugged tight in a sweetheart top. My eyes land on her red-stained lips and outrageously blue-green eyes. Her hair is straight and blown out to frame her face. It is as if time stands still. I feel like it is for her too because once she is in full view, her eyes go wide, staring at the towel, my arms crossed over my chest, and my face as if she doesn't know where to look first.

"I, uh, here." Aria holds out my bag, trying not to look me in the eyes.

"Thanks." I grab the bag from her, tossing it behind me. "You look stunning."

You always hear about 'the little black dress number,' but that would have nothing on the angel I see before me. Seeing her squirm at the sight of me is also a nice perk. I must thank Lee for all the extra days of physical training this week. The way my compliment makes her blush makes me feel more confident than ever under her watchful gaze.

"Thank you. So do you." She winces like she didn't mean to say that out loud.

"Oh, really? You like the practically naked look then." A corner of my mouth quirks at the thought.

"I mean. I." She stutters, trying to find her words. I decide to come to her rescue.

"Let me get dressed, and then I want to hear about the wedding. We may have to talk to Chris and Scarlett."

"Why is that?"

"The way I see it, I can't let you look that good and not take you out on the town on my arm. It's a sin, I think."

"Wouldn't want to let the devil win that one." Aria sneers, giving me a wink.

She turns to walk away, and I stand with my arm propped up in the doorway, admiring the way the dress shows off her backside.

I am in a world of trouble with this one.

I close the door as she is out of sight. I get ready as quickly as I can. Thankfully, I brought a short-sleeved, black button-up shirt and a pair of khaki pants. I leave the shirt partially unbuttoned and add a brown belt. I know we all planned on a night in, but after seeing her, I must show the world this beautiful woman on my arm.

I drop my bag in the guest room and head to the living room. Aria's back is to me, standing at the kitchen island. Scarlett and Chris stand opposite her, staring at me, confused in their T-shirts and baggy sweatpants.

"Well, geez. You didn't have to dress up for me." Chris says, mockingly placing a hand to his chest. Scarlett pushes him on the shoulder playfully.

Aria turns around, and her mouth slips for a millisecond before regaining her composure.

"Ok, I know she was at a wedding, but what are you dressed up for?" Scarlett asks.

"Because we are taking this night in, out," I state.
"And where to, might I ask?" Aria says, placing her hands on her hips with a sly grin.

"I need to get this woman out to a dance floor," I say, moving closer to invade every inch of her personal space. She doesn't flinch or back away.

"Oh my gosh, yes! Clubbing! It has been forever since we have been to a club! I'll get an Uber for us. Chris, come on." Chris's face has the look of dread. Scarlett grabs him by the arm, whisking him to the bedroom, mouthing,' Help me.'

Then there is just Aria and me, merely inches from each other. It is taking everything in me not to pull her close and kiss her like our lives depend on it. Instead, I brush a hair behind her ear and trace a finger down her arm. I see her tremor slightly at the contact, but her head instinctively inclines in my direction. I sit on the barstool behind her, leaning back on my elbows. My knees knock softly into her legs. My body doesn't know how to keep away or give her space.

"So, tell me about this wedding you went to."

CHAPTER 9

ARIA

I am going to have to repent for the multitude of illicit thoughts that ran through my head at the sight of Antonio's almost naked body. Then again, when he came out, he was dressed to impress.

Talk about getting yourself a man who can do both.

I didn't feel like going out after having to spend hours at a wedding, but how he makes me think fills me with pure adrenaline. The thought of our bodies swaying and moving together is the perfect motivation to not let this night end with a simple hangout in the house.

The wedding was for one of my childhood friends, Aubrey. My mom and her mom stayed close friends through the years. It was a beautiful wedding. I was my mom's date for the evening. My dad isn't the touchy-feely wedding guy, so he stayed home. We stayed for dinner and cutting the cake, but we left when it was time for the dancing. I generally do not dance unless it is coordinated. Hence, the anxiety prickles my thoughts at clubbing.

Scarlett comes out of the room at a full-on sprint. Her royal blue mini dress flows behind. Her matching heels clack against the hardwood floor as she stops before me. Her hair is curled in long ringlets past her waist. The deep V of her dress pushes up her breasts, making me jealous since I am significantly flatter. She jumps up and down, gripping my shoulders.

"I am so excited. We haven't been clubbing in forever!" She shrieks.

"There is a reason for that." Chris grumps walking in. Antonio stifles a chuckle behind me.

Chris is wearing a halfway open, white button-up shirt and blue jeans. A pair of brown cowboy boots peeks out from underneath. If Scarlett is on level ten on the excitement scale, then Chris is a negative five.

"The car is here! Let's go." Scarlett says, walking to the front door and dragging Chris along.

Antonio opens the car door, allowing Scarlett and me to slip into the backseat. I sit in the middle, and Chris climbs into the front passenger seat. Antonio gets in beside me, closing the door. His leg brushes mine. He places his hands lazily on his knees, and I am suddenly urged to hold the one closest to me, but think better of it.

"Hey, my name is Eric. Where are we going tonight?" The driver asks, introducing himself.

"Let's go to Dueling Pianos," Scarlett says promptly.

"You got it," Eric says. "Where are you guys from? I hear some northern accents up in here."

"I was born in Islip, Long Island, but I have been here since I was about two," I say.

"Islip. You'll think I am crazy, but I thought you said Iceland last week." Antonio admits turning a bright shade of red.

"Bro, what?" Chris doubles over in a fit of laughter.

Antonio slaps Chris's back as we exit the neighborhood and move towards the city.

We spend the car ride belting out songs on Eric's radio. To our surprise, he isn't totally annoyed by us. In fact, he joins in the singing and rolls down the windows. He even offers to pick us up when we are done. We thank him and get in line to be let into the club.

Waiting in line is taking longer than expected. The longer we wait, the more self-conscious I get. The women in line all look like models. They are all showing way more skin than I am. Scarlett is busy talking Chris's ear off. Chris looks like he is trying to find an escape route. Antonio can feel the tension because he breaks the silence.

"Has anyone ever told you, you look like a celebrity?" He asks.

"I don't think so. I know who you look like, though." I laugh at the question.

"And who is that?"

"A young Vin Diesel."

"What?" Antonio belts out a laugh. "I don't see it, but it is true. 'I don't have friends, I have family.' You looking for a guy to 'ride or die' for you?" He places a hand on my lower back, sending chills up my spine at the contact. His impression is spot on.

"I mean, besides Harry Potter, the Fast and Furious franchise is my favorite movie of all time."

"I can work with that." Antonio winks at me, and I nearly trip over my heels as we move up in line because of it. "I do think you look like someone, though. I'm thinking of young Cameron Diaz. Back when her hair was brown."

"No way. I appreciate the compliment, though." I smile, shaking my head as we finally reach the front of the line.

We walk through the doors, and there are shoulder-to-shoulder crowds. The large bar outside the dance floor is packed with people shouting orders. All the yelling, loud music, and people make me feel claustrophobic. Bright neon lights strobe to the beat of the music. Antonio is tense at my side. His military persona is coming out because his head is on a swivel. His hand has a permanent fixture on my back like my personal security guard.

"Let's go dance!" Scarlett says, already shaking and moving to the beat.

"I think we are going to grab a drink first," Antonio says, taking my hand.

His fingers lace through mine, as if my whole arm catches fire. Antonio looks down at our intertwined hands shocked at what he sees. His eyes reach mine. A slight grin creeps out of the side of his perfect lips. A sense of comfort and protection washes over me.

"Yeah, don't you want to…" Chris starts, but doesn't get to finish. Scarlett grabs his shirt collar and pulls him to the dance floor. Chris tries to reach for Antonio's hand to no avail.

"Thank you for that," I say, leaning into Antonio's ear. "For someone so new to knowing me, you seem to pick up on my vibes fairly easily."

"I know "overwhelmed" when I see it. Plus, I feel very protective of and connected to you. I do not want to ever see you in discomfort." Antonio finds a small table for two for us to sit down, far away from the dance floor. He sits across from me, still eyeing anyone within an arm's reach of me.

"Let's play a game." He says, pushing his sleeves up and clasping his hands together on the table before us.

"What kind of game?"

"Question for a question. Get to know each other a little better."

"I don't think that's a game." I laugh nervously about what his questions could be.

A server comes by with Jello shots, and Antonio grabs two from the tray, passing her a crisp ten-dollar bill from his wallet.

"Ok, fair. What if you have to take a shot if you don't want to answer a question?"

"Deal. You ask first." I say, shaking his hand in agreement.
"Do you like sports? Football perhaps?"

"Yes. I am a die-hard Panthers fan. What about you?"
"Raiders. Born and raised."

Thank God he isn't a Pats fan. I would never live it down with my family. We have been Panthers fans my whole life. I even remember sitting outside in the snow, cheering them on as a kid, the first time they went to a Super Bowl. They had a parade before they left. We went downtown to watch them leave. My brother plays the bass drum for their percussion section. Two people get to go to every game and sit in the family section. Football is family for us. Raiders are acceptable. We only play them every four years.

"Is this the typical Marine's weekend scene? A club or maybe a strip club?" I hope this forces him to take the shot before questions get too deep.

"Our reputation precedes us. Actually, no. Not for me, at least. Granted, I'm not going to lie to you, I've been to dance clubs and strip clubs. I even asked a dancer to the military ball once." He says sheepishly.

"No." I gasp. "What did she say?"

"She rejected me. Turns out she was already going to one with her Navy boyfriend." He shakes his head in defeat. "So, I took my mom instead."

"Stop, that's adorable," I say, placing a hand on his and quickly pulling it away when I realized what I did. He smiles, clearly unbothered by it.

"Next question. What would it be if you could purchase one thing right now?"

A smile pulls at my lips. I stare around the room, thinking about my answer. "I would say, a friend for Dianna. I hate that she is all alone while I work all day. I would probably get a German Shepherd or a pomsky."

"I am all for a German Shepherd. I would love an all black one. What the heck is a pomsky?" He chuckles, spinning his shot around on the table.

"Only the cutest fluff ball you have ever not seen." I quickly search for one on my phone and hold it up. It is a husky, pomeranian combination. Small and fluffy like a pomeranian with a curled tail. However, it has the color markings and coat thickness of the husky.

"Ok, I am not remotely a small dog fan, and I can't deny that dog is adorable." He grabs the phone as if he could hold the dog in his hands before giving it back to me.

"If you could pick a nickname for me, what would it be?"

Antonio's lips part as if he is going to speak. His eyes catch mine. The heat and intensity of it make me smile before looking down at my shot. He lets out a small laugh and slams back his shot. "It will take me a little more time to figure out one word to summarize all of you." He winks.

Holy swoon.

"My turn." He says, leaning back into his chair, propping one arm behind him. "Is this a date?" He grins wickedly at me, looking from the shot to me.

My heart picks up pace. I look into his blue eyes, pick up my shot, cheer it to his sitting on the table before slurping it back.

He laughs. "I had a feeling you would do that."

"Then why even ask the question?" I say, biting my bottom lip.

"Because." He says, leaning forward until he is so close I can smell his mahogany scent. "I am the only thing I want to make you a little nervous." Antonio looks down at my lips.

I hear my name over the music boom when I think he will kiss me. Scarlett comes rushing over, grabs my arm, and pulls me to the dance floor. I look over my shoulder. Chris takes my seat. Antonio leans back in the chair. A mix of emotion clouds his face. He looks like part of him is enjoying the view while the other half is about to slice down anyone who comes close to me.

I look up to the stage and see a DJ between two multicolored pianos. His large table of gear and lights is pulsing to the beat. Scarlett and I start to dance. We aren't even halfway through the first song when two men approach us. They are both wearing various shades of black on black. One has shaggy black hair, and the other a tousled blonde.

"You ladies care if we join you?" The tousled blonde asks, coming up behind my rear, placing a hand on my hip.

"Actually, we do mind." I hear from behind me as I try to rip the man's hand off my waist.

"Sorry, man. Didn't see your name on her."

"Yet." Antonio growls. Scarlett puts her hand over her mouth.

Chris walks over, placing an arm around her shoulders. "Last I checked, I don't see your name on her either. She doesn't want you on her, so back off."

The two men back up, throwing their hands in the air in surrender. The blonde winks at me, blowing me a kissy face. Antonio's face turns lethal. I put a hand on his chest, stepping in front of him. He is still staring down the man, who is batting his chest, egging Antonio on. I place a hand on his cheek and pull his gaze down to mine. I slowly see the rage slip from his darkened eyes. He pushes his head into my hand. Pulling my hand away, he kisses the inside of my palm. My heart soars.

"Let's just dance, ok?" I say, grabbing his hand.

We spent the next hour bumping and grinding to every song. Scarlett and I belt out verses until I am sure my voice will be gone by tomorrow morning. Antonio has his arms wrapped firmly around my waist. Occasionally, I turn to face him, throwing my arms behind his neck. The proximity and his scent are so hard to resist; I keep having to turn away.

By the time the hour is up, we are all so sweaty and exhausted, we all agree it is time to call Eric back to get us.

"I should get my own ride back. That way, you guys don't have to drop me off first." I say as we wait outside for Eric to pull up.

"No way," Scarlett says, hooking her arm through mine.

"Yeah, it's after midnight. I am not a big fan of sending you home with some stranger." Antonio says. Eric pulls up to the curb. "Hey Eric, I'll give you an extra tip if you can drive this one home first." He says, pointing to me.

"Sure, no problem." Eric unlocks the car, and we all get in as we did before.

"Trying to impress me with your extra tip?" I whisper to Antonio once he gets in the car.

"No, your safety is just worth everything to me."

I look at him. I have never met someone so naturally protective or so much of a gentleman. A sudden rush of anxiety fills me that this could all just be how every relationship seems to start. The knight in shining armor becomes a bleak reality once you get to know them. However, something about the honesty gleaming behind his eyes makes me think I could be wrong. The car ride back is quiet. The city lights pass us by, and I find my head resting on his shoulder. He places his head on mine and a hand on my knee. Scarlett grabs Chris's hand, which he reaches back towards her. It all feels so natural. Like the four of us have always been a thing together.

When we arrive at my house, Antonio gets out, holding my hand to help me.

"So, are you ever going to answer whether this is a date?" He says, walking me to my door.

"How about this? We probably need to be on our own for a real date." The look crosses over his face like a little boy being told he is getting a puppy for Christmas.

"I am absolutely ok with this. Another night in the city, maybe. Next weekend?" He asks, rubbing a thumb on the back of my hand.

"Actually, nights like this are not my ideal date situation. I'm not exactly the city type of girl. Don't let the address fool you."

"Thank God, because this isn't exactly me either." Antonio takes a deep breath as if he is at ease for the first time. "I tell you what. You pick the date and I'll be back next weekend. I want to learn what type of woman you really are."

"Deal."

"It's a date." Antonio's smile could break his face in half; it is so big now. "I'll check in later to see what you come up with."

"Give me your phone then. No more app messaging." I grin, taking his phone that he hands me and add my number.

Antonio steps forward, pulling me in for a hug. We linger in it for a moment. My head tucks perfectly under his chin. We pull away, and I so badly want to kiss him. Instead, he places a soft kiss on my forehead. Warmth fills me all the way down to my toes.

"Goodnight, Aria."

With that, he turns away, walking back to the car.

"Until next week," I say to myself, unlocking the door and waving as I go inside.

I don't understand how I got from being one-hundred percent ok with dying alone as a dog mom for life. Now, I am knees wobbling, leaning against my door, and hyperventilating at our physical contact. But. Here I am. We didn't even kiss; I only wish we had.

CHAPTER 10

ANTONIO

APRIL

Still on a high from the weekend, my mind is reeling. The almost kiss we had at the door made me realize that any thought I had about getting out of the Marines and traveling along the Appalachian Trail is a goal of the past. I haven't even kissed yet, and I know I couldn't leave to go on a trip like that without knowing how far whatever this is with Aria could go. It would take months to hike the trail. Then what? Stay in New York, knowing a woman like Aria exists in a world without me. No. This weekend has changed everything. I have a new goal, a new peak to conquer, a new relationship to chase.

"Wait. Let me understand here. First, I was right, and it was not clearly a date initially." Lee says putting his weight down on the gym floor the following evening, back at base.

I scoff and wipe my face and neck with my gym towel.

"Knew it. Second, you walk her to her door and still do not kiss her." Lee's voice grows louder as he clips out every word.

The thing is, Scarlett and Chris said the same thing when I got back in the car. They couldn't believe I didn't kiss her. I'm pretty sure Scarlett wanted to film it.

"Why don't you spray paint it on the wall? I don't think everyone in the gym heard you." I snap back, throwing my sweat-drenched towel in his direction.

"I'm just saying. What exactly are you waiting for?" Lee catches the towel and throws it down at his feet.

"I will find out this weekend when we go on our first official. Both recognize it as a date." I say, grabbing my phone from my gym bag.

"Where are you guys going?"

"I told her she could pick."

"You are whipped. Haven't even gotten a kiss in, and you are already a goner." Lee shakes his head as we grab our stuff to head back towards the barracks.

"At least I have a date, you lone wolf! I can't help but think you are so grumpy that nobody wants to date you." I say to Lee's dismay. He mumbles something under his breath. "Barrack bunnies don't count." He scoffs in response.

I pull out my phone to send Aria a quick text. Hopefully, she has an idea of what she may want to do.

Antonio

Hey, beautiful, I had another great weekend seeing you. What would you want to do on our first date?

I don't expect to get a text back right away.

I am sure she has plenty of other things she does on a Sunday evening before the school week starts.

Lee and I reach our vehicles, throwing our bags in.

To my utter surprise, she texts back immediately.

Aria

Hey, handsome, I also had a great time seeing you again. I would like to know if you could come stay at my house this weekend because my ideal, more like dream date, has always been for someone to take me on a hike. I just figured if you stay at my place, we can wake up early and go on Saturday morning. We can always hang out with Scarlett and Chris on Friday night when you get in, or Sunday before you leave.

My mouth hangs open reading her text. Not only did she pitch the most glorious date idea I've ever heard, but she also invited me to stay at her house. She called me handsome.

"Trying to catch some of these bugs in your mouth?" Lee asks, watching me quizzically as a swarm of June bugs surrounds us.

"She's it."

"She's it what?" Lee asks, confused.

"She's the one. She said her dream date has always been to be asked to go on a hike. She even invited me to stay with her."

"Congrats, man. A city girl who wants to be asked on a hike. She asked the right guy for sure, with all your backpacking experience. Let me know when the wedding is."

Lee pats me on the shoulder and climbs into his green Jeep Wrangler while I stand against my truck reading the message repeatedly.

"Maybe you can have that first kiss at the altar," Lee shouts out his rolled-down window, pulling out of the parking lot. I shoot him the finger back.

Antonio

If you are comfortable with me staying at your house, I am more than happy to. Your dream date and my dream date are one and the same. I will come to your house right after work on Friday. I will probably be there around six if that works.

Aria

That sounds like a plan to me. I'll have dinner ready when you get here.
She is going to cook for me, too. This woman is something else.

Antonio

If you cook for me, I might not ever leave. You know what they say, the way to a man's heart is through his stomach.

Aria

Maybe that's all part of the master plan.

Antonio

I'm ok with this. I will see you on Friday.

Aria

See you then.

Friday couldn't come soon enough. Everything has become robotic and mind-numbing because my every waking thought is about what to expect this weekend. I spend the rest of the time leading up to it planning which mountain range we can go to and which trailhead we should start at. I text her ideas for it throughout the week. She is excited, but I can tell there is a bit of nervousness. When I get there, I can put her nerves at ease.

∗∗∗

I am amazed when I pull up to her house on Friday after work. The house has a six-foot privacy fence. The house is a quarter-acre corner lot, but it is gigantic. It is a soft yellow color with a black door and shutters. The house is a little older but has two stories with a large pine tree in the front yard. Aria opens the front door with a wave as I step down from my truck. She leans back and forth on her bare heels as I walk up her driveway. Her straight hair flows lightly in the breeze behind her. She wears blue jean shorts and a pink T-shirt that says Charlotte across her chest.

"Aria, your house is huge. It's beautiful." I say, pulling her into a hug with one arm and holding my bag with the other. I stare at the house in disbelief at the woman standing before me.

"Thank you. Welcome to my home."

Aria opens the door to a large, yellow-painted kitchen. Light brown wooden cabinets line the walls. A small white bistro table and two chairs sit in front of a large bay window. Dianna comes in wiggling with excitement. I place my bag down by the door and bend down to pet her.

"This is the kitchen, obviously, and Dianna, as you know." Aria snickers as Dianna nearly topples me over with her enthusiasm.

"Yes, I certainly remember this one." I look up to Aria and can tell she is a mix of excitement and nervous energy. "Listen, are you sure you are ok with me staying here? I can call Chris and Scarlett. I don't mind."

I watch her whole demeanor change. She goes from the cheery, upbeat personality I have quickly adored to a stone-cold stoic. Aria takes a seat. She isn't looking me in the eye. Her hands are wringing each other out in her lap. Her feet are rubbing against one another on the floor. She is nervous, but why? I take a seat across from her.

"Listen. I've never been one to be able to hide my emotions well. I am not someone who holds things in. I tend to word vomit. I didn't want to say all this immediately, but I just want to clarify." I start to get nervous, but I give her an encouraging smile to continue. She takes a deep, cleansing breath but continues. "I haven't really done this before like this. I've kind of grown to hate dating. I've seen people be one way while dating, then another once real commitment is involved." She pauses like she is trying to keep from crying. I stand up, grab her hand, and run my thumbs over the back of her hand. "I don't do casual hook-ups. I get attached, and I value commitment. If you want a fling, it isn't me. I've… I've been through too much for that." She looks down at Dianna as if she is ashamed of her emotions.

"Aria. I signed a dotted line when I joined the military to be willing to die in the line of duty to protect you, before I even knew you. I only know how to commit. When I do, I obviously will lay my life down to protect what's mine." I say, placing a hand on her cheek.

Her eyes lift to mine, and the urge to kiss her nags away at me. I lean in, waiting to see if she will allow it. Aria's breath catches, and she closes her eyes, leaning in. Our lips meet as she stands up. It's electricity and heat all at once. My hand cups the back of her neck while her hands rest on my waist. I turn her back against the door, leaning my opposite arm above her head. I kiss her tenderly. I couldn't ask for more out of a first kiss. It feels like my heart is exploding. I pull away, putting my forehead to hers. Her pulse is pumping rapidly under my hand. She bites her bottom lip with a small smile.

"Yeah, I'm not going anywhere. I should've done that last week." We smile at each other, and my hand intertwines with hers. "You want to show me around? Although I'm content with standing here all day, too." I wink.

"Did I say this is the kitchen?" We both laugh, and I shift my weight, allowing her to lead me.

As we pass the stove, I see she has several pots on a low boil. The smell of pineapple and curry fills the air.

"What's for dinner?" Something about being so domestic makes me feel right at home here. I can picture coming home from work like this every day. Not that I expect her to be barefoot cooking in the kitchen all day, but just being in her presence after a long day to do something as simple as eating a meal together fills me with joy.

"Pineapple chicken curry. I know it sounds weird, but don't knock it 'til you try it." She says, holding my hand, leading me into the next room.

"I trust you." I've never said a more factual sentence.

"Good. This house was built in the eighties, so unfortunately, there is no open floor plan. It's basically all carpet except the kitchen and bathrooms."

The next room we walk into is the living room. There is a dark brick fireplace, a fifty-inch TV on an entertainment center, and a brown leather couch set. Two French doors lead out to a concrete slab outside for the backyard.

"Nice! A fireplace."

"Yeah…you can't really use it. It would need repairs unless burning down the house is your goal."

"Note taken."

There goes that romantic idea.

She continues down the adjacent hallway, where a half bath and laundry closet sit to the left. On the right, I see a lavender set of walls.

"This is my happy place." She says, entering the room, twirling in a circle with her arms out like a little kid.

"What makes it your happy place?" I say, running my hand along the bookshelves.

"Well, my murder shelves for one."

"Your what now? Should I be concerned?" I quickly pull my hand away from the shelves.

"No." Aria laughs, covering her mouth. "I like to say that instead of trophy shelves for my books. You see, I only buy books that I read and think 'this author absolutely killed it with this one.'"

"You are such a nerd." I love learning these little details about her.

I've never been one to date studious, wise women, but I am starting to understand that I have been missing out.

"Thank you." She says, gripping my hand and walking me into the room at the end of the hallway, completely unbothered.

"This is the master." My mouth hangs open once more.

A California king bed with a cream and tan colored comforter lay in the middle of the room with a high tan and dark wood headrest. Two dark wooden nightstands are on either side. She has matching dressers. It curves around to a large master bath with his and her sinks, a glass shower, and a walk-in closet.

"This house is amazing."

"Thanks, but we aren't done."

"There's more?"

"This way." She smiles coyly.

We go back down the hallway and through the white double doors. To our right is a formal living and dining room. The dining room has a brown table and chairs, but the formal living room is empty.

"I have to be honest, I don't know what to do with these rooms, so this is where you start to be able to tell this is a one-income household." Aria nervously grapples with her hands.

"You are twenty-five and have a house. I don't think anyone can say anything to you. You will figure it out over time." I say, rubbing her shoulders.

She nods and leads me up the white carpeted stairs. Upstairs, there are two more bedrooms and a full bath. One bedroom has a couch. The other has a full-sized bed and a white dresser.

"Is this where I should put my bag?" I ask, plopping down on the bed.

Aria turns around but keeps her eyes on the carpet.

"I think you can put your bag in my room. We can be adults

about this." She looks up at me, confirming this fact.

I take a second to gather my thoughts because I genuinely thought and was content with staying in another room. Shocked in an understatement.

"Are you certain? I would never want to make you uncomfortable." I pull her into me, clasping my hands behind her back.

"I'm sure." She rises onto her toes and kisses me softly. "Let's eat."

My stomach grumbles in agreement as we head back downstairs and into the kitchen. She plates two bowls of white rice with pineapple chicken curry on top. It smells delicious, and the bright colors of the peppers and pineapple are eye-catching, like it should be in a food magazine. I take a bite, and rich flavors fill my mouth.

A guy can get used to this.

"Aria, this is incredible," I say, taking another bite.

"I'm glad you like it. I've only made it a few times."

"I love it. I love your house too. I am beyond impressed. Do you mind telling me about how you came to buy a house on your own so young?" Her smile falters, and I regret my question.

"I bought it myself, but I wasn't alone when I bought it." She sets her fork down on the table and pats Dianna on the head. "I was engaged."

I put my fork down. I want to ensure she knows I am in this conversation and ready to support her. Chris and Scarlett told me about her ex, but I want to hear from her. They didn't give me many details, so there is much to unpack to fully understand Aria. I can see the depth of the pain etched deep in her eyes.

"I never liked the idea of renting. My parents did it for years and wish they had never done it. They allowed me to stay home through college and not give them a dime as long as I agreed to save as much money as possible. I took on part-time jobs and saved. I met my ex, we got engaged, but my goal never changed. I bought the house in January and, to his dismay, didn't include him on the title."

Smart. That's my girl.

"I think your parents sound very wise. That's sound advice and good on you to accomplish this." I say, lifting my hands, gesturing around the house.

"It doesn't bother you that I was engaged only a few months ago?" She asks, looking down at the table.

I ponder my response for a moment. My biggest concern is if he still comes around and what the dynamic was. The more I think about him in this place, the angrier I become that he didn't value her spirit.

"The only thing I care about is that we are together here now, and my hope is that he stays long gone because I am not going anywhere." I grab her hand. "If you want to talk about it, that's fine by me too."

"I feel like you should know." She stares at me with glassy eyes.

"I'm right here with you. Tell me whatever you think I should know."

CHAPTER 11

ARIA

My head is already spinning with all this day's different highs and lows. I invited a man to stay at my house, whom I had only met weeks ago. Not only that, but I already word vomited to him and offered for him to stay in my room. Now, I sit across from him discussing my abusive ex. I can't wrap my head around it, but I want him to know all of me. I want him to know it now. Maybe it is part of protecting myself. Tell him everything up front so he can run now instead of finding out gradually over time, then leaving later. I have this unnatural sense of trust and yearning for him that I have *never* felt for anyone. Generally, when I meet a guy, we are just friends, and I can't picture them as significant other material, so one day, I just give in. Antonio, however, it's taking everything in me to keep my mouth shut, thighs together, and my hands to myself. The kiss we shared earlier still makes my toes curl at the thought. We couldn't wait any longer to wonder what it would be like.

He must know about my ex. Though I have my ex blocked on everything I can think of, I never know if we could run into him. His role in my life has significantly affected the way I am today. So, I decided to tell him every minute detail. Now.

"Let me start by saying he wasn't always bad. When we first started dating, I met him at the gym. He and my dad bonded over being in the military. He was an Army vet. My dad introduced us, thinking he would be a stand-up guy. He was your typical city guy when it came to dates. Always wanted to go to bars, dinners, etc. It was going fine. He proposed in my parents' living room by telling me he didn't want to be my boyfriend anymore. He let me sit there believing it. I started crying and walked away. He chased after me. He knelt, proposing, saying, 'It's because I want to be your husband instead." I look out the window at the memory flashing in my mind. "I should have known then. I didn't want to say yes, I just felt like I had to. It felt wrong immediately."

"That's how he proposed? By making you think he was breaking up with you first?" Antonio rubbed his hand over his head.

"Yes, it was emotional turmoil. That's when it all started. He drank more and more. He would crush twenty-four packs of beer in two hours like water. Not long after the engagement, I found out he was abusing steroids. He would take them in cycles. Every time he was on them, he would be angry for weeks. His lease had ended, and he had moved into my parents' house with me while I was still saving up. One night, he was on a roids cycle, we got into an argument, he got in my face and said, 'Do you know what I could do to you?' I got scared and pushed him away because he was so close to me, saying that. I thought he was going to hit me." I can feel myself start to tremble. Antonio's hands are clenching into fists on the table, but he reaches down to stroke my knee. It encourages me to continue.

"This is why I blame myself so much; I put my hands on him first. I pushed him away from me." Tears start to fall down my face. This is my most significant source of guilt.

"Aria no. Stop. You can't do that. You were trying to protect yourself. The fact that you tried to protect yourself against a guy like that speaks volumes to your bravery." Antonio wipes stray tears from my cheek.

"I'm working on it. So many things happened after that. Every argument seemed to get worse. He tried to flip the bed mattress over with me on it. He put his hands around my neck in an argument, too. That's when I knew I had to get him out of my parents' house. I was afraid he could hurt them, so I moved up my goal of moving out. Then we moved in here." I look up at Antonio, and his eyes have grown dark. His back is leaning against his chair, and his hands grip his knees. Absent mindedly, I stroked the back of my neck as if Adonis's hands were still there.

"He had pills from the VA for sleeping. One day, I came home from work to an empty bottle of them. Three days prior, he had just filled it. It had thirty pills. I panicked and ran to our room. He was passed out on the bed. I tried to wake him and couldn't get him to wake up. I called his dad because he told me this happened last time he was on the pills in a prior conversation. His dad informed me he was on the way but was thirty minutes out. I grabbed his keys and hid them in case he woke up because I knew he would drive and get alcohol." I feel my breath start to pick up. My nightmare races in front of my mind. I take a few deep breaths.

"You don't have to tell me, Aria. It's ok. I understand." Antonio says soothingly.

"No, I need to get this out." He nods and grabs both of my hands. "He woke up screaming for his keys. I told him I wouldn't give them to him because he took too many pills and didn't need to drink. I didn't want him to get on the road and hurt someone. He ended up picking me up and throwing me down on my back. He kicked a hole in the office wall and threw open the door of the master's so hard that the doorknob went into the wall. He flipped the coffee table and broke glasses in the kitchen. It was a mess. By the time his dad arrived, he began to simmer down. It took us almost five hours to get him calm enough to sleep. At one point, his dad fell asleep on the couch, and Adonis sat beside him, staring into the darkness, smoking a cigar. When I had to pass it on the way to work the next morning, he had dropped it onto the carpet, and it burned a spot in it. I went to work without sleep, and his dad informed him of everything that occurred when he woke up. I told his dad before I left that I wanted Adonis out. By the time I got home, all his stuff was gone." I say it so fast that I can tell Antonio struggles to keep up with all the information.

"Wait, his dad had to inform him when he woke up? So, he didn't remember?"

"No, evidently, he was so high off a cocktail of sleeping medication, alcohol, and his steroids, he didn't remember any of it."

"Did you ever tell your parents any of this? How was he not dead?"

I shrug. I've always wondered the same thing. "Yes, my mom found out after his dad left with him the next morning. His dad drove him to the VA and had him committed for two weeks."

"Geez. Aria. You understand that you are a survivor, right?" Pain washes over his features. "That night could have ended much differently. Why didn't you call the police or an ambulance when you saw him passed out to begin with?"

"I blamed myself for everything. That's what he always had me believing. I thought I would somehow get in trouble. I drove him to drink, abuse his pills, etc. Plus, like I said, his dad said this has happened before, so I thought he could take care of it." Antonio places his forehead on mine.

"Please tell me you cut off communication, got a restraining order, something."

"I blocked him on everything. I didn't get a restraining order or ever have the desire to press charges. I don't want to see him again in court. I just want it all over. So far, I have never seen or heard from him again. He has run into people I know and asked about me, but there has been no direct contact." Antonio lets out a breath like he has been holding it all day. He lets his head tip back, looking at the ceiling.

"And he has never shown back up at the house?"

"No, supposedly, he told one of my friends he ran into that he couldn't even remember where our house was. That's how drunk and out of his mind he was when we moved here. I'm not sure what to believe, though. He lied a lot."

"Come here, please," Antonio says, standing. "Thank you for telling me."

He pulls me into a hug, wrapping me tightly in his arms. My head rests on his chest. I can hear his heartbeat beating so hard and so fast, I am afraid he will fall out on the floor. His hands softly trace up and down my back. He kisses the top of my head and leans back.

"I need you to know that you never have to worry about that with me. I'm sure there is still more for me to know. I will be right here any time you need to let it out. I don't want you to hold these things in. You will not scare me away. I need to know that you are safe and ok, always."

When I look at him, everything in me calms. My heart rate begins to slow. My mind goes quiet. He has taken this so well. He is still here. He still wants me. He doesn't blame me. He isn't acting like I will go insane at any moment. He is supporting me.

I lean up and kiss him. Kissing my ex never felt this good. All my ex cared about was being a frenzy of arms and legs. The more aggressive he is, the better. Antonio kisses me with slow and deliberate movements. This is savoring. Worshipping. Appreciation. It's intoxicating.

His hands wrap around my waist while mine are intertwined behind his neck. Our kiss deepens. Red, hot need crashes through me. He kisses the side of my neck but abruptly halts, pulling back to look at me, clearly fighting his urges.

"Why…why did you stop?" I ask, trying to catch my breath. Bitter disappointment wafts over me. I don't know if I was ready, but I wanted to find out.

"Because I'm not here to rush or take from you, Aria. I only want us to give and provide for one another when that happens. You've been through enough. That moment will change everything for us. Trust me, I want to, but it won't be after we just talked about your ex."

If that is any indication of what could happen when he is in my bed tonight, I am in for a master class of self-inflicted pain if I try to resist his advances.

We decide to sit back down and finish up our dinner. We continue to talk, making plans for the evening. We settle on playing old GameCube games and having a few beers. Evidently, the first time truly 'on her own Aria' results back to tomboy when it comes to suggestions for things to do on a weekend night before an early morning. To my surprise, my suggestions only served to delight Antonio. Never in my wildest dreams would I ever think a guy would be down for all my very unsexy ways of planning.

We clean up dinner and settle in the living room. I pop in Super Mario Kart and grab some Mike's Hard Lemonades. We sit on the floor to be closer to the split screen.

"I feel like we need another wager," Antonio says as the game flashes.

"Oh boy. What will it be this time?" Selecting the epic combo of Princess Peach and Mario.

"Whoever loses has to say something the other doesn't know about yet. It can't be surface-level. Something real."

"You just want to know all about me, right?" I shimmy my shoulders towards him.

"I do, and I intend to find out." Antonio selects Donkey Kong and Luigi with zero hesitation.

"Fine."

The game begins. There are three rounds. Each round is on a different track with five laps. The first round is dinosaur-themed. I won this one by a landslide. Antonio's characters kept being knocked off the tracks into pools of water, making him fall behind the pack.

"Man, you really love to lose," I smirk. "Let's go, handsome. Tell me that dark family secret."

"Slow down, killer." Antonio grins. "Ok, it is only fair since you told me about your latest ex to tell you about mine. Her name was Danielle. I knew her through mutual friends. I threw all my eggs in one basket. Helped her get to a place closer to me and the base. Ended up shooting myself in the foot on that one because it also got her closer to other Marines. She cheated on me. She ended up pregnant with the guy she cheated on me with." Antonio looks down at his controller, fiddling with the toggles.

PREGNANT?! Being cheated on is already heartbreaking enough. For her to end up pregnant from another man is next-level torture.

"Oh my gosh, I am so, so sorry."

"It's ok. I had a feeling it wouldn't work out. I had never gone for a relationship like that before, so I thought it would be returned if I just committed heavily. Guess I just committed to the wrong woman." Antonio leans over and kisses my shoulder, making me blush.

I want to know more, but he isn't ready to share much more. I don't want to push it if he is not prepared. Just because I felt the need to word vomit all my traumas doesn't mean he is able or willing to do the same all at once.

The next round begins. This time it is space-themed. It is my absolute worst course. I used the speed boost, but it constantly sends me flying off the rainbow tracks. I come in dead last. Antonio fakes yawns as I finally reach the finish line.

"Ok, I already told you a lot of deep stuff tonight, so how about something funny about me and my family?"

"Fair enough. I'm listening."

"My family celebrates Groundhog Day," I say as Antonio sips beer.

"What?!" He says, choking on his beer. "How do you celebrate a groundhog?" He laughs.

"Well, we all get together at my parents' house right down the road. We watch the movie Groundhog Day. Each of us brings something from the diner scene when he orders one of everything on the menu."

"That is amazing. I want to go to the next one."

"If you don't decide to go on your little backpacking trip," I say. I mentally slap myself for saying that.

Antonio's smile goes from face-splitting to non-existent in about two seconds flat. Before he can respond, the next game begins. This round is haunted house themed. We are neck and neck the entire race. On the final lap, we are both within arm's reach of the finish line. Antonio's car is slightly ahead of me. Out of nowhere, a green turtle shell bounces off a wall ahead of us and slams into his car, making him fall back into a spin. I raced by winning the final round.

"Yes!" I scream, fist-bumping the air.

Antonio throws his controller down on the carpet and throws his arms across his chest, pouting.

"Lucky shell ricochet." He grits out. "Ok, so something you

clearly don't know about me is that my plans of wanting to go hike the Appalachian Trail ended the moment I dropped you off on your porch after the club. Walking back to the car away from you that night was an awakening. I just knew. You are my new inspiration. I have new dreams now, and every single one has you involved. I don't need to do that right now. Right now. What I need is to see where this goes." Antonio eyes me nervously, waiting for my response.

I turn towards him. This man had made me feel more secure and comfortable in a few weeks than anyone I have ever been with. The crazier part is that we aren't even an exclusive couple, and here I am willing to give him even the tiniest parts of me because in my head and my heart, I know it will be protected as valuable.

I waste no more time thinking. If living in the moment is what I am supposed to be doing, then I am ready for an A+ on the assignment. I move so I sit on his lap with my legs firmly around his waist. His hands wrap around me, and he rubs the small of my back. My hips roll into him. We kiss softly first before it turns into something more. His head folds into my neck, kissing and sucking as I moan. With unimaginable strength, he rolls me over, still hugging him, and comes to a stand. I kiss down the side of his neck as he walks us to the bedroom and lays me on the bed. He stands back, putting distance between us and leaning on the dresser. His eyes scan every inch of my body in thirsty appreciation.

"You have to tell me what to do here, Aria. It's everything I can do right now not to take this any further." He says, rubbing the back of his neck, clearly aroused.

The fact that he hesitated is giving my overthinking brain time to do its primary purpose in my life, ruin reckless decisions.

"I...I don't know. I don't normally do this. It normally takes me a long time to get to this point with someone." I stumble over my words, trying to get my body to stop moving.

"Ok. Let's just take a beat. Like I said before. We don't need to rush this. We need to get up early, maybe we should just try to sleep it off." He suggests returning to the side of the bed, placing an arm on each side of my head, and leaning over me.

"Can we at least cuddle?" I ask, feeling like a little kid.

"Definitely." He says with another kiss.

He removes his clothes, stripping down to a pair of blue boxers. His body is a work of art. His olive skin and toned chest work down to a deep V that disappears into his briefs. His thighs and calves are built like he runs ten miles daily for fun. His biceps are sculpted and might be one of my new favorite features on him. A line of curse words runs through my mind.

I usually wear a t-shirt and sweatpants when I sleep, but that will not cut it tonight. I dig into my drawer for black silk sleep shorts with a matching silk lace top. I excuse myself to the bathroom to change. By the time I return, Antonio has already climbed into bed and is lying with his hands behind his head on the pillow. When I open the door, he is propped up on his elbows. His Adam's apple bobs as he swallows.

Clearly, I made the right outfit choice.
I slide into my side of the bed. Before I can get in, he is already wrapping an arm around me, pulling me to him. My back is flush against him. He gently kisses behind my ear. My hands find his, gliding up and down his arm.

"Goodnight, Aria," Antonio whispers in my ear, making every hair on my body stand on end.

"Goodnight, Antonio," I whisper back, settling into him even more before falling into the most restful sleep I've ever experienced.

CHAPTER 12

ANTONIO

I have never had to have so much self-control in my entire life as I did last night. Waking up, still clutched to her, does not help. Her nearly bare backside, occasionally rolling back into me, is torture.

Can a man die from this magnitude of anticipation?

"Coffee," Aria mumbles, turning to face me. Her face burrows into me with an arm coming to lay on my waist.

"Good morning to you, too," I say, kissing her head. "I tell you what. It's six AM. How about I prep the coffee pot and have you get dressed?" I suggest into her mess of hair.

"You are a saint and a scholar, sir. A real gem amongst men." Aria continues to mumble, trying to lift her sleepy eyes.

I roll out of bed and grab a pair of black sweatpants out of my bag. I slip them on and make my way towards the kitchen. Dianna follows me from her pink dog bed, so I let her outside before entering. I fill up the pot of coffee, and a sweet aroma fills the air. I look at the bag of coffee sitting next to the coffee maker, Utica Coffee Cinnamon Bun.

Getting up was the best idea because I didn't trust myself if I continued to lie beside her. I walk to the French doors and watch Dianna as she prowls around the backyard. We have about a two-hour ride ahead of us, so I need coffee, too.

"Is that my primary food group I smell?" Aria says, walking up behind me.

Aria's hair is pulled into a ponytail and a blue New York Yankees cap. She is wearing a gray active tank top with a tight-fitted pair of three-quarter-length black yoga pants. She has a thick pair of hiking socks on.

"Coffee is not a food," I say, facing her and eyeing the curve of her hips.

"I'm offended," Aria says mockingly.

"I think today's dream date will make up for it," I say, tilting her hat to kiss her on the cheek. "At least we have one team in common. I'm a Yankee fan too." I point to her hat.

"Good for me, but bad for you. If you ever meet my dad, just don't tell him that one. He is a Mets fan. Almost got me kicked out of the 'circle of trust' when he found out my Yankee love runs deep." Aria shrugs and heads into the kitchen.

I would have been mistaken if I had thought Scarlett and Chris were huge coffee drinkers. Aria's giant insulated mug would put them to shame. She doesn't even use creamer, just a dash of milk. I walk over and pour a cup of coffee, which is black, correctly. All natural for me. I blame the Marines for this one. No luxury in the desert. I may not have been overseas, but Twenty-Nine Palms, California's desert warfare training, is tried and true. It is monotonous and lonely.

"We'd better get on the road. Get Dianna all strapped up, ready to go." I say, checking the clock, six thirty.

"I just hope she doesn't pull me down the mountain or off a cliff." Aria gripes.

"Like I would let that happen to either of you." I scoff.

We get Dianna ready and get in the car. We spent two hours learning the most minor details about each other. I found out she is from a conservative family. They attend church and have weekly family dinners, and her parents' marriage roles are pretty traditional. She likes conventional roles and plans to do the same when married. Having a family of her own one day excites her. She tells me about how her older brother heavily influences her dating life. She has seen him go through some heartbreaks, and it made her cognizant about how she, in turn, treats guys when in a relationship. We even cover nicknames. I tell her my family mostly calls me Ant. Her name is short, but after she tells me her middle name is Jade, we settle on AJ as her newfound nickname. For now. I'm still thinking of better ones.

When we pulled up to my surprise hiking trail, I knew so many details about her life, down to her favorite candy and snacks, that it felt like we had known each other for years. The trail I picked is in Pisgah National Forest. She doesn't know this, but I hope we are an exclusive item by the end of the hike. There are still a lot of unknowns about where this will go due to my impending opportunity to re-enlist or be discharged. I hope she can overcome that uncertainty and allow us to figure out a future together. Now that I have decided not to do the Appalachian Trail, I have to figure out my next move, sooner rather than later.

"This is gorgeous!" Aria says Getting Dianna out of the vehicle. "Have you been here before?"

"Yes. I have a friend back at base, Lee. We have been here backpacking a few times. Chris has come too."

"I still can't get over the fact that you have been to visit them before, and I never met you. Granted, it was probably now if there was ever a time to meet. I've been through enough serious relationships and life events that opened my eyes more to the world. I grew up sheltered, so I needed to go through some things to mature myself." Aria says, lacing up her hiking boots and grabbing Dianna from the backseat.

I ponder this for a bit. There is something to be said about timing. If we had met growing up, she probably would have hated me. I was not a bad kid but went to my fair share of wild parties. I did dumb boy things like throwing ice balls at passing truckers' windshields, and I loved all things fearless. According to our conversation on the ride here, she was the captain of the color guard in marching band, an honor roll student type. She loved sports and being outside, but that would have been our only connecting pieces.

"I had to go through my things, too. Maybe all the things we have gone through put us here together. A mutual destiny." I squeeze her hand as we start to walk towards the trailhead.

Aria's lips form a soft smile. I love watching her eyes absorb the scene around us. The trailhead's beginning is always busy, but there are so many paths here that the further you go, the more the people get spread out. Tall grass nips at the back of our knees on the path's edge. All around us are red and yellow blooming wildflowers. Balsam fir trees stretch out, and peaks can be seen far ahead. Wild blackberries blow gently in the breeze. The path is rocky as we start our ascent to the first peak. I am amazed at how well Dianna is doing. For a pit bull, she hikes this like a pure-bred working dog. Aria trips over a rock and slams forward. I catch her arm right as she is about to smack into a boulder ahead of us.

"Here, let me take Dianna. You are in my church now." Reaching for Dianna's leash and helping her stand up.

"Oh, your church, huh?" Aria says, trying to play off the fall.

"I am a believer, I just don't go to service. I grew up Catholic like you. I haven't been able to attend church service in a long time. Since the Marines Corps, it's hard to sit like that without getting nervous. This is where I come to feel close to God."

"God isn't just in one place. I can respect that. I mean, look at this creation." Aria gestures to the scenic views all around us.

We get to the most strenuous part of the trail, where it is a straight push to the top over rocks with zero switchbacks. We take it slow, allowing the people coming down to ease past us. Dianna doesn't even seem winded by the time we reach the top. When we reach the top, we find a small meadow to sit down and rest in. Purple wildflowers surround us. All you can see for miles are mountains, flying hawks, and endless green trees. I lean against a rock and throw an arm around Aria's waist. Dianna lies down at Aria's side, taking a sip of water out of a collapsible bowl we brought. She leans back with me and lays her head on my shoulder. I started to get nervous as I realized now would be the perfect moment to ask her to be exclusive with me. She must sense the change because her eyes shift to look at me.

"Hey," I say breathlessly, trying to calm my rapid heart rate.

"Hey." Aria kisses my cheek, reassuring me enough to ask my question.

"Aria, I don't want to date anyone else. I know you just went through a hell of a time not that long ago. I don't need any type of drugs; your smile is enough of a high. I don't need to be drunk all the time; your laughter can be my swig of whiskey. I don't need steroids because your touch and just knowing you are mine is strength enough for me." Aria is sitting up now, staring at me, glassy-eyed. "Will you be my girlfriend?" I say, trying to lighten the mood in case I came on too strong.

"Ant, I would love nothing more than to be your girlfriend. I don't want to be with anyone else either."

"I know we have a lot to figure out. I know I have to make an official re-enlistment decision. I know I don't live here, and you do. I just think we can figure it all out together."

"I am a planner. I am not good at the unknown. It makes me extremely nervous, but I just know in my heart that I can trust you. I'm in this. We can figure it all out."

I remove my fleece top layer, throw it over her shoulder as the wind picks up, and use it to bring her closer. We kiss, and something about it feels like a flash-forward in time. Something about this kiss makes me feel like this is it. This is the last woman I will kiss for the rest of my life.

During the rest of the hike, we smile so hard that everyone passing us thinks we are two hormonally charged teenagers, not twenty-something-year-old adults who just agreed to go steady. Aria's vulnerability astounds me. We discussed anything and everything we could think of as we went over peaks and valleys before deciding to head back. It is well past lunchtime. The sandwiches and snacks we packed before heading out the door are already gone. The sun will set soon. We conclude that we must go home and get cleaned up because we are now covered in dirt and grime. That's when I realized one day it could be our home together.

CHAPTER 13

ARIA

We get back to the house, and my jaw aches from the number of smiles and laughter we shared today. My mind still reels at his asking me to be his girlfriend. I have *never* had a guy say the things that he said to me on the top of that mountain. He took my dream date and made it a reality. Never in my wildest dreams did I picture him asking me to be exclusive on what has always been a date I've desired to do. His fleece is still wrapped around me with his heavy scent. Dianna jets off into the house, claiming a spot on the sofa. I head to the master bedroom to strip off these sweaty clothes. Antonio is approaching behind me.

"You want to take a shower first?" He asks, reaching down to grab his phone charger from his bag.

My palms sweat, and my breathing intensifies as thoughts flood my mind. This is another first for me. I've never lusted this hard for someone. It usually takes months, sometimes even years, to get to the point where I am comfortable enough to feel this way.

While Antonio's back is still turned away, I quietly strip out my clothes and throw them into the laundry hamper until I am in nothing but my undergarments. I roll my shoulders, waiting for him to turn around.

Antonio turns around, and a look of pure shock covers his features. His eyes dart between my heaving chest and my face, unsure of what to focus on.

"I was thinking maybe we can shower together." I giggle out

of nervousness.

"Have I ever mentioned how much I love that mind of yours?" Antonio says, inching forward, pulling my hips to his. "What happened to 'we can be adults' about staying in the same room?"

"I can be an adult, see. Adults are responsible, and I want to be responsible for a whole list of things right now." I say, trailing a hand lightly down his chest.

"You are sure this is ok?" Antonio says, kissing my cheek. "Are you protected?"

"Yes. I want you, and I am on the pill. I take it every day." I try to say between breaths.

He is done waiting. That was all he needed. I turn on the water in the shower, waiting for it to warm. His fingers travel down my body with urgency.

How is that for living in the moment?

***

After the shower of a lifetime, we lay on the bed, somehow still sweaty. I am not even bothered that my soaking wet hair is seeping through my pillow. Our chests are busting at the seams as we try to catch our breath. My former level of intimacy is almost non-existent. I have always been overthinking how the guy feels or if I look awkward, which I never really enjoyed much. Antonio is the first guy to truly make me feel confident. I feel like I am combusting from bliss.

"That was…" Antonio says with one hand behind his head and the other on his rapidly rising and falling chest.

"I know." I snicker, rolling to my side to look at him.

"Come here," Antonio says, putting an arm underneath me.

I shimmy over to him, wrapping a leg around him. We lay there, cuddled up for a few minutes, soaking in the euphoria of what we just shared.

"How much time do we have?" Antonio asks with his eyes closed.

On the way home, we called Scarlett and Chris to invite them over for dinner. We told them we are officially dating exclusively. Had we known this level of intimacy was going to happen, we would have spent the night reliving that new core memory repeatedly until morning.

"Oh my gosh, they must be almost here by now. We have to get up." I sit straight up and run into the bathroom.

Antonio gets up sluggishly, slipping on a pair of boxers. I

quickly blow-dry my hair and throw it up in a claw clip. I grab the first pair of sweatpants and a green deep V-neck crop top. Antonio is in basketball shorts and an Adirondack Mountains t-shirt. The doorbell is already ringing when we go to the living room.

"Well, hello to the newest couple!" Scarlett yells, pulling me into a hug.

"Scarlett made us get cake; otherwise, we would have been here earlier." Chris said, handing us a cookie cake with the word 'congratulations' written on the frosting across the top.

"Thank you?" Antonio says, grabbing the cake and setting it on the counter. "AJ and I thought you and I could grab some Chinese. The girls can hang back here." Antonio says, pointing from himself to Chris.

"AJ, huh?" Chris says as they come further into the house. "What's that stand for? Amazing jugs." Chris brings his hands up to make fake breasts, pretending to motorboat himself.

"Apologize." Antonio grinds out, rushing over and putting Chris in a choke hold.

"Chris, geez! I want a nickname." Scarlett pouts as the two continue to wrestle.

"I got it. Scar." Chris chokes out from under Antonio's arm.

"Your nickname for your wife is after the villain in The Lion King." I try to contain my laughter.

"You're done. You two idiots, go get the food, please." Scarlett says, giving them a disapproving glare.

Antonio and Chris call a truce. He leans in, giving me a quick peck before they race out the door.

"I have so much to tell you," I say, turning to Scarlett and leading her into the living room. "Some may be a little TMI."

"You know what I always say. TMI just means, tell me immediately."

By the time the boys return, Scarlett's mouth still hasn't been picked up off the floor. I told her what we did when we got back from hiking today. She was shocked and amazed that I had even let myself go there.

We spent the next two hours eating, talking, and watching reruns of Friends with the boys. By the end of it, Antonio and I are so exhausted from the entire day that we practically fall asleep on the couch. Scarlett and Chris decide they should let us rest. We hardly make it all the way into bed before the two of us pass out with me cuddled into his chest.

***

"I don't want to go back to base." I hear Antonio groan as we wake up. My body is sore from hiking yesterday, and I can't move.

"Me either. I was thinking about something you said yesterday about having never been deployed. Does it bother you that you haven't?" I say, wiping sleep from my eyes.

"No. It used to bother me, not being deployed. Then I realized, if we didn't have personnel here, who would protect the home front? We all have a job to do. We all serve a greater purpose than ourselves. You change in this career regardless of where you go. Once you are trained to protect the person next to you, no matter the cost, there isn't any coming back from that mindset." His voice fades out, lost in thought. "If I had deployed, who knows if we would have met. I firmly believe everything I have done or didn't do led me to you."

He is making me into the mushiest person I've ever met. I can't even think of what to say because everything he says is how I feel. I just don't know how to word it like him. "Ant, thank you for your service."

"Thank you for being worth serving for."

We take our time getting out of bed. It is almost as if we are trying to find time to stop, and we won't have to keep seeing each other only on the weekends. We drink our coffee snuggled up on the couch, trying to find excuses for him to stay a little longer. In the end, we know he has to return, but he will be here again next weekend. I asked him if he would want to meet my family. He knows how close we are. It would help ease the blow of them finding out I am in a relationship again if they got to meet him. He goes rigid. You can practically smell the anxiety in the room, yet he agrees it would be a great idea.

Is he nervous they won't like him? That's impossible. They will be protective, but I am sure they will love him. Maybe he hasn't met many other girls' families. Now, I just have to tell my family about *us*.

We kiss goodbye, and he gives Dianna a quality belly rub before he grabs his bag. I stand watching the door as he pulls out of the driveway.

***

"Hey Aria, I need to tell you something." My brother, Gio, says later at the family dinner. "Can you come with me outside?"

"Sure?" I walk outside to our parents' back deck.

Their deck overlooks a pool they put in and has two large navy-blue umbrellas opened to create some shade. As peaceful as this spot should be, I can tell whatever Gio has to say to me will not be fun to hear. His brows are stitched in concern. His hands are in his pockets, and he isn't looking me in the eye.

"What is it?" I ask, my anxiety growing by the second.

"I saw Adonis. He is still in town." Gio looks up at me with eyes full of emotion.

Gio never liked Adonis. Nor did Carly. They harbored great parental concern about his presence around Cam. Adonis was always lovely to Cam, but his ability to get angry and his state of constant drunkenness were unacceptable. Deep down, I knew these things were major red flags. Gio never questioned why I didn't call the cops or get away. He could tell something bigger was going on. I didn't know if Adonis would track me down if I forced him away. I had no plans to evacuate the area. It's easy to say 'why doesn't the victim leave' or 'just go to the police' when you aren't in the situation. I got lucky that he doesn't remember where the house is. I've been fortunate that I have never run back into him.

"Ok. Where?" I ask, trying to remain calm. It's not like I expected him to leave town, but knowing he's nearby is unsettling.

"He is working at the local sandwich shop."

I'm sure he is also acting like a God amongst subs there. Show everyone how to make a proper Greek twelve-inch.

"You didn't say anything, did you?"

"Are you kidding me? No way. I high-tailed it out of there so fast you would think I had wings."

"Good. Thank you for telling me."

"Of course. You needed to know."

Stay calm. You haven't run into him yet. Maybe you won't. I attempt to positively talk through it, but it is not helping. My body feels stiff with worry. It's hard to breathe. I can't tell if I want to get in my car and go home or find a tight corner to curl up in. *What would happen if we ran into each other?*

We walk back inside. Cam runs at me, so I scoop him into my arms. I spin him around, putting him back into his highchair, so we can eat.

"Anything new this week?" Mom asks, grabbing a helping of salad.

Better just get it out there. I'm already a nervous wreck anyway after Gio's news. *Why not keep it going?*

"Well, I have some news," I say, fiddling with my fork.

"We are listening," Dad states, grabbing the bowl of mashed potatoes.

"So, I have been hanging out with Scarlett and Chris's friend the past few weekends."

"That's not news," Mom says, not understanding where this is going.

"Well, he took me on my dream date to go hiking and stayed the weekend at the house. He asked me to be his girlfriend. I said yes. He wants to meet all of you. I wanted to see if you could all be here next Saturday instead of Sunday to do so." I don't think I took a breath. If they managed to understand all of that, I will be stunned. I fork a mouthful of green beans into my mouth, smiling sweetly.

Everyone is staring at me around the table, except my nephew, Cam. The wonders of being a blissfully unaware toddler. My sister- in-law, Carly, has stopped mid-chew, Dad is looking up at the ceiling, Mom is looking at me with her head crooked to one side, and Gio is stifling a chuckle behind his hand.

"Your dream date is a hike?" Gio asks, breaking the silence with his best attempt at helping me. I may prefer country, but my brother is all city.

"I think it is sweet," Carly says, nodding a seal of approval. She knows how hard it is to keep me from the outside.

"Oh, I will meet him, alright." Dad gruffs.

"Meet, not kill." Mom chimes in.

"I'm not going to kill him. Then I would go to jail, and I have to be here in case your ex shows his face anywhere near any of us. Or have we forgotten about that?" Dad cuts his pork chop. He is one hundred percent serious.

Mom shakes her head in dismay about Dad's attitude. "We will meet him. I'm not fond of the idea that he is already staying at your house for the weekend." She raises an eyebrow in my direction. "But I trust your intuition."

Dad scoffs at that. She knows I have learned my lesson because she learned hers in the past. She glares at him menacingly. "You forget I met you not long after my life experiences, Gigi. We talked, and she was not looking for a new relationship. That's normally when you find the one you were supposed to be with. Wouldn't you agree?" Mom dares him to answer otherwise with a grand stare down.

Dad takes a bite of beans in response and nods silently, muttering under his breath.

"So, it's a plan then. Dinner next Saturday?" I ask sheepishly.

"We will be there." Carly pipes up excitedly.

"And we will all be open to it," Mom says, still staring at Dad.

***

"So, tell me about your week." Dr. Shots says after I got done with work on Monday. We used to meet in person, but meeting virtually has worked better. I look around at the lavender walls of my home office.

I proceed to tell him everything. There is no detail missed about the entire weekend. That is the wonderful thing about therapists. There is rarely anything you can't say to them. They aren't there to judge.

"Wow, so much to go over here. First, I am impressed with how open you are with him. Honesty and being vulnerable will only serve you both in the long run. How does it feel to be like that with him?"

"It actually feels terrific to have someone to whom I can reveal those parts of myself."

"How does he react?"

"He will, in turn, tell me something about himself or offer me comfort through words and physical affection."

"Do you see how healthy that is?"

"I do." I smile shyly.

"Now, did you initiate physical intimacy because you felt like that is what he wanted or because it is truly how you felt?"

This was a problem for me in the past. Not only did it take me a long time to get to that point with someone, but once I got to that point, I often felt like I did it just to make the guy happy because I thought that's all they wanted. This was different, though. I want every piece of Antonio. I can't get enough.

"For the first time, it truly felt like it was something I wanted to do. I felt it and just went for it. He asked me many times if I was ok with it."

"It sounds like you two are starting this relationship from a great point. There are open lines of communication, you obviously find unmeasurable comfort with him, and he seems to address your hesitations with a calming grace. How about your concerns with his zip code?"

I shift in my seat. Here comes the discomfort.

"We agreed to figure that out as we go along. He did say he is putting his dream to hike back to New York on hold, though."

"I think figuring it out together is a great idea. You do not have to have all the answers right now. You can make plans, but plans change. He could be deployed at the last minute. You could get in a car wreck. Plans are great, but take things a step at a time. It will reduce stress. I know you are religious, so I know, you know, you or he is not in control here. There are greater things at work."

"I needed that reminder. Thank you. It's hard not to fall back into the habit of planning to protect myself."

"You can't protect yourself from life. It will find a way to ruin or grant plans one way or another. Our time is up, but the same time next week?" Dr. Shots says, closing his notebook.

"Talk to you then."

CHAPTER 14

ANTONIO

"Meeting the fam already, huh?" Lee asks on Tuesday morning after we finished running a 5K around base.

"Earth to Marine. Most guys in our unit would already have the girl pregnant or married in base housing. In our world, I'm moving at a glacial pace." I say bent over with my hands on my knees, trying to catch my breath.

Of course, Captain Marine-ica over there isn't even breaking a sweat.

"Yeah, well, those Marines aren't getting out in less than a year, or is that no longer your plan?" Lee takes a sip from his water bottle from his gym bag.

"Depends. Am I talking to a sergeant or my puked-in-my-dresser-drawer drunk friend?" I say, raising an eyebrow to a reddening Lee.

"That wasn't my fault. You kept handing me shots of liquid marijuana. You know, blue curacao is my weakness. Besides the point, I have something to tell you. Well, two things, and as a sergeant."

And here we go…

"First, they have an offer for you to re-enlist. Pick of the station."

My ears perk up to that one. I could pick anywhere I've ever wanted to go. I could choose Hawaii if I wanted to. As much excitement washes over me, a sudden crashing wave of anguish hits me, too.

What about Aria?

"What is the second thing?" I say to a dismayed Lee. He definitely thought I would be happier about this. I know Lee doesn't want me to leave him behind. He gets out a year after me.

Lee sighs, looking out at the water of the Port Royal Sound shifting with the wind. His hands are on his hips. His broad, chiseled chest takes a breath and holds it before it caves in, letting it out slowly.

"We leave in six months for ITX. Twentynine Palms. It's a month and a half." He does not look me in the eye. Instead, he leans against his Jeep as if the run didn't take his energy, but having to tell me this news did.

ITX is supposed to test a unit's readiness level for warfare. Twentynine Palms is the military's version of hell on Earth. It is nothing but weeks of baking in the hot desert sun, isolation, and intense training. It is in California, on the opposite side of the country from where I live.

"I am supposed to potentially be discharged four months after that. You have to be kidding me. I can't get an exemption?" I throw my bag furiously into the backseat of my truck.

Part of me feels like I might hyperventilate, while another side wants to punch a hole in a wall. Equal parts anxiety and anger.

What does it matter if I might not even be here four months after it?
"I know I just threw a lot at you. Just think it all over." Lee gets in his Jeep, giving me a pat on the back, knocking me forward a step with his heavy hand.

I watch as he pulls away. Dread is not enough for what I feel about discussing this with Aria. We have been texting since the moment I got back to base. We don't even text goodnight anymore. It is more of a long-winded conversation piece that never ends until we see each other again. I don't want to tell her about these things over the phone. I want to say this to her in person.

The only thing that could make me feel better right now is knowing I can put a smile on my girl's face. I get in the truck. I picked up my phone, which I had left on the console, and looked up flower arrangement deliveries near Aria's school. In one of our many conversations, I found out she loves sunflowers. I ordered a bouquet to arrive at her school within an hour. I think I know my new nickname for her.

***

"Hey, Dad," I say once I return to my room. I decided to call my parents to tell them the news about me and Aria.

"Hey, son. What are you doing?" I can hear the lawnmower stop in the background.

"Just getting ready for tonight. I have a twenty-four-hour shift. I have some good news."

"Oh yeah, what's that?"

"I have been going back and forth to Charlotte the last few weeks after I met that girl I told you guys about."

"Aria?"

"Yes, Aria. Well, we are officially dating. I am meeting her parents this weekend."

"I think that is great! Granted, I'll never hear the end of it now from your mother about her being right." Dad chuckles. "When do we get to meet her?"

"I was thinking about surprising Mom for Mother's Day. She can meet everyone then."

Going back home means Aria would meet everyone. And I mean, everyone. Mom, Dad, my last remaining grandparent, and lifelong friends. I have one older half-sister, but she is traveling the world. My family is huge on truly experiencing everything the world has to offer. My parents own a hundred feet of lakefront property with about an acre of land that my dad's parents sold to them on their property. I loved growing up with my grandparents down the driveway. I want Aria to see and feel how I grew up, even though they are no longer living.

"We would love that. Looking forward to it. Don't worry, I won't tell your mom about the surprise visit."

My phone buzzes, and I can see I got a message from Aria.

"Perfect. I have to go, but I'll talk to you guys soon. Love you!"

"Love you too. Bye, Ant."

I hung up and opened the message from Aria. It is a photo of her with the sunflower bouquet, teary-eyed and smiling in her classroom. She sent a message too.

Aria

Thank you so, so much for my flowers. They are gorgeous. Your note was so sweet. I have not stopped thinking about this weekend either.

She sent a winky face, and I remembered the note I added. In the note, I told her how happy I was that she said yes to being my girlfriend and how unforgettable this past weekend was. That I couldn't stop thinking about it. It is true. It is all that is on my mind. I think of the hours of conversations covering everything from religion, politics, and family dynamics to simple things like favorite colors, sports teams, etc. I've never met someone more open, nor have I ever been so vulnerable with someone in my entire life. We've had deeper conversations in a few weeks than with friends I've known for years.

Antonio

I just wanted you to know I was thinking about you. Sunflowers always turn to and follow the sun throughout the day. Perfectly, it is your favorite flower because you always turn to the bright side of life. You constantly look for the good. I am glad that I could make you smile even from miles away.

Guess I found my nickname for her?

The rest of the week goes by in one exhausted blink. When I am on the road to Aria's, I drink multiple coffees to keep me vertical. When I walk up to her front door, I get a feeling I only have when I visit New York. It feels like the comfort of coming home.

Aria opens the front door, which leads into the kitchen. An all too familiar scent brushes against me, pasta. I don't see any on the stove, but the oven is on with ten minutes left counting down.

"It smells amazing in here," I say, placing my bag down and pulling Aria into my arms.

"Thank you." Aria flips her hair over her shoulders. "Sticking to our roots. It's stuffed shells. No homemade sauce, I'm afraid."

"I'm sure it is perfect. You are the only woman who has ever cooked for me like this besides my mother." That makes Aria giggle. "I appreciate it. I missed you."

I kiss her, wrapping her into me as tightly as possible. Every second of holding her makes the exhaustion shift into a ball of insurmountable lust, though having to drive here and back every weekend is already taking a toll. However, it is worth everything in me for this slice of heaven.

"You want to take this greeting to our room?" Aria says, leaning away, tugging towards the door of the kitchen.

I look at the timer on her meal. Eight minutes. She said, "Our room" already has me in all my feelings. It is her house, which she calls "our room."

"Aria, the things I want to do to you right now will take much longer than the eight minutes you have before that food comes out." I kiss her collarbone.

Aria turns as red as the tank top she has on.

"I think I am the one who owes you after that bouquet you sent me. The number of husbands and boyfriends you got in trouble that day is unreal." Aria says, pointing to the sunflowers I didn't notice sitting on the bistro table.

"What do you mean?"

"The flowers came during lunch to the front office. Our secretaries were freaking out about how cute and sweet it was, so they came running into the cafeteria with it. Two grade levels' worth of kids, teachers, and other cafeteria staff witnessed the whole thing. All the other teachers were so mad that their significant others had never done something like that. My students came running over and everything. You caused quite the uproar." Aria says, blushing again.

"Good. Let everyone see. You deserve to be made a spectacle of."

"What did I do to deserve you?" Aria says, placing her forehead to mine.

"You did nothing to deserve me. I must have done something right to be rewarded with you."

CHAPTER 15

ARIA

Prior to Antonio walking through the door, I felt like a mass of anxiety. With the family dinner pending and some hard decisions at work, this week felt like a giant adrenaline rush. I probably spent most of the week crying if it wasn't for the flowers. I am not someone who cries when I am sad. If I am crying, I am more than likely anxious, overwhelmed, or in absolute rage. At some point this week, I went through all three.

As if on cue, Antonio asks me how my week is going as we devour the stuffed shells.

"It was not the best, honestly. Your flowers were my only highlight, so receiving them made me even happier. I suspect one of my students is being abused. I had to call social services." I say, unable to look him in the eye.

This is the part of the job that is hard for a lot of people to hear. As a mandated reporter, making the judgment call that could strip a child from their family is not one that I take lightly. The girl I am referring to missed several school days this week. When she came back, she had a physical handprint across her face that you could see was disappearing as if it had been there for days and was fading away. I already had suspicions because she always had the same three tattered, dirty outfits, was never bathed, and would steal food whenever possible. Maybe her family just needed help, so I tried reaching out, but got no response. I bought her clothes, toothbrushes, hair supplies, etc. This was the last straw. I notified my administration multiple times, so they were fully supported. I explained all this to Antonio.

"I told you before. I don't know how you guys do it. I think you made the right call. I hope everything turns out ok. I will never understand parents like that. When I am a dad, I know my kids will be loved beyond measure. There won't be a doubt about it."

I'm pretty sure my ovaries just screamed, "I volunteer." Our eyes lock on one another. A slow smile creeps across his face at the realization that we are discussing kids. *Possibly one day, our kids? Focus Aria. Stay present in the here and now.*

"I know. I don't understand it either. Thank you. How about you? How was your week?"

Antonio wipes his mouth with his napkin. The energy shift is heavy. Clearly, I wasn't the only one who had an off week.

"I got a lot of news this week. My friend and sergeant, Lee, told me some things about my upcoming re-enlistment, amongst other things." He fiddles with his utensils, uneasy.

"By all means, leave out the details. Why don't you?" I tease, trying to lighten the mood. He smiles slightly, but it fades quickly.

"They told me I could pick stations if I re-enlist for another four years. I could go to any Marine base I want. I also discovered that even though I have less than a year left, I have to go to ITX for a month and a half in six months.

To go from a dream of a weekend to this mess of a week is one heck of a rollercoaster. Hearing this news, I want to scream. It's one of my biggest fears. The up in the air feeling of his location, career decision moves, and extensive time away from one another in a new relationship. However, "once a marine, always a marine." The military isn't just a career. It's a mindset, it's a lifestyle, you cut them, and their blood practically pours out scarlet and gold. This is something he must decide. I won't stand in the way of that.

"I will not tell you what to do about this decision. I am not even going to tell you what I think. I've watched how important this career and lifestyle are for my dad. I've seen that grown man who has never cried, cry over retiring. Whatever you decide, we can find a way to make it work. As for ITX, women out there kiss their husbands goodbye daily as they fight wars for months. If a month and a half break us, we weren't meant to be anyway." I grip one of his hands in mine and use the other to lift his eyes to mine so he can see that I mean every word.

"Oh, we are meant to be alright. I'll prove that right now."

Without hesitation, Antonio kicks the chair back and swoops me into a cradle hold, bolting for the couch.

"Let me show you," Antonio says tenderly, placing me on the couch.

***

We spent the rest of the night showing each other how right we are for one another with every square centimeter of our bodies. I even thanked him for the flowers he sent me this week. We were so tired we couldn't move from the living room to sleep in the actual bed. We threw down several blankets and couch pillows onto the floor. I giggle nonstop as we cuddle up to one another. Dianna nuzzles in next to us. At one point, she is lying entirely across Antonio's legs, pinning him in place. I convince her to move down, so she sprawls across the excess blankets near our feet. Before long, we both fall asleep cradled against one another.

***

Today is the day he gets to meet my parents. Part of it feels natural because I have lived at home for so long, and my parents have met everyone I have dated. A completely different side of me knows this will not be an easy feat for Antonio. My family is recovering along with me from my ex. I know he'll have to win them over in a big way for them to gain his trust. I'm just not sure how to help him prepare for it.

Antonio doesn't know yet, but the best thing I can do to calm my nerves is to get outside. Last week, he took me to one of his favorite hikes, and this time I want to take him with me to mine, Crowder's Mountain. This mountain has got me through the breakup of my college sweetheart, the escape from my latest ex, and has been my ultimate hangout spot with my friends for as long as I can remember.

I shimmy from under Antonio's arms. I let Dianna out into the backyard and tiptoed to the bedroom. My clothes from yesterday are all over the living room. I slip into a lilac athletic set before returning to the kitchen to prepare my most crucial day's meal, coffee.

Lorelai Gilmore would be proud.

When I sneak back into the living room, the blankets are neatly folded on the couch, our clothes are folded next to them, and the pillows are back in their appropriate spots. The scent of coffee permeates the air. Frank Sinatra is playing softly. I walk into the kitchen, arms crossed over my chest.

I might have an essential new meal for the day.

Antonio is shirtless at the stove with his sweatpants on. As much as I would love to say it's the smell of bacon making me drool in the doorway, it's not. It is him.

"You already won the boyfriend of the week award. You can chill for one morning and let me be the one to surprise you with coffee and breakfast." I say, placing my hands on my hips.

"I'm going for more than boyfriend of the week." Antonio winks my way. "I'm going for the best you've ever had. I intend to ruin all other men for you. Read into that however you prefer." He smirks slyly.

"You won that award in more ways than one." I wink back. "Guess you get a prize or something. Speaking of which, I am bringing you on a date before we meet my parents. We are going to my favorite hiking spot."

"Oh, you are bringing me on a date? Bring me up to the highest peak before my downfall and demise, meeting your parents. How kind of you." Antonio flips the bacon onto a plate.

I swat him in the stomach, making him drop a piece of bacon. Antonio had let Dianna back in earlier, so she caught it in her mouth before it could hit the floor.

We eat as I tell him about what to expect on the trail. I prepared a quick picnic lunch for us. We load up Dianna, food, and plenty of water.

We spent the ride with the windows down, blaring various music. Everything from *Bohemian Rhapsody* to my rendition of *This Is It* by Scotty McCreery. I don't know who loves life more: me, Antonio, or Dianna, blowing in the breeze with her head out the window.

We park after a nearly forty-five-minute drive. We waste no time as we venture on our way to the trailhead. After witnessing my clumsy nature last time, Antonio takes the lead with Dianna, trying to balance basic walking skills with her innate pulling uphill abilities.

Our time climbing the trail is filled with conversations about our childhoods. When he was younger, he loved to play baseball. He was a pitcher, but any hope of wanting to play futuristically ended with a hurt shoulder. His cousin was married to a Marine when his military exposure began. We are nearing the peak when he tells me how he stunned his parents with his news of being recruited. His parents were on vacation, thinking he was away at community college. The next thing they knew, they were getting a call from him letting them know he had dropped out and would be attending basic training soon. When you hear about surprises and the military, it is usually a happy surprise homecoming. Not, "surprise, I am leaving the state and won't be able to talk to you for a few months unless it's by mail." I couldn't imagine making or receiving that phone call.

"This view is something else. You can see the city from here." Antonio says, pointing to Charlotte in the distance when we reach the top.

Large boulders jut out from the bright orange clay around us. Pine trees stand tall, stretching to the sky, while hawks fly directly over us. You can see far into the horizon where the city peaks from the tree tops miles away. The vibrant blue of the sky contrasts with the lush greenery around us. It's a straight drop down from where we sit, but it only adds to the glory of reaching the top.

"Welcome to my other happy place. I will be here or in my books if you want me. There isn't much in between." We sit on a large rock away from enough of the other hikers to get some semblance of solitude.

I pull out the picnic lunch. We eat like we haven't eaten in days. Hiking can do that to you.

"I do all my best thinking up here. This mountain has heard my prayers, absorbed my tears in its dirt, echoed my laughter, and given me an escape from city living." I bite my sandwich while watching Dianna lap from her collapsible water bowl.

"I can certainly see why. I would be here all the time if I lived here." Antonio says, taking a swig of his Camelbak.

A heaviness hangs in the air at the reminder that he doesn't live here, and we don't know what that part of the future could look like.

"How about you tell me a little more about your family? What should I expect tonight? Give it to me straight. Don't sugarcoat it for me."

"Well, you will meet my mom. She is the older-looking version of me. Think of Jennifer Garner and her daughter. My mom's name is Tula. She is what we would call your typical southern belle. She takes her chicken fried and her water as lemonade. My dad, Giovanni, on the other hand, you can call him Gigi. You have heard a little about him when we met at the White-Water Center. Remember? The para-weatherman who spent over thirty years in the Air National Guard. He will be the tough one. He took things the toughest. He and my mom had encouraged me in different ways at different points in my last relationship. They have taken on some responsibility for what happened because of that. They didn't know what was happening, though. I hid it well. He isn't much of a talker, so don't be surprised if he doesn't talk much."

"Great. World's shortest relationship on account of me being killed by your father." Antonio scoffs with a smirk, playfully bumping into my shoulder.

"He isn't going to kill you." I laugh. "He said he can't go to jail in case my ex ever shows up." I shrug matter-of-factly.

"Thank you for that calming sentiment," Antonio says, playfully pushing my shoulder.

"You will also meet my adorable nephew and godson, Cam. He is the smartest two-year-old you will ever meet. My sister-in-law, Carly, is the most creative person I know. She can figure out how to make just about anything. She is one of the best cooks and bakers around. My mouth is watering just thinking about some of her dishes. Show her a photo of anything you want made, and she will build, cook, or draw it. My brother, Giovanni junior, is called Gio. He is a jack of all trades. He is great at everything you wouldn't even think about. He plays the drums, is wicked good at cornhole, and can debate you on any topic any time."

"They sound like fun," Antonio says, throwing Dianna the last piece of his sandwich.

"They are the best. My brother has always been my best friend. Other than Scarlett, of course. We talk about everything. Nothing is off limits. He's the first person I call for advice. I've always looked up to him." I smile, looking out into the vast expanse of mountains. "Speaking of which. We should finish here and head back to get cleaned up before we go."

We spent the rest of our picnic finishing our food and looking at the world. Hawks soar overhead. Dianna lifts her head, enjoying the breeze. Once we finish our food, we pack up and quickly head back down the mountain to the car.

Time for him to meet the Italians.

CHAPTER 16

ANTONIO

I would never admit this to anyone, but I am freaking out over this family meeting. This is not your typical meet and greet. This family has been put through the ringer. They are going to be protective. They will be three times as protective because she jumped into a relationship so soon after the fact, with yet another military member. I am not even an inactive Marine. I am a full-fledged, active-duty Marine who can deploy at any time.

On the way, we stop to pick up some cannolis, a bouquet of flowers, and a new small soccer ball for Cam. We approach the house, an inviting ranch with blossoming pink-flowered bushes framing the front entrance. Aria squeezes my hand with a reassuring smile. She leans over the center console and kisses me on the cheek.

"Let's do this," I say, grabbing the goodies.

We walk up to the door. Aria doesn't knock. She doesn't ring the doorbell. She just walks right in, holding the door open for me to walk through. I give her a confused glance. Aria waves me on to come the rest of the way in.

"We're here," Aria calls out into the house.

"Zia!" Cam shouts, running into Aria's outstretched arms.

"Hey, guys," Carly says, walking up behind him with Gio trailing her.

"Guys, this is Antonio. Antonio, this is Carly, Gio, and Cam." I shake their hands and give Carly her half of the bouquet I picked out, pink roses.

"Aw, thank you so much. Very sweet." Carly says, smelling her flowers.

"And Cam, this is for you, buddy," I say, handing him the soccer ball.

"What do you say, bud?" Gio prompts.

"Thank you!" Cam grabs the soccer ball and jumps out of Aria's grip. Cam takes off with Carly and Gio behind him, mouthing apologies for the shortened greeting.

"Hey, honey!" Aria's parents come out of their bedroom. I suddenly feel overdressed. Everyone is in shorts or blue jeans with T-shirts. I am the only one in khaki pants with a blue collared shirt, other than Aria, in a yellow floral maxi dress.

"Mom, Dad, this is Antonio," Aria says, hugging each of them.

"Pleasure to meet you both. You have a lovely home." I shake their hands and give Tula her flowers.

"These are beautiful. Aria must have told you about the roses. You can call me Tula." Tula chirps as she heads to the kitchen for a vase.

Gigi eyes me with an intensity so strong I am tempted to bolt out the door.

"I don't think Aria told me anything about roses," I say, trying to initiate conversation.

"I buy roses every year for Aria on her birthday. One rose for each year she has been the biggest part of our world. I'm the man who bought her roses first." Gigi says curtly. "My name is Gigi." He extends his hand to shake. I shake his hand, but feel like his tight grip will rip it clean off my arm. I quickly pull away.

Already stepping on toes. I am on a roll.

Aria smacks herself in the head and mouths "sorry" to me behind her dad's back.

"Let's sit. You can tell me all about yourself." Gigi says, heading to the dining room table.

Let the grilling begin.

"Well, my life has been pretty mellow," I say, sitting beside Aria, who rubs my thigh reassuringly. "Grew up with my mom, dad, and half- sister. She is older and currently traveling the world. My family is full blood Italian. I was raised Catholic and regularly attended until my confirmation. I went to community college. One day, I decided it wasn't for me and joined the Marines."

"What is your military occupational specialty?" Gigi asked before I had a chance to say anything else.

"I am a motor transport operator. I did a few months as military police, too."

"What are your intentions with my daughter?"

It is like my brain is a train that has gone off the rails, flipped over, and caught on fire. Though I partially expected this and prepared some mental notes, I am taken aback by the utter fury with which Aria's dad spits questions. He doesn't process one before he is ready with another. It is like a dang question machine gun. He just dropped a bomb.

"Give him a minute to breathe," Tula says with the rest of the family trailing behind her.

"Yeah, dinner still has a few minutes. How about we grab a cigar out back while the ladies relax inside. You like cigars?" Gio asks, pulling a few nubs from his pants pocket while his son continues to play with his new ball.

"I do," I say, standing up and accepting one. "Thank you."

"Come on, there, killer." Gio pats Gigi on the back, handing him a cigar as well.

Aria squeezes my hand. Worry and anxiety plague her eyes. She is worried about how I am taking this. I can tell. I lightly kiss her forehead and whisper, "I got this. It's ok" in her ear before I head out back with the guys.

We each take a seat overlooking the pool in the backyard. Cam comes out with us and is busy with a bubble machine.

"I am not trying to be off-putting. I am sure Aria has told you about her past. Her mother and I feel partially responsible. We always encouraged her to see the good in others. With her ex, it was the equivalent of telling her to see the good in the Devil. I promised myself the next man would know I will not make the same mistake twice. If I suspect anything is wrong, my presence in your life will be well known." Gigi says, biting the end of his cigar.

Who bites the end off their cigars? Where is the cigar cutter?

"She told me a lot of what happened. I am sure there is stuff I still don't know about. I have every intention of being the man she has been looking for. Your daughter is intelligent, genuine, caring, and beautiful. She doesn't need a man in her life. She is self-sufficient. You asked about my intentions. My intention is to date your daughter. Show her that she deserves respect and love and that somebody can protect her. My intention is to be her best friend. The person she calls when she has the best day of her life or the worst. My intention is to show this family that they never have to worry about her again because I will never hurt her or let anybody do anything to her again. This isn't a fling for me. It is serious. Neither of us was looking for this. It just happened. I feel like that's how I know this is something special. Does that answer your question?"

Gio takes a puff of his cigar, but I can tell it is to keep from laughing. He nods his head and lifts his cigar towards me with approval. Gigi doesn't even notice because he is staring at me. The muscles in his jaws tick. I swear I see him fight back a tear.

"Seems like the payback of his questioning technique got his tongue, so I will answer for him," Gio says, handing Gigi a lighter. "After that, I will let you date my wife and tell Cam to call you daddy. Geez, man."

Clearly, I said something right because the next thing I knew, we were giving each other a hard time over everything from sports teams to Gigi making all the typical military rivalry jokes. By the time we head back inside, the ice king of a father has turned into a boisterous, laughing giant. Aria is sitting on the couch with Carly and Tula, looking at me, confused when we walk back in, smiling ear to ear.

"Told you they needed that time," Tula says, looking at Aria.

"I guess they did." Aria smiles.

I sit beside her on the gray sectional couch, putting my arm around her shoulders. She leans back against my arm. I instantly feel her melt in comfort.

"Seems like you won him over. What did you do?" Aria whispers to me while everyone starts getting dinner sorted on the counter for a buffet-style meal.

"I was just honest about every single one of my intentions towards you. Plus, when all else fails, there is nothing like bonding over a mutual rivalry between branches or baseball teams." I smirk while Aria stifles a giggle.

Relief crashes over me, and I realize I've just taken my first deep breath since stepping over the house's threshold. Cam comes over with the ball and playfully tosses it my way. I pretended it hit me like a ton of bricks, grasping at my chest and falling onto Aria's lap. She laughs and fakes concern over me. Cam giggles as I roll the ball back to him across the floor. We spend the next few minutes in a back-and-forth game of this. Carly watches on, smiling at Cam from across the room in one of the armchairs.

"Everything is done, people. Let's eat!" Gigi shouts from the kitchen.

Shouting is Gigi's normal talking voice. He really is your typical New York Italian. Cut that man open, and I am sure his mom's pasta sauce and limoncello pour out instantaneously.

We all sit at the table and pray over the meal, holding hands. Aria is to my left, and her mom is to my right at the head of the table. Gigi is at the other end. Cam, Gio, and Carly sit across from us.

"Can I just say it is refreshing to see Aria with someone who actually enjoys doing what she likes to do?" Carly says as we eat and pass plates around.

"True. I was losing hope." Gio says, handing Cam some fried chicken from his place.

The table is filled with typical southern cooking, from fried chicken to collard greens. Aria hit the nail when she said her mom was a southern belle type.

"You? I believe I was firmly set in my resting biscuit face that told every man to leave me alone. I never thought I would see the day." Aria bites her corn on the cob.

"Biscuit?" I question.

"It's my stand-in word for a certain b word I can't say around Cam," Aria whispers. "We have a lot in common. I know more about him in weeks than guys I've dated for years. We have discussed a lot. It's easy to do when all you can do is talk on the phone or text due to the long distance. We've covered a lot of ground."

"Oh, really? Carly says with a mega watt smile.

"Here we go," Aria says, rolling her eyes.
"Dream dog?" She says, beginning an endless question round.

"Easy. Same for both of us. Though Dianna is the best. We both want a German Shepherd." I answer without hesitation. "Although she did mention something called a pomsky?" Aria nods her head with approval.

"Nicknames for each other?" Carly quirks an eyebrow.

"And please, nothing from the bedroom." Gio chimes in with his two cents.

If. Looks. Could. Kill.

Gigi is glaring at me from the head of the table. I think I feel a hole burning in my cheek. It is as if he is daring me to say it. The grip on his fork has me wondering how many different ways he could kill me with it. Aria is so red I wonder if she is choking because she can't breathe. Tula sits with a hand to her forehead, questioning her life choices. Carly smacks Gio in the back of the head, giggling, making Cam copy the motion on his other side.

"He calls me AJ or my new favorite, sunflower," Aria says, trying to break the tension, but I can tell she is wrecked by how hard she squeezes my hand under the table.

"Why sunflower?" Tula asks genuinely interested.

"Like the flower, she always turns to face the bright side in every situation. She radiates beauty and rises above the rest." I say, smiling in Aria's direction.

"And you can water her seeds," Gio says, biting into his chicken.

"Ok, that's enough with the Q and A session." Tula gives Gio a disappointed glare.

"I think next time I'll just set your dinner up outside with the gutter since that is where your mind has a permanent residence anyway." Aria bites out.

"It was a joke, people. Relax." Gio rolls his eyes.

CHAPTER 17

ARIA

Thankfully, Antonio's nickname answered, we got dinner back on track, and we finished without a hitch. I'll give it to him. The man has a way with words. He completely swooned my mother and semi-won over my father. Gio and he are comfortable with his willingness to bring up "jokes" during an initial meeting dinner.

Overall, I would call this a successful night. Watching Antonio play with my nephew tonight too....

Oh. My. Ovaries.

After dinner, we say goodbye and head home. As great as tonight was, I am suddenly feeling a pit of anxiety boiling in my stomach. My brain feels as if it is attacking itself, waiting to see what Antonio thought about my family.

Was my dad over the top for him?

Were Gio's jokes too much?

Was it too soon to meet them?

Are we going too fast?

Hello, spiraling thought storm of doom. It's me again.

I realize how quiet I am.

"So, that's the family." I laugh nervously. "When you return to base, please lock my doors first."

"You don't have to do that." Antonio pulls the truck out of my parents' neighborhood.

"Remind you about my safety?"

"No, you don't have to try to joke because you think I am

going to leave or that I didn't have a good time."

Who is joking?

"I just know it can be a bit much meeting any family. Especially mine. You didn't mind the jokes from Gio?" I look down at my hands on my lap.

"Aria, did you forget my occupation? If that's bad, remind me not to let you around any sizeable group of Marines. If it wasn't for your dad plotting ways to end me, I would have been dying laughing." Antonio unbuttons his collared shirt's top few buttons and partially rolls the windows down.

"Right. My dad wasn't overkill?"

"I'm alive, aren't I?" Antonio looks over with a smirk. Dimples are set to kill shot. "He is a protective, Italian father. It's in his DNA. Wait until you meet my dad. He may be fun-sized, but he is scrappy. Speaking of which, I have something to ask you."

"Go for it."

"How would you like to meet my family? Feel down for a road trip to New York for Mother's Day?

My brain is high-pitched screaming in fear and saying yes simultaneously. I am going to need a serious therapy session this week. My mind is unhinged.

"Yes." That is all I can manage.

"Don't throw a party over it." He quips sarcastically.

"Sorry. I am just feeling very anxious. Not sure why. I would love to meet your family. That is several weeks from now, though. What are your thoughts about seeing each other before then?" Anxiety builds and builds at the idea of not seeing him for weeks in such a new relationship.

"You don't need to be nervous. They will love you. As for next week, I was going to see if you would want to visit the base."

"How would I get on? I don't have a dependent card for your base. Plus, I am not dependent on you anyway to get one."

"Yet." Antonio looks over at me, dead serious.

"One step at a time, killer." Deep down, the hint of a possibility of us ending up together for the long haul is somewhat settling my nerves. The way his mouth quirks up on one side makes me swoon in my seat.

"I will meet you at the gate. Just make sure to have your license ready. I will book a hotel for us for the weekend. Could I try to sneak you in? Yes. Do I feel like getting demolished on a surprise field day? Absolutely not. With my luck, it would be Lee. Just to mess with me, he would white glove test my room because of you."

"Earth to Marine. Civilian speak. My dad didn't live in the barracks while I've been alive. Explain, please." We pull into our neighborhood. For the first time, I almost slipped into my mind, thinking, 'our neighborhood.'

"Every Thursday, my unit has a field day. We have to clean our rooms spotlessly. Friday, they come and check our rooms for cleanliness. Some people will wear a white glove and run a finger over your furniture to check for dust. They find that you, and possibly your whole unit, pay for it with excessive physical training. Or as I call it, physical torture."

"That doesn't sound like the field day I am used to. Where is the fire truck coming to spray you all down with water or the class competitive games?" We burst into fits of laughter, pulling into the driveway.

"Fire truck at the school, huh? I bet the teachers all go crazy over the firefighters."

Do I hear a tinge of jealousy?

"Yeah, but I already have a man in uniform." I lean over the console and kiss him with enough passion to stifle his jealous thoughts. "Next weekend, when I see you in it. I'll show you how 'crazy' we teachers can be." I wink, edging out of the truck. I wave him on teasingly to follow me inside. "I want to show you my version of field day," I call over my shoulder as I sprint inside.

***

The early morning sun peeks through the blinds. Antonio has his arms firmly wrapped around my shoulders. My leg is draped over him as I am nestled into his side. The only thing ruining this spectacular moment is my work email popping up on my cell phone.

Why did I add work emails to my phone? It's probably a parent.

Antonio must get used to being with a teacher and the students' parents. I have received emails as late as ten at night on weekends and as early as five in the morning. They all want an email back immediately on what they deem essential. However, those critical emails end up being questions about wanting to know if I have seen a missing jacket or water bottle. Apparently, kids aren't the only ones who think teachers live in the school. As a matter of principle, I make it a firm mission to not stay at work longer than necessary. We are paid too little, with no overtime, to stay at school as late as I have seen teachers. I would rather get to work a little early every day than be emotionally and mentally depleted trying to stay focused enough to be productive after the kids go home.

"Whoever is trying to get hold of you so early on a weekend morning needs to get in line." He grumbles, turning to face me, and clutches me into his chest.

"I have to check that." I push out breath, attempting to pry my way out of his firm grip.

Antonio grumbles, letting me go. I grab my phone and open the email. Scarlett is up to date because she is on the email already and has sent a message.

To: AriaJ.Pecorelli@uhes.k12.nc.us

CC: ScarlettM.Benning@uhes.k12.nc.us

Subject: Monday Morning Meeting

Good morning,

I hope you are having a restful weekend. I need to see both of you in my office as soon as you arrive on campus on Monday morning. I have an essential request to ask of you both.

See you tomorrow!

Grant Tanner, M. Ed

Principal

University Heights Elementary School

Can I not get one day from the crushing panic of what-ifs?

I roll my shoulder like I am about to be the first at bat in the World Series. Antonio went into the bathroom, leaving me to answer back. Scarlett responded, saying she would be in by six-thirty. After the taxing morning commute in Charlotte, it can take me anywhere from thirty minutes to an hour to get to the school. I decided that I was going to shoot in the middle of that.

To: GrantD.Tanner@uhes.k12.nc.us

CC: ScarlettM.Benning@uhes.k12.nc.us

Subject: Reply- Monday Morning Meeting

Good morning,

I will be happy to meet you as soon as I arrive. I should be arriving by six forty-five. I look forward to hearing about your request.

Thank you for your time,

Aria Pecorelli

2nd-grade teacher

University Heights Elementary School

I groan, turning my face into my pillow.

"What's wrong?" Antonio sits beside me on the bed, rubbing

my back. If I wasn't slowly experiencing my chest getting tighter by the second, I would pull him back down to the bed with me after peeking enough to see his black basketball shorts and bare chest.

"My principal wants to see me and Scarlett in his office bright and early."

"Ok. And that's bad, right? Is it bad if you're an adult and get sent to the principal's office?"

I try to bite back a laugh, turning to face him. "It can be."

"Ah. It can be. Doesn't mean it will be. Where is my sunflower?" Antonio coos, brushing his lips against my ear. "Think with facts. How often have you been called to meet him, but it turns out to be some trouble?"

"Once. If even."

"See. He said it is a request. I doubt it is anything horrible."

"You are right. Probably taking on another student or having to help with test proctoring."

"Would you look at that? The sunflower found the sun again." Antonio kisses my forehead. "I hate to say it, but I must get ready to go."

I unwillingly get up and get ready for the day. We take our time cooking breakfast together and drinking coffee on the patio. Minus the massive amount of pollen, Carolinas in April and May are the equivalent of Heaven on Earth. It is a beautiful Carolina blue sky day with a slight breeze to keep it cool. The steam of our coffee waves in the wind.

When we finish chit-chatting, Antonio gives me a lingering kiss goodbye. He leaves, taking a piece of my heart with him. Something about this weekend feels like a game-changer. Watching him fit seamlessly into my family was like watching my life in an out-of-body experience. I revel in it. I am not just liking and crushing on Antonio anymore. It's bigger than that.

***

"Aria!" Scarlett called down the hallway of the front office the next morning. She leaned against the wall, her hair in a messy bun, spinning her Syracuse University lanyard and wearing a yellow striped dress.

"Hey. Did you go in yet?" I point to Mr. Tanner's office.

"No, he has been on the phone since I arrived."

"Any idea what this could be about?" I pull on my retractable pencil lanyard repetitively.

"No clue."

"Mrs. Benning, Miss Pecorelli, come in, please." Mr. Tanner swings open the door as if on cue. "Hope you ladies had a good weekend."

"I know Miss Pecorelli did." Scarlett quips, holding back a grin.

I shoot Scarlett my best 'not right now' glare, but she bites her lip, holding back a laugh.

"That's great. Let's jump right into it. I have a student teacher, and I want you two to share the responsibility for showing her what University Heights and teaching are all about. She will get to see two different grade levels and teaching styles. It's perfect."

"I am not off my probationary license yet." I am confused about how to perform such a task when I am not experienced enough.

"I'm aware. My usual candidates I would ask to do this will not be available. Mrs. Yates will go out on maternity leave here soon. Mr. Kent is going on medical leave for surgery, and Miss Davidson…well, she said it's her last year before retirement, so no. You are in your third year of teaching and already outscoring most teachers beyond your tenure. Your students' growth scores are exceptional. You are timely, lead many different functions of the school, and I think you are fully capable of handling yourself, Aria."

So it is not really a request. It's more of a must. Oh, and I was the last choice. But a good one. I agree with him there.

"If we are handing out compliments, then waiter, I would like to order a round, please." Scarlett chimes in, breaking the ice, swirling a finger in the air.

"Of course, Scarlett. Your students have also always performed with above-average results. Their growth is phenomenal. You can form true, lasting relationships with your students. You can be a teacher, mentor, and, dare I say, a friend."

"When you put it like that. I obviously must accept." Scarlett clutches her chest, pretending to shed a small tear. "I'll make this sacrifice for the sake of education. It's my duty."

"Me too. What's her name?" I shake my head at Scarlett's antics but can't help smiling.

"Cassidy Adams. She starts tomorrow. She will be finishing out the year between you ladies. It will be great for her to see what Miss Pecorelli is doing in second grade and then go to Mrs. Benning to see how that transfers to third."

As he finishes explaining logistically how Cassidy will be splitting time between us, the bell rings to start the day. He wishes us a good day and sends us on our way. I check my phone to see that Antonio messaged me at exactly six forty-five when the meeting started.

Antonio

Good morning, sunflower. I hope you slept well and had an even better meeting this morning. I will call tonight to see how it went, but I feel it was great. Talk to you then.

I sent him a quick message to let him know it went better than expected, and I look forward to talking tonight.

"Nothing like an ego boost before work. If I had a confidence inflation session from the boss every morning, I could probably teach sixty kids how to read Chinese at once." I tell Scarlett as we walk down the hall towards our classes. Our classrooms face each other from across the hall.

"You don't read Chinese," Scarlett says, confused.

"Exactly. But having a nice ego boost now and again could make me." I turn into my room, ready to greet my students.

I tell my students all about the idea of having a student teacher in the room with us. I love the radiant positivity of children. You would have thought I told them a Disney princess and Spider-Man were coming to join us for the rest of the year. The more they ask questions, the more excited I am.

As a teacher in the middle of a state-wide shortage, knowing there are still young, bright, creative minds that want to join us is a blessing. Accepting being a mentor will help the fact that we do not have full-time assistants. I wish I had her at the beginning of this year, but April to June is still a long time.

***

"Aria, nice to see you again. Tell me about your week." Dr. Shots grabs his notebook behind him via Skype.

I tell him everything from Antonio meeting my family to his possible re-up. I explain the massive amount of anxiety that has settled over me, that lingers at a low hum.

"Do me a favor. Tell me your, let's say, five-year plan."

"I want to be married, have a kid or two by then, and excel at my job."

"Ok. What if you or your partner are unable to have kids?" He jots down notes.

"Geez. Harsh." I am in disbelief at how off-the-cuff he is.

"I'm trying to prove a point. You can plan everything, but what if Antonio isn't the one, and you don't meet the one within that time? If you do, what if you can't have kids? What if you get in a car crash and can't work for an extended period?"

"Can we get to a happier point? I thought therapy was supposed to lessen anxiety."

"Aria, part of your anxiety is that he may mess up this unspoken plan of his staying around. Possibly moving in is a thought, right?"

Not that I want to admit it, but it has been a nagging subconscious thought that Antonio could take the honorable discharge and move in at the end of his current contract.

"I think you also worry that his being away at ITX for a month and a half could make him lose interest. To me, this is more about seeing your own worth. Do you think you are worth coming back for and staying faithful to?"

"I struggle with that," I admit, hanging my head. "I think I am struggling with the idea of us getting closer. I've never been in a long-distance relationship like this. It challenges everything in me to deal with my trust issues. It's funny, though." I ponder.

"What's funny?"

"Physically, the relationship is forced to slow down in a sense, but the head and my heart. No way. My head and heart are first out of the plane. They are skydiving to the ground with no parachute. No safety net."

"Say it." Dr. Shots arches an eyebrow with a sly grin.

"Say what?"

"You are falling in love with Antonio. That's what scares you. You are feeling more and therefore have more to lose. It's fear."

I haven't said this out loud yet. I've also never been the one to admit that kind of emotion first. The only other time I've ever felt anything close to love was in college. Not even my most recent ex. Even back then, it didn't feel like this. I've never hit it off with someone so easily and felt so understood. It is as if he understands my very soul. I guess that's what happens when distance forces you to do nothing but talk and get to know every part of one another.

"I am falling in love with Antonio."

***

"Hi, I'm Cassidy."

I'm shaking hands with the peppiest blonde with chocolate brown eyes. For a second, I thought my favorite actress, Hilary Duff, graced my doorway with her presence. When I arrived at my usual time this morning, she was already waiting at my door with a large tote hung over her denim jacketed shoulder.

"Hey! I am Aria. Nice to meet you." I shake her hand and unlock the door. "I cleared a table for you to make a work area for yourself. Feel free to make the space your own."

"You're so nice. Thank you so much! Anything you need, I'm here to learn, but I'm also here to help. You need copies, a bathroom break, whatever. I'm your girl. I'm ready to hear every scrap of advice you have."

The golden retriever of student teachers. Live and in person.

"I'll do all I can to teach you what I have learned… and unlearned." I let out a small chuckle. Granted, this is only year three for me, so take it with a grain of salt. Mrs. Benning will also be a significant source of knowledge for you."

"What's first on the to-do list this morning?" Cassidy places her tote on the rolling chair behind her table, placing her hands on her hips.

I hand her a box of unsharpened pencils. We start getting the room prepped for the student's arrival. As predicted, you would think I told my students that Bluey was a new teacher in our room. They were so excited to meet our student teacher and asked her way too many invasive questions about her life. By the time we got to lunch, I knew she was single, owned a cat named Phil (*funny name for a cat*), and was a big-time country music fan.

When we got to lunch, a handful of students had already convinced her to eat lunch with them. She needed to warm her lunch, and I needed a bathroom break. I show her to the teacher's lounge. It is small with two fridges, a drink machine, a snack vending machine, a small table with chairs, and a single bathroom. I head into the bathroom while she uses the microwave. I hear two people enter and greet Cassidy.

"Hello, who do we have here?" I hear the voice of Ms. Taylor.

Ms. Taylor teaches fifth grade, is a widow, and is vocal about her nearing retirement. We only see each other at staff meetings because she teaches upper grades in a separate building. Our class schedules never cross. If she is in here, then Mrs. Finley is not far behind. They are two peas in a pod. Same grade level, same retirement plan, but Mrs.

Finley has been *unhappily* married for thirty years.

"Haven't seen you before." I hear Mrs. Finley. I can practically hear how she scans Cassidy's whole frame searching for flaws.

"I am Cassidy. I am the student teacher for Miss Pecorelli and Mrs. Benning." Cassidy says brightly. I try to hurry out of the bathroom when I hear what is said next.

"Ah. Miss Pecorelli." Mrs. Finley sneers. "Have to mind what you learn from her, I'm afraid."

"Yes, I overheard her and Mrs. Benning one day discussing how she just got out of an abusive relationship. She is already in another rebound relationship. I saw it on social media. Poor guy probably doesn't even know he is the rebound. Suddenly, it seems she is all interested in the outdoors." Ms. Taylor hisses.

"Changes with the wind, that one. Seems she is just looking for marriage. If she makes those life choices, who knows what kind of teacher she is? Know what we mean?" Mrs. Finley continues.

It is like someone stabbed me in the chest while stomping on my foot. You can hear a pen drop. I take a few deep breaths and edge out of the bathroom door into the lounge. Cassidy is facing me with a face like she has seen a ghost. She is so visibly uncomfortable, her shoulders nearly surpass her ears. Her hands rigidly clasp her steaming meal. I know the back of Mrs. Finley's brown bob and Ms. Taylor's long gray hair.

"Cassidy," I say calmly. Ms. Taylor and Mrs. Finley stiffen before turning to face me as their faces redden. I pretend not to notice them. "You mentioned how you wanted advice earlier. I thought of my first bit. Keep to your room and your students as much as possible. Avoid the lounge as much as you can. It's something I learned far too late and obviously recently." I eye the two elder staff members, but they look away as our eyes meet. "The lounge is often filled with unwarranted and unfounded gossip. The students were excited to have lunch with you. Why don't you go ahead? I'll meet you there."

Cassidy doesn't waste another second. She lowers her head and rushes out the door toward the lunchroom. I wait a second for shame to fall over the teachers before me.

"Thank you," I say, utterly confusing them. They look at each other, dumbfounded.

"For?" Mrs. Finley says, crossing her arms over her chest.

"Saved me time telling someone my life story. Now, I can focus on training the next generation of students and teachers instead of reliving my past. Way to show her what not to do." I wash my hands as I say it, staring them down through the reflection in the mirror. "You ladies have a great day." I dry my hands and walk out without bothering to look back.

***

"I'm sorry I wasn't there to help you," Antonio says through FaceTime later that evening. He is lying in his bunk with his arm leaning back on his headboard. "It sounds like you handled it well, though."

"It's not true, you know. I don't want to just find someone and get married. I was literally thrown around in my own home. I had no intention of any of this. You're not a rebound." I fight back tears.

"Aria. I know that. I know what I feel and see. I don't need convincing. Don't let two jealous gossips fill your head with nonsense. Also, give me some credit here. You think I would have stuck around if I suspected that?"

"I know." I sigh, lying back on my bed.

"How did the student teacher handle it?"

"Well. She apologized six thousand times. I kept telling her she didn't have to apologize, but she kept saying it anyway. Until it was Scarlett's turn to have her, in which case Scarlett told her, 'My first piece of advice is to stop apologizing.'"

"Ah, Scarlett. This wisest of us all." Antonio jokes.

"Beyond her years smart for sure. Anyway, I am excited for this weekend." I smile at the thought of being next to Antonio right now.

"Me too. Just remember, it's the Marines. I am not responsible for any obscene, vulgar, or idiotic things you hear from anyone this weekend. Especially Lee." Antonio wipes his hand over his face as if mere thought is already stressing him out.

"I can handle myself."

"Yeah. We will see, I guess."

CHAPTER 18

ANTONIO

I stand waiting at the base gate for Aria to arrive. I am pretty sure I am making our military police concerned for my mental state as I pace back and forth on the small bit of pavement. A few minutes pass, but I see her blue Chevy Cruise turn onto our road.

I wave, grinning so hard my jaw hurts. I see her excited wave through the windshield. One of the military police steps outside the guard shack and asks for her license as she pulls up next to us. She hands him the permit. I slide into the passenger seat. He lets us through. I lean over and kiss her cheek.

"Hey, sunflower." I squeeze her hand, giving it a soft kiss across her knuckles.

"Hey." She smiles sweetly. "Where to?"

"My room. I need to change out of my cammies." I pull at my green, tan, and black camo uniform.

"Wow. At least take a girl to dinner first. I know it's a fantasy of mine to finally see you in this uniform, but dang boy." Aria says sarcastically.

Aria slams on the brakes as a tall frame runs in front of the car.

Lee.

"You have a death wish or something, you moron?" I shout at Lee as I roll down the window.

Lee only laughs and invites himself into the car, hopping in the backseat. Lee grabs my shoulders from behind and shakes me.

"So, this is Aria?" Lee says, looking at Aria like she is a snack.

"You must be Lee. Nice to see you are exactly as I thought you would be." Aria says, catching her breath and continuing to drive forward.

"She just got here. You couldn't have waited to be introduced for a few minutes?" I ask, annoyed.

"Ah, that's as long as you can last?" Lee says with mock sadness for me.

Rage. Pure rage. He is lucky we are friends at his point, or I would be getting myself a nice disciplinary write-up for fighting a sergeant. Aria speaks first before I can even think of something to say back.

"Aw, Lee, are we already having our first 'who hurt you moment?'" Aria touches her heart.

Lee sits back in his seat and smirks.
"Oh, too close to home for this guy. We wouldn't have enough time to go down the list." I say, looking over my shoulder as we near my barracks room. "Not that you would know. He doesn't exactly open up to many people."

"I'm just making sure our girl here can handle the lifestyle. You know, for when you decide to re-up." I sense Aria's tension as her shoulders go stiff and her knuckles whiten on the steering wheel.

"I can handle the military. My dad spent over thirty years in the Air Force and the National Guard." Aria tries to maintain composure.

Lee laughs so hard and loud that I think my eardrums will burst. "Honey, we are Marines. They have nothing on us. When we get called in, the Devil runs with his tail tucked, screaming."

I point out where Aria needs to park and whip my body around to face Lee. "The only person's honey and woman I see is mine. Don't you have somewhere to be or something? By the way, her dad deployed just like you have. In fact, he was a special forces soldier at one point. Don't be a jerk to my girlfriend."

"Touchy. Just wanted to make sure she isn't one of those city slickers who manifest their way through a good life. Looking out for you, man. We don't need any surprises like last time." Lee says. He is still doing his worst with a charming smile.

"No, Lee. I don't manifest. All my manifestations are just a long series of prayers that God said no to before he gave me the yes that made my life better." Aria looks at me with an understanding nod.
This woman.

"You know what? I will give you some time. Guess I will see you cuties later." Lee winks at Aria, playfully slaps me in the back of the head, and jets out the door.

What the heck was that all about? I've never seen him act like that before.

"He is a world of fun. I can see why you are friends." Aria's tone drips sarcasm.

"I warned you."

"That you did. Now I need to know the story of how you two came to be such an *item*."

"At least let me change first." I groan as we park by my barracks building.

"You need help with that?" Aria bats her eyes flirtatiously.

"As much as I would love that, I can't. I don't need to get in trouble if they randomly check the rooms, remember? Let me change and grab my bag for the hotel. I'll be right back." I kiss the back of her hand and jog to my barracks room.

The room is nothing special. Light wooden dressers, a tall metal cabinet, a small bathroom area, an old couch, and a wooden dorm room-style bed. I change into a pair of blue jeans and a Boston Celtics shirt. I grab my bag for the weekend and head out the door.

I rush back to the car. I am excited to show Aria around the area this weekend. Let her experience just a little bit of my current life.

"You have to be one of the fastest people I've ever met when it comes to getting ready," Aria says as I get back in the car.

"I packed my bag, and getting ready when you have no hair is not hard." I laugh, throwing my bag into the back seat.

"Good point. So where to?"

"Waffle House."

"Waffle House?" Aria asks, not understanding.

"I have to give you the true Corporal Ranaldi experience. You have books. I have video games and Waffle House. It's a dinner delicacy."

"Fine, but I hear your Lee story of friendship," Aria says, holding a hand for me to shake.

"Deal." I shake her hand as she pulls out of the parking space. "One time at pre-deployment training." We laugh, like I am recounting my American Pie band camp story. "There is a portion where they run a simulation of something that could happen when overseas. It's a startling wake-up followed by three days of intensity. His unit was attached to mine, so he took the lead. Nothing special happened that made us friends; we just liked many of the same things: riding motorcycles, playing football, playing video games, etc. We more or less met and trauma-bonded over the mutual misery inspired by desert warfare training. It's how he was a friend to me later that made us brothers beyond the current occupation status."

I pause. I have never told anyone all that occurred after my ex cheated. The only person who truly knows the ins and outs of how it affected me is Lee. I owe him everything. I take a deep breath. I don't want hidden secrets between us, and certainly don't need anything that could come up later. I'm surprised she didn't question me about what "surprise" Lee was referring to earlier.

"Everything ok?" Aria asks as I give her a few directions. I didn't realize how rigid my body had become or how white my knuckles gripped my knees.

"Yeah, I've never told anyone else but Lee and my parents this next portion." I take a deep breath and continue. "When I told you Danielle got pregnant, there is a little more to the story." I glance at Aria, who has lost all coloring in her usually pink blushing cheeks. "She tried to say I was the father initially. We had to get a paternity test and everything. She tried to make me pay for appointments, but I told her no until we knew if I was the father or not, since she had cheated. I have the court documents and everything if you want to see them. It turns out that I had zero chance of being that little girl's father. I had to go through the pregnancy and birth before I found out in February. That's another reason I decided to come up to Charlotte. I was celebrating in a sense."

Aria doesn't say a word. I give her a few more directions as we pull into a spot outside Waffle House. She stares without blinking at the building in front of us with her hands still on the wheel. I continue to talk, trying to explain myself.

"The thing is. There was a chance I thought I could be the dad the whole time. Danielle was mixed. When the baby came out, she was light-skinned. The guy she cheated on me with was dark skinned. It could still go either way at that point. As time passed, the baby got darker, and the results returned. At first, I was angry and scared, but when you go that long thinking something like that. Especially since she was born, Danielle sent me photos. I couldn't help but be a little excited. I fell a little in love with the idea of what I thought could be my daughter. When I found out I wasn't the dad, I had a reaction I didn't expect. I freaked out." I start wringing my hands together. I can feel my heart rate begin to pick up. "I kind of lost myself." Aria's head whips in my direction. Her eyes that had grown dark were now full of clashing emotions. I wish I could hear what she is thinking.

Aria's hand quickly covers her mouth; tears roll down her

cheeks. I feel something cold hit my own when I realize I've started to tear up, too. She grabs my hand.

I have to get this all out.

"So, you called Lee." Aria finishes for me, already knowing where I was heading.

"So, I called Lee," I confirm. "He met me in the parking lot, and we sat in his truck. I told him everything. We ended up falling asleep in the truck. He stayed the rest of the night to keep an eye on me to ensure I would be ok, but also to ensure I didn't try anything stupid. Danielle eventually reached out and apologized for what she put me through. She knew I would have never stayed in the relationship even if I were the dad. However, she wanted it to be me because she knew I would support my kid to the end of the Earth. I would never let her go without."

"Antonio, I am so sorry all of that happened to you. That was unfair to you. I wish I knew you then so I could have helped you through it." Aria hugs my hand to her cheek while rubbing my arm with her other hand.

"I'm glad you didn't see me like that. We met at the right time. You are here now. You are helping me see there is a road to a bright future ahead. You know how many things had to fall into place for me to have met you. If you really think about it, the circumstances we both went through to meet each other are insane." I kiss her, and it hits different.

I knew after last week that I was falling in love, but after telling her my darkest moment and seeing her reaction, I know it's more. I think about the way she handles every situation. Even the idea of me re-enlisting. Part of me wanted her to be upset to make my decision easier. The way she handled it only caused me to fall deeper. It is as if the kiss has put everything in slow motion. Allowing me the chance to realize that this is it. I am in love with Aria Jade.

"Did you ever talk to a professional after all that?" Aria asks.

"Does Lee not count?" I chuckle.

"Most certainly not. Hard pass." Aria laughs. "If you ever want to, I'm sure Dr. Shots wouldn't mind taking you on."

"Thanks, I'll consider it. As of right now, how about we go clog some arteries? I am starving. All these emotions do something for my appetite." I say, grabbing my grumbling stomach.

That's right. Ladies don't have the trademark on stress eating. Guys do it too.

CHAPTER 19

ARIA

Sugar, carbs, and a chance to develop diabetes are all I smell walking into Waffle House. I feel as if I am still coming down from the whirlwind of emotions after hearing Antonio's trauma. I don't think I've ever felt more trauma-bonded to someone when we haven't even experienced the exact scenarios. I like what he said about the events that brought us together more. That butterfly effect is something else. Scarlett and Chris had to decide to move from New York to North Carolina to meet. I decided to stay home for college to attend UNC Charlotte, which helped me meet the professor who recommended hiring me to my current principal. Scarlett was working there, and we were in the same group for a staff ice breaker during summer planning sessions, and we quickly became best friends. Antonio decided to join the military and was stationed in South Carolina. His situation with his ex and his mother's suggestion to visit prompted him to visit North Carolina. Now, here we are after meeting through our mutual friends. Maybe this really is destiny after all.

"There's my favorite couple." We hear him before we see him. Lee, *again*. "I knew it was only a matter of time before you ended up here."

An older waitress behind the counter shakes her head at Lee punching in a payment on the register.

"Hey there, honey. You two go take a seat, I'll be right over." She points to an empty table by the windows.

"You heard her, let's go, Ant." Lee throws his arm around Antonio's shoulders, propelling them towards the table.

The waitress gives me an apologetic shrug and smile.

"I'll let it slide," I say.

"Probably for the best with those two." She grabs some menus and follows me to the table.

"Ruth, this is Aria," Antonio says as I slide in beside him, placing an arm around me.

"Pleasure. How did you two meet?" Ruth says, putting the menus down in front of us.

"A lot of stars aligned." Antonio kisses my shoulder. Lee fakes gagging across the table from us.

"They usually do." Ruth smiles, but there is a hint of sadness behind it. "Dare I even ask what you guys want? Is there even a point?"

"Ruth, I'm offended. It's like you have forgotten all about us. You know how we like it." Lee mocks.

"Yeah, yeah. I got it. Aria, what about you?"

"Chocolate chip waffle with plain hashbrowns, please."

"You got it, sugar." Ruth goes back behind the counter.

"Chocolate chip waffles. What are you five?" Lee laughs.

"I blame the students. Their preferences rub off on you after a while." I say unbothered.

"Plus, last I checked, you display the many antics of a two-year-old." Antonio jokes.

"Ha, hilarious. Take that act on the road, you two." Lee rolls his eyes, fiddling with his utensils.

"I have to go to the bathroom. I'll be right back. Lee, I won't tell you to be normal, just be…humane. I don't know." Antonio kisses my cheek. I slide out to let him by and slide back in.

Once Antonio is away, I figure now is my time to talk to Lee. "So, Antonio told me about how you guys became friends. I guess I just wanted to say thank you. For helping him. I can see why you are… protective."

"Yeah, well, he was pretty messed up. I am not going to let him be another statistic for the military. There is enough to feel guilty about with our occupation." His gaze fails to meet my eyes as he says it. I get the sense there is something more behind his words. "Just do me a favor and take care of him. I don't mean to come off like an arrogant jerk. Let's just say I have plenty of reasons to be protective that I haven't even told Antonio."

So why would you tell me that?

"I will care for him, but he may decide to re-up. There is still a chance." Now I am the one who can't look him in the eye.

"Doubtful."

I don't get to dig into that response. Ruth comes back with glasses of water, and Antonio slides next to me.

"Did he behave himself?" Antonio asks. Ruth starts bringing our orders one at a time.

"I'll let him pass this round." I shrug, still curious about Lee's reasons for his protectiveness.

"Good. There is a first time for everything."

The side of Lee's mouth quirks up. Lee isn't bad. He just has ten-foot walls with barbed wire and electric shock. As we all begin eating and talking, I find out he is single. It has been over a year since his last deployment. He is so tall and muscular that his frame barely fits in the booth seat. As an educator, I know he is the definition of when there is more to the story with someone. But that story is for someone else to figure out.

We continue our meal. Lee and Antonio swap stories of all their most humiliating times together, from waking up in other people's barracks rooms without remembering how they got there, to Lee drunkenly dancing on tables in clubs. Turns out Antonio really is a homebody. It always took Lee practically dragging him out of his room to get him to go out. When they did go out together, it was a series of mass chaos. Growing up sheltered as I did, I don't have any stories like that to share. I've maybe been drunk two or three times so far, and nothing crazy happened. I just sit back listening and laughing along with them. Before long, it was time to head to the hotel, so we made our way outside.

"It was nice meeting you, Aria. I will let you guys have the rest of the weekend to yourselves this time." Lee pulls me into a tight bear hug. Just when I think he will let go, he keeps holding on. "Antonio, keep this one. If not, I'll steal her." I playfully push Lee away from me, hitting him in the stomach. He can't keep from laughing. "I apologize again for the way I came across."

"Only because you are one of my best friends will I let that slide." Antonio wraps me up in his arms in front of him. "Only once, though."

"Oh, I'm so scared." Lee throws his hands up in surrender, smirking.

"Whatever, moron. See you later, loser." Antonio bumps Lee on the shoulder, making our way to the car. Dimples on full display.

***

"This bed is the softest bed I've ever been in, in my life," I say, face-first in the crisp linen sheets of our hotel room.

The hotel room isn't anything special. Just one queen-sized bed, a green couch, brown dressers and night tables, with a TV hanging on the wall. The bed, however, feels like lying on the fluffiest cloud in the sky.

"Oh yeah? Move over." Antonio flops on the bed, stomach first, shaking the whole thing. "You aren't wrong. That's very nice."

He pulls me into his chest. I tangle my legs up with his and breathe in his scent. He kisses the top of my head. We lay like that for a few minutes before he speaks again.

"I'm happy you and Lee eventually got along and that he apologized for his initial idiocy."

"That big, ole teddy bear. Please. With that award-winning personality, what is not to love?" I joke, making Antonio laugh with me.

"Eh, he has his quirks like the rest of us, but as I said before, in the depths of his soul, he is a good one. He would do anything for the people he cares about."

"I can sense that," I say truthfully.

"Speaking of which. Turn over." Antonio says, suddenly excited.

"But I am so comfortable." I groan onto his chest.

"It will be worth it. Let's go. On your stomach."

"Geez, alright, bossy. No wonder you are a corporal." I roll onto my stomach, laying my face on my folded arms.

"I. I want to try something." Antonio stutters.

"Oh, kinky." I giggle.

"No, seriously. I will draw on your back, and you must guess what it is."

"Ok?" I am so confused about why he wants to play this little game.

I feel Antonio's finger start to move across my back. Three lines. Two horizontals with one on the top and one on the bottom. One vertical line in the middle.

"I?"

"Yes."

He continues one letter at a time.

"L."

"O."

"V."

"E."

My breath catches in my throat. My heart skips a beat. My brain comes to a halt.

Is he telling me what I think he is telling me?

My voice shakes as I say the rest of the letters, trying to hold back tears.

"Y."

"O."

"U."

"All together now," Antonio whispers in my ear. His hands stroke my back.

I roll towards him. We are looking at each other in the eyes. Never has anyone told me they love me in such a unique way. Never has saying those three words made me feel this level of joy in a relationship.

"You." I struggle to speak. "You love me."

"I do. I think I've known, but after meeting your family. Realizing I can tell you about things I don't talk to anyone else about. I can't go on without you knowing how I feel about you. You are the most unexpected thing that has ever happened to me. I want you to know how precious you are to my soul. I truly believe you are meant to be in my life. Not just for a season but for a lifetime. God aligned our paths so I could be with you."

A tear slips down my cheek. Our lips crash into each other. His hand cradles the back of my neck. His other hand pulled my leg up to his waist, caressing my thigh. I pull back, feeling the sudden need to affirm my feelings, too.

"Antonio."

"Yeah, sunflower."

"I love you too," I whisper as if admitting it in return could change his mind.

The smile that spreads across his face is captivating. If I had my camera, I would have snapped a photo to capture it forever. His mouth crashes into my mind with a balance of tenderness and desperation. We spend the rest of the night in a tradeoff of show and tell on how we love one another. Never has my heart been so whole.

We wake up early the next morning. Though neither of us wanted to leave the comfort of the bed, we decided to visit a coffee shop so my no-coffee gremlin wouldn't appear. Antonio hasn't seen that side of me yet. Right after we confessed our love to one another, it would not be the time he did if I could help it. I'm not necessarily mean, but the headache from the lack of caffeine is enough to drive me to insanity.

We arrive at the most southern charm coffee shop I've ever seen. Everything is pearly white, and small bunches of wildflowers are in vases on each table. The mint green accents go perfectly with my peach dress. I keep catching Antonio's eyes on the small cutouts on both sides of my abdomen. We ordered our coffees and some baked goods. We find a seat by the window to wait for our order.

"I have something for you," I say, reaching into my purse.

My fingers rub across the house key in my bag. I hadn't planned on doing this, this weekend, but something about our admissions last night is driving me forward. I want him to understand how serious I am about this. I want a physical sign of how much I have trusted him.

I take the key out and slide it across the table. My hand lies on top of it, so his look is bewildered as I edge it closer to him. "You didn't have to get me anything, Aria."

"I didn't exactly," I said, edging my hand off the key. "I want you to have it."

I don't even have to say what it is to. He already knows. His eyes turn to saucers, going back and forth between me and the key. "Aria, I. I don't know what to say."

"We gave each other part of ourselves last night. I don't want to just tell you with words how I am feeling. I want to show you the level to which I trust you. I hope you consider it home the next time you pull in the driveway." I nervously look down at my dress.

There is something more terrifying about this moment than when we said we love each other. It lets him access a part of my life that I created, worked for, and protected myself. It's letting go of the past, allowing him fully into my present, and trusting an unknown future.

Antonio's hand wraps around the key. He takes his keys out with his other hand and adds them to the key ring. He reaches across the table and grabs my hands in his.

"Thank you for trusting me. I have already considered it home because you live there. Every weekend has felt like a homecoming. I live here." Antonio places a hand above my heart. "I will protect our home. I will protect it because it shelters what matters to me most. You. Your creative mind, caring heart, kind soul, and God given magnificent body."

I lean across the table and kiss him lightly.

"And Dianna," Antonio adds with a smile. "She is part of what makes our house a home, too."

The word "our" echoes in my head like an angelic choir. Such a loaded, beautiful word. *Our* house, *our* dog, *our* love.

CHAPTER 20

ANTONIO

MAY

The rest of the weekend was a blur. After our coffee, we walked around town and talked about *our* home. I can't believe our house's key is in my pocket. We talked about everything we want to do in the backyard, getting Lee to stay for a visit sometime, and what we could do in the empty rooms. Aria knows I still have to make up my mind about reenlisting, but her willingness to put so much trust into me to give up some version of control over the house and admit she loves me as well has nearly made up my mind. Part of me feels it is unfair to accept a key, given my inability to decide. I only need to see how well she gets along with my family. My family is a big part of me, and I couldn't imagine making a life-changing decision over someone who didn't get along with them. It seems highly unlikely that she wouldn't get along with anyone. She worries so much about how everyone around her feels she could befriend a crocodile.

When she leaves the next morning, I realize just how heart-wrenching this is turning out for me. It is getting increasingly complex for me to constantly leave her every few days. Something about her being the one to drive away this time makes it that much worse. Especially knowing how we both feel. I can't fathom what it will be like to leave her behind for a month and a half to train in the desert. I can barely stand being without her Monday through Thursday.

I drive home every weekend for the next few weeks leading up to Mother's Day.

Home.

We hang out with Scarlett and Chris, take Dianna for a walk in various parks, and spend time with Aria's family. Cassidy has become a fifth wheel when we are with Scarlett and Chris now. I am growing increasingly close to Aria's family. We have our weekly dinner on Saturdays now. We always end up playing some type of board game. I am pretty sure her nephew thinks I am his real uncle. Aria's brother is quickly becoming one of my new best friends. His jokes have me doubled over in laughter every time, since I am now comfortable enough to laugh about it in front of her parents. There is something special about watching Aria with her family. Her interactions with her nephew give me a glimpse into how she would be as a mother. She would be caring and fun teaching them so much in the process. Even though Aria acted embarrassed at her brother's jokes the first time, I am quickly learning her jokes are just as dirty sometimes. Sometimes they may even be worse. Aria, Gio, and Carly are a trifecta of humor and closeness. You can see how much they value, respect, and love one another.

Regarding Cassidy, I have never met a more bubbly, positive person in my entire life. Watching Aria, Scarlett, and Cassidy in action is practically unbelievable. It is as if Cassidy has been around us all for years. All three of them finish each other's sentences. If one needs something, I swear one of the other girls is already getting it before they even have a chance to ask out loud. It's borderline creepy.

Every weekend brings Aria and me closer together. When I think I've found out all I can or have reached the depth of my love for Aria, I am wrong. The depth of our love is like the universe itself. Ever growing, evolving, and extending. I have Friday and Monday off duty for the Mother's Day weekend. Aria asked for it off, and she was also granted the time. I never realized how much went into asking off for a teacher. She had to spend hours over the weekend before making class copies and writing substitute plans just to be able to have the time off. I tried to help as much as possible, but the only thing I could do to help was staple packets together. To top it all off, she was required to find her own sub.

On the Thursday before Mother's Day, we decided I would come up after work, and we would continue the rest of the drive to New York overnight. Thankfully, the twenty-four-hour shifts I occasionally pull have given me an upper hand at being overtired. I don't know what I am more excited about, seeing Aria, my family…or their combination.

"Woman, what in the world are you wearing?" I pull into the driveway to pick Aria up.

It's become our standard greeting to see her at the front door as I pull in. We use an app, so she knows when I am getting close. I have never seen someone wear what she is wearing for a nearly eleven-hour car ride. It's more than twelve hours after stops.

She stands before me in a navy-blue A-line dress. The midsection has small, knitted sections with cutouts. The neckline is squared. She has done her makeup and hair as if we were going on one of our typical dates. Dianna is sitting at her side, tail wagging, looking up at her as if she is giving enthusiastic approval.

"You don't like it?" Aria pouts. "I thought it was cute."

"First, you can wear whatever you want. Second, of course, you look good. When do you not? Third, I will take a break from driving long enough to see what is hiding under those cutouts before we go." Aria's face reddens at that. "I am just saying, a dress seems mighty uncomfortable for this long ride. It is overnight, too."

"It's called 'air flow and ventilation.' It's also called, 'I want to make a good impression.'" Aria twirls in the dress, making the hem flow around her like Marilyn Monroe. I stop her spinning, grasping her waist with both hands.

"You know what I call it? Easy access." I scoop her up, tossing her over one shoulder.

Just a quick break.

***

"That was just the right amount of motivation I needed to continue this drive." I pull Aria's dress back down to rest on her thighs. She still lies on the bed with her hands on her stomach, taking deep breaths. "You know what? Wear what you want. I may need more motivation on the road."

Aria shakes her head, giggling at my utter nonsense. "I bought my motivation for the road."

"Oh, kinky." I help her off the bed, but receive a swift arm to the gut in response.

"Not like that, perv. I brought the traveling seeds." Aria makes her way over to her light pink suitcase.

"You aren't helping your case here."

Aria rolls her eyes at me, reaches into her purse on top of her suitcase, and whips a jumbo bag of sunflower seeds.

"That's not all." She bends back over, coming up with a bag of Dove milk chocolates.

"Are you trying to tell me something? Something I need to know? If so, let me know now." I tease at the possibility of her being pregnant.

"Ha, ha, you're a comedian. No, it's a travel tradition for me. People have lucky socks or underwear for games. Why can't I have special snacks for safe travels?"

"You can have whatever you want." I kiss her head, reaching down to grab her bags. "Let's go sunflower."

By the time we hit the road in my truck, it is almost seven PM. Dianna is sleeping in the back seat. Aria and I chat about random things. Initially, it is simple stories about our childhoods. I tell her about how much snow we used to get. So high that it used to touch our roof, I would jump from the roof into large snowbanks on the side of the house. I tell her stories about snowmobiling and about friends she may get to meet while we are visiting. I hope she meets at least my friend Kelsey from high school and Noah. I have known Noah since we were in the same class in elementary school. Those two make up my chosen family.

Aria tells me about weekend band competitions in high school, Friday night football games, and all her family's holiday traditions. I discovered that her family attends midnight mass on Christmas Eve, her dad cooks the seven fishes for Christmas, and they all participate in at least one Panthers' football game yearly. I thought I was a huge Raiders fan, but she has me beat between her brother being on the Panthers' drumline and the number of games attended.

I don't know how it happened, but before long, we discussed what kind of traditions we would want for our kids. As in, hers and mine. Together. Even with everything that happened with my ex, we *never* discussed these things. I've never even considered kids with anyone. When I thought I was going to possibly be a dad, I didn't want to talk about anything until I knew with certainty. It's not that I don't like or want kids; it's just not been on my radar other than when I thought it had to be with my ex. However, talking about it with Aria seems natural. Something I can picture and would want one day. She would be a nurturing mother. Her job as a teacher would help our kids as they grow and develop. They could go to school with her once they are old enough. We talk about wanting them to attend church, but not forcing them to do it, so it doesn't discourage them. We discuss how our different upbringings will influence them and what kind of kids they could be based on our personalities. We talk about our expectations of each other. Before long, we are talking about what being married would look like. We rode the rabbit hole all the way down.

"Is that something you would want?" I ask nervously. We are about three-fourths of the ride in, and I can tell she has gone the distance trying to stay awake for me.

"What do you think?" Aria yawns and scrunches down into the passenger seat.

Ah, the old, put the ball back in his court, so you don't show your cards trick. Oldie but a goodie.

"I think if you know, you know. I think waiting is just to appease other people's expectations. We are pretty aligned on what we think and expect out of being married. Heck, we are even in agreement on many parenting ideas." Aria is quiet. "What do you think?" I look over when she still doesn't respond. She is fast asleep, curled into a ball against the side of the truck door.

How can you fall asleep at a moment like this? My heart rate is so high that it feels like I drank at least two energy drinks.

Disappointment fills me. I want to know her answer. I am not asking her to marry me, but I want to see if we are heading in that direction. It would help my decision considerably if I knew she was on that path. She calls her house our home now, but does that mean she can see us married necessarily? I grab a blanket from behind the back of her chair that I keep with me. With one hand on the wheel, I lightly place it over her.

"Goodnight, Mrs. Ranaldi." I can't help it. All the conversations tonight made me say it once just to see how natural it felt. But man, am I screwed. It didn't just feel natural; it rolled off my tongue like she was my wife. As if she had been for a long time.

The next few hours, I listen to music quietly. We are approximately two hours from home when Aria groans and stretches her body. She sheepishly looks over at me. Her once straight hair is now in a matted mess. She looks in the truck mirror in horror.

"Oh my gosh, I can't meet your parents looking like a troll!" Aria screeches in horror, pulling at bits of her hair.

"Good morning to you, too, sunflower." I grin.

"Where is my purse?" Aria shifts through luggage in the backseat, making Dianna grumble in protest.

Aria grabs her purse, pulling out a navy-blue hat, and

slamming it on her head. "Purse hat comes in handy again."

"Not going to lie, if I were a woman, a purse hat sounds like one of the most brilliant ideas I have ever heard. I would do the same."

Aria beams with pride. "I also always keep a large pack of gum on me. I blame the coffee addiction, and my Grannie Annie never left home without her Juicy Fruit gum."

"I like it. You know. My parents wouldn't care about your hair. They are so excited to meet you. You could have shown up in sweats and a shirt with holes. They still would have been over the moon to see you. My mom will be so shocked and surprised, I doubt she would notice if you wore a brown paper bag."

"That's all good, but I am determined to make a good first impression. I hope you know what this means." Aria pauses.

"You just woke up and need your coffee fix."

"Wow. I trained you so quickly." Aria mocks reaching to the back to scratch behind Dianna's ears.

We stopped one last time for coffee and let Dianna out again for a bathroom break. Aria prunes herself in the gas station bathroom; before we know it, we are back on the road.

***

"We are here," I say, turning onto the gravel driveway.

The driveway is on a slight hill. On the right is where my grandparents used to live. It is a small two-story house. A large deck extends across the front of the second-story house. My parents' dark green barn has a black roof and white trim to our left. You can see the lake spreading out behind their brown and white house. Their large, white garage is almost as oversized as their house, where my dad keeps his prized possessions, a vintage red Corvette and an old Harley Davidson motorcycle. I can already hear the last one of the beagles my dad ever bred barking as we approach the house.

Aria is leaning forward in anticipation. Her eyes are wide as she takes in the lake and acreage. Her face is one of pure awe. It's not a mansion, but it is home. It is beautiful and filled with love. I enjoyed every second of growing up here. If I had to choose to do it all over again, I would in a heartbeat. Same house, exact location, same family. Nothing changes.

My dad steps out onto their screened-in front porch as we pull to a stop. He is about the same height as Aria. Fun-sized. His salt and pepper hair is the only thing that gives away his age. His height will fool anyone, but he has stiff muscles hidden away. A scrappy little Italian man. He is wearing a complete outfit of Real Tree camo. He waves, adjusting his glasses on his face. Aria waves back, and I swear she is about to jump out of the truck window in pure excitement.

"Hey, guys." My dad, Joey, says as Aria hops down from the truck, letting Dianna out.

Dianna barrels up to my dad, nearly knocking him over as he comes down the few steps of the porch.

"Sorry. She has been cooped up in the backseat. I'm Aria." Aria grabs Dianna's collar and extends her other hand to shake.

"Bring it in." Dad wraps her up in a hug. Dianna jumps up, wrapping her arms around both of their waists. "I'm Joey." He chuckles, patting Dianna's head.

"Hey, Dad," I say as I walk over, helping get Dianna down. Aria let dad go. I pull him in an embrace.

"Hey, son. Marine Corps is still doing you good, I see. Nice and lean. Put on some muscle, too." He eyes me up and down, taking me in.

"Yep. Although this one's cooking is going to pack on some pounds." I wrap an arm around Aria's shoulders while a blush creeps across her cheeks.

"Nothing wrong with that." Dad smiles. "Let's go inside and say hey to mom. I told her I was going out early to hunt this morning, but we had someone 'coming to work in the garage' so she needed to be up. It will be the perfect surprise."

The property is stunning. The long driveway drops down a small hill from the road, giving the house a sense of solitude. The vast expanse of the lake stretches far beyond what the eye can see from left to right. Across the lake, you can see another town. Antonio's parents have flowers and bushes in full bloom around the small ranch-style home. They also have a white detached garage and a dark green barn. A large rock wall lines their barrier to the lake overlooking their neighbor's boat dock. Lush green grass contrasts with the dark blue water sparkling in the early morning sunrise.

Dianna relieves herself and follows us inside. As we walk in, we are immediately hit by the strong smell of coffee. We enter through the kitchen. The whole house still looks the same as when I was a kid. An old gas stove, beige walls, and all-natural wood dining furniture handed down through generations. They still have the old Hoosier cabinet with a pasta roller on the side. My mom is in her gray bathrobe. Her short blonde hair is straight, and her glasses are slightly crooked.

My mom is not a morning person; she is awake at seven A.M., which is a miracle. She is in the process of warming up her morning tea.

"Happy early Mother's Day!" I shout, coming in the door, making my mom jump, clutching at the opening of her robe.

"Antonio?!" My mom yelps, turning to face me. "What are you doing here?" Tears gleam in her eyes. Pure joy.

"Came to surprise you. Brought along a stray." I reach back, grabbing Aria's hand and pulling her into my body. Her arms firmly wrap around my waist before extending one to shake hands with my mom.

"Oh my gosh, Aria. We have heard so much about you. No wonder Joey insisted on making way more coffee than was needed. I thought it was for the repairman or his hunting buddies. Grab yourself a mug." My mom shakes Aria's hand before giving her a mug from the cabinet.

"We brought along Dianna, too." I turn towards my dad behind us, who is holding onto her collar.

"We need to introduce the dogs before we do anything else," Dad says, knowing my mom's fear of dogs fighting one another. "I'll take Dianna around back to see Sadie. She's on the tether."

"Thanks, Dad."

Aria and I grab a cup of coffee and sit at the table. We can hear the dogs barking outside in the front yard. Thankfully, it doesn't sound aggressive. I look out the living room window to see if they are within view. I take in the ripple effect of the wind going across the lake. My parents' garden is flourishing to the left. The lush green grass blows in the breeze, but the dogs are in the side yard, so we can't see them.

"Thank you both so much for coming and surprising me. Aria, I'm sure your mom will miss you for Mother's Day, but I appreciate you coming up with Antonio. We don't see him often, as you can imagine." My mom, Tiffany, smiles, taking a sip of her tea.

"Of course. I am happy to get the opportunity to meet everyone. Your son is so caring, compassionate, and fun to be around, so I know the people who raised him must embody those same qualities. It made me even more excited to be here. Why wouldn't I want to come celebrate the mother of the man who's brought so much positivity and quality back into my life? I thought I would never find it. So, thank you."

My heart is bursting at the seams. To hear the woman I am in love with tell the first woman who ever loved me these glorious sentiments is a full-circle moment. How did I go from calling my parents terrified to reveal I could be a father, to a woman telling my mother these things about me? As I look at Aria, I am filled with love and admiration. She just met my mom and is already willing to be so open. Someone who, once again, has every reason to be closed off or emotionally unavailable continues to embrace openness. It's inspiring. I place my hand on her thigh under the table, giving her a light squeeze.

"Wow, Aria. I don't think you understand how much that means to me as his mom. He really is special. I don't just mean it as his mom. I truly believe I would think that even if I wasn't. Between the surprise visit and what you just said, those were the best presents you could've given me for Mother's Day." My mom wipes a tear from her eyes.

"I told you she was pretty special." I kiss the top of Aria's head. My mom looks back and forth between us.

The only other woman I have ever brought home in a serious manner was Danielle. My mom was not a fan of her out of the gate. She has a great read on people; she is trying to understand how well we go together now. By the tears gleaming in her eyes and the soft smile playing across her features, I know Aria is making a great impression. It goes beyond excitement about our surprise.

"I've heard so much about you already from Ant, but tell me about yourself anyway."

Aria tells her all about Dianna, teaching, and her family. She explains the crazy butterfly effect of how we met, and even I didn't realize everything that made us come to fruition. After my mom agreed that we were meant to be together, Aria excused herself to help my dad outside with the dogs.

"Oh boy." Mom sighs, standing up after Aria walks out of the back door, leading out towards the lake.

"What?" I ask.

"She's it, isn't she? She's the one."

I look out the window, watching Aria tilt her head back, laughing at something my dad said. The dogs are chasing each other around the lush yard. Everything in me is screaming yes, but I also hear the nagging from the depths of my brain screaming about the impending doom that is my re-enlistment.

"I think that depends on how well this visit goes," I say jokingly, knowing I'm too far gone for Aria. Nothing can change the love I have for her. Hopefully, she feels the same.

Tiffany raises her brows at me. She shakes her head.

"Well, you already know how this visit will turn out. You have to get out of your own way. So, give me a real answer this time."

I remind her of everything Lee told me, the upcoming training, our mutual baggage of the exes… It's all a lot to consider. Loving her is easy. Figuring out if that means life-changing decisions that alter my career and where I live are not. Even if every time my heart pounds, it calls me an idiot for considering anything but Aria.

"If you can find someone who treats you right, loves every part of you, and can handle the hard times with grace, you would be denying a life I'm afraid doesn't come around often. You may never find it again." Mom places her hand on top of mine, giving it a soft pat.

"Ant, get out here and help me with this." I hear Dad yell from outside the window.

"Didn't I just walk in the door? He already has chores." I groan. Mom chuckles, but I get up anyway and head out the door, weighing everything she said.

CHAPTER 21

ARIA

What in the smut is this? I swear I've read many, many books about this.

I grin mischievously while staring at Antonio. He climbs on his dad's teal blue and white Harley-Davidson motorcycle. Watching him get on the bike with a full-faced gray helmet, blue jeans, and his dad's black leather vest over his black T-shirt is heating me up. His dad suspects something is wrong with the bike and wants him to take it for a quick drive down the road to check.

This is just what my mind needed to stop my ridiculously overthinking brain. Once I left the table after my initial greeting with his mom, I couldn't help but feel like I laid it on too thick. She seemed very pleased with me, but my mind always does what it wants with me. The only time my brain has remained with its tiny neurons to itself was when we admitted we loved each other. It is probably the only time since my ex that my brain ceased. I had gone to Dianna to ground myself. Thankfully, Antonio's dad is hilarious. We spent the whole time laughing over stories of Antonio's pre-Marine Corps days. Evidently, during a going-away party, he ran off the neighbor's dock fully clothed and dove into the lake after a glow stick, screaming, "I'm a Marine. I'm amphibious." It quickly refocused my mind. His dad, Joey, also told me I'd better prepare for a complete schedule. Evidently, Antonio keeps himself busy while visiting family and friends.

Now, I stare at Antonio as he backs out of the garage. He motions for me to come over.

"I will be right back. We will get the rest of our stuff in from the truck when I return. My grandpa is going to come over for lunch today." Antonio lifts the entire front portion of his helmet.

Placing two fingers under my chin, he kisses me. Red-hot need washes over me. He is lucky we are in his parents' driveway because the fact that he can drive a motorcycle is an unlocked fantasy I didn't know I had.

I'll be his old lady any day.

With that, he slams the helmet back down. He revs the engine, edging up the driveway, carefully navigating the gravel. Slowly, the tension dissipates, and a new feeling creeps in. Fear. Having a dad who was a former EMT pre- military days means I've heard all the stories of motorcycle crashes. As if on cue, Dianna comes running up to my side for a pat on the head with Sadie trailing behind her.

I give them both a scratch behind their ears. Making my way towards the yard, I take in the breathtaking scene. A near-constant breeze makes small waves across the expansive Oneida Lake. Across the way, you can see homes and mountains. I can see a storm rolling towards the far south side of the lake with thick, dark clouds. I walk all the way down to the rock wall. I've never felt more at peace than listening to the waves crash against the shore. I think I found my vacation reading spot.

"In the winter, this entire lake freezes over. This rock wall will be covered with ice from the waves crashing against it." Joey comes up behind me. He picks up a ball and chucks it back towards the house, throwing the dogs into a frenzy to get to it first.

I look back at the lake, imagining how this whole thing could be frozen. "No way."

"Yep. Ask Ant. He used to tear this lake up on his snowmobile."

My jaw hangs open. We have Lake Norman, sure, but it is nothing like this lake. We also do not get snow in Charlotte. It is mostly ice with a kiss of snow on top. Oh, and then more ice. There is no way we could ever be cold enough or have the amount of winter precipitation to freeze the lake with measurable thickness to drive over.

"I can't even imagine. I don't think I've ever known anyone who has snowmobiled."

"Oh yeah. We used to have one, but when we started snowbirding down to Florida in the winter, we had no use for them, so I gave them to my nephews. Ant and I used to ice fish all the time, too."

"I would love to see snow like that just once."

"I have a feeling you will get that chance. The way he has talked about you. Yeah, you aren't going anywhere any time soon."

Here I go blushing again. It's just my permanent skin color at this point.

"I'll stay as long as he keeps me." I smile, picking up the ball Dianna dropped at my feet to throw again.

We hear the rumble of Antonio's motorcycle. We turn towards the noise. The dogs take off in his direction. We make our way to the garage. My heart is pounding, and I am excited to see him on the bike again.

"What do you think, son?" Joey asks when Antonio stops before us, putting the kickstand down.

"You're right. Needs a tune-up." Antonio lifts the helmet off his head, swinging one leg over like hopping off a horse.

"I knew it." Joey puts his hands on his hips, shaking his head. "Pull it into the garage for me. After you both get your stuff in, let's help Mom prepare the house for her dad to come over."

"Sounds good." Antonio hops back on the bike, putting it back in its spot in the garage. I follow him in as he closes the garage door.

"I am learning so many new things about you already." I place myself between Anthonio's thighs after he repositioned to one side.

"Oh boy. I don't even want to know what stories you were told." His hands come to rest on my hips. I wrap my arms around his neck.

"Let's see… You are an ice fisherman, you snowmobile, oh, and you can ride a motorcycle. I thought the uniform was hot, but this is next-level torture."

Antonio stands quickly, pushing me onto the bike and leaning over me, placing his hands on either side of me.

"No, you on this bike is next level torture." Antonio's lips quirk to one side. He leans slowly and kisses the side of my neck, making me feel weak in the knees.

"Come on. We should get our stuff in the house." He pulls back, grabbing my hand to lead me out of the garage.

Motorcycle fantasy pending.

***

"Are you sure?" I'm holding my bags, perplexed.

Antonio's parents informed me that we would stay in his old bedroom. Granted, he has not had to stay with my family, but it will be a rude awakening for him when he realizes my family does not allow sleeping in the same room unless you are married.

"Of course." Tiffany nods, showing me towards Antonio's childhood bedroom.

We continue to organize our bags and supplies into the bedroom. Pictures hang on the walls of Anthony's backpacking parts of the Adirondack Mountains in feet of snow. Photos of him with his grandparents line the natural wooden dresser. His bed's comforter is fishing themed with stripes, fishing rods, and jumping fish. Two nightstands sit on either side, matching the bedframe with more natural wood. The window in his room looks out towards the lake. They keep their windows open most of the time, allowing the fresh, cool air to fill the house.

"So which one am I meeting today?" I ask, pointing to the various photos of his grandparents.

Antonio stares at the photos. A sudden sadness fills his eyes. "Well, the thing is, there is only one left."

"I'm so sorry. I had no idea."

"It's ok. My dad's parents passed when I was in high school. They both had esophageal cancer. My grandmother went first, and a few months later, my grandfather. It was tough to navigate and watch. I didn't handle it well. Growing up with them on the property, I spent just as much time running to their house as I did here. Maybe even more. They were my favorite people in the world." He grabs their photos, looking at them as if lost in a torturous memory.

In the photos, Antonio stands to the right of each grandparent. His grandfather was a slender man with graying hair and a mustache. He wore a blue button-down shirt and khakis. Antonio wore a white shirt, blue tie, and black dress pants. It was weird to see him with hair. His hair back then was a shaggy reddish blonde. He looked like a young Jeremy Sumpter when he played Peter Pan. He wore the same outfit in the photo with his grandmother. She had on a pair of black glasses that matched her short black hair. She had a sweet smile with a purple shirt and a skirt combo.

"Cancer is the worst. My grandfather also passed away from cancer. It started in his shoulder and went to his bladder. It kind of runs in my family. I have two uncles and a cousin who are cancer survivors."

"I'm sorry to hear that as well. It's hell on Earth to watch them suffer through that."

"Do you mind if I ask what happened to your other grandma?" I ask, looking at the next photo.

Antonio looks over to the next photo. His other grandma reminded me more of my Italian side of the family. Dark features, stout, and a kind smile. "I don't mind. She had dementia. She was so calm all the time. One day, when she started to get bad, she yelled at my grandfather, and I was shocked. I had never seen them yell before, much less argue. It's unfortunate to me that all my grandparents had to suffer to rest in peace. I try not to think about it too much because it bothers me."

I can tell Antonio is at a breaking point when discussing this. His eyes are shining with the beginning of tears. I need to break the tension.

"What about this handsome guy? Don't let my grandmothers find out about him. I may end up with a new step-grandfather." I laugh, trying to ease the mood.

Anthonio blinks away the memories and grabs the last photo of the grandfather I will meet today. He smiles, looking at the headshot. It is black and white. If I didn't know better, I would say he looks like Robert De Niro in Meet the Fockers with his black sunglasses.

"This man is a saint. No matter how difficult it got with my grandmother, he stuck by her until the bitter end. He took care of her the whole time with the dementia. She never went to a home or anything. Some medical personnel would come to the home to help, but it was he at the end of the day. You will love him." Before I could respond, Antonio's phone rang in his pocket.

"Hello." A brief pause while someone on the other side is talking at max volume, detailing something that sounds a lot like someone in trouble. Antonio rolls his eyes. "You have to be kidding me. How late was he?" Another pause. "Great, that's a mile hump for every damn minute. Throw in an extra one for making me curse in front of my woman. I don't care why he was late."

My woman.

It's one thing to see a man say that in the movies or read about it in a book, but to hear it told from this man's mouth is doing all sorts of things to me. Nothing prepares you for the real moments of hearing the man you love say that. Antonio looks at me and winks.

I should have brought more underwear.

Between the motorcycle moment and now this. I'm not going to have any left. Antonio angrily hangs up the phone, sliding it back into his pocket.

"Idiots, man. All of them." He grunts.

"Do I even want to know what a mile hump is?" I ask, confused and amused.

"It's basically a mile hike in full gear. It's grueling."

"Geez. All because he was late? How late was he?"

"10 minutes. Said he got stuck in traffic. Idiot. Should have checked before leaving and adjusted accordingly. Left earlier. Something. I swear it's like I have to hold their hand." Antonio throws his hands up.

I think about the number of times I was late to school because of something as stupid as picking up a coffee when I knew I had no time to do it. Thank you, God, for my career choice. I don't think I've seen him this flustered yet.

"Well, if it makes you feel better, you can return to that, my woman, comment anytime you want." I wrap my arms around his waist, pulling him into me.

He is stiff initially but softens. Antonio wraps his arms around me. He kisses me lightly on the forehead.

"Right now, I want to continue to introduce *my woman* to the rest of the most important people to me. Screw anything else right now. Let's see how much longer until my Papa Joe gets here." Antonio kisses me, grabs my hand, and leads me back out of the bedroom.

CHAPTER 22

ANTONIO

"What a surprise you managed to pull off!" Papa Joe claps me on the shoulder, sitting beside me on the living room couch.

Aria sits across from us on a reclining lounge chair. My parents are busy prepping some light snacks and lemonade for everyone in the open kitchen.

"About time he grants me a good surprise." Mom teases, referring to my, 'surprise I joined the Marine Corps and am moving to South Carolina' phone call a few years ago. "You missed him yelling at a Marine earlier. I could hear you outside on the deck."

I didn't realize my voice was raised earlier, talking on the phone, handing out punishment. Aria covers her mouth, suppressing a grin.

"I wasn't yelling. I was talking about what punishment to give a lower-ranking Marine with an inspired purpose."

Papa Joe shakes his head; Aria can't contain herself anymore. Laughter burst out of her. My parents shake their heads as they hand us lemonades and set a plate of assorted meats and cheeses on the side table near the couches.

"Remind me to tell my students' parents that next time I want to inspire them to do their work."

"Ah, that's right, you are a teacher. I don't know how you guys do it. Especially math nowadays. What do you think about it?" Papa Joe asks Aria as he grabs a slice of prosciutto.

"Well, it is extremely challenging for the parents who never got to study the new strategies. They have difficulty helping the children at home because they weren't taught the new methods. I will say, though. I have seen kids do things with numbers in their heads that adults would need a calculator for. Even I have become a better math whiz after using the strategies for so long."

"Hm, interesting. Can you show me some of the new strategies?"

"Sure! Do you have something I can write with?" Aria asks my dad.

"Here you go." Dad hands Aria a notepad and a pencil.

Aria leads my Papa through various strategies to solve simple two-digit addition and subtraction. I can tell how good a teacher she is because of her patience with each question, and how she explains it all makes sense to me. School was extremely difficult for me. I always got good grades, but it took me an enormous amount of time and energy. It's funny now to even think of me as being with a teacher because school for me was straight-up torture. Watching her talent with teaching makes me remember the one teacher in high school who helped me finally break through my own learning difficulties. I can easily see her being that person for other people.

Watching my Papa, I can see he is just about as awe-struck by Aria as I am. I can also see a tinge of nostalgia, or is that sadness?

"I can certainly see why you are a teacher. Even I understood that." Papa Joe jokes.

"Me too," Dad says in surprise, leaning against the couch.

"You know who she reminds me of, don't you?" Papa Joe looks at Mom.

"Mom." She smiles back.

"You got it. She was so smart." Papa beams with pride at the fond memory.

Aria glows with the compliment.

"Do you have any favorite teachers from movies or shows you like?" Dad asks.

"Oh. That's a good question." Aria ponders. "I grew up wanting to be the female Mr. Feeny from Boy Meets World. I loved his wisdom and teaching students about real-life issues. I also grew up with Mrs. Frizzle and Bill Nye, who used hands-on learning and the students' natural curiosity to spearhead their science curricula. More recently, I came to love Elizabeth from When Calls the Heart. She builds her curriculum based on student interest while building relationships outside the classroom. Though every teacher wants to be a version of Ron Clark."

"Who is that?" Mom asks, biting her cheese.

"He is a teacher who opened a school in Atlanta for students in high-poverty areas. He shows teachers nationwide how learning should be fun and more interactive. He maintains high expectations and standards, making the students' leadership skills unmatched. His work and that of the teachers he employs are known worldwide. He is the golden standard for teaching. Districts send teachers to their school all the time. I got to go once. It was amazing. Districts just don't realize that they get in their own way of allowing that type of learning to exist." Aria shrugs her shoulders in defeat.

"I think just knowing teachers out there feel this way is comforting. Those are great examples of teachers to look up to. Is that why you decided to teach?" Papa Joe asks.

Thinking about the memory Aria told me about her, it makes my blood boil. I remember the day we met and her telling me about the teacher who targeted her. It is always the purest-hearted people who are meant to make a meaningful impact on the world around them, who always get the most beaten down by it. Aria tells them why she studied education. Initially, the room is quiet. It's not often you hear someone say how something so horrible caused them to want to enter the same scenario that should have broken them. All for the sake of making it better for the next person.

"Wow, Aria. I don't even know what to say. You take the hits and keep on going, don't you?" Dad says.

I reach across the space between us and gently squeeze Aria's knee. "I've tried to tell you how unique and awe-struck I am by her." I muse.

"You aren't so bad yourself, Mr. America," Aria says, grabbing my hand, rubbing her thumb lightly back and forth.

"I bet you have some funny stories too," Mom says.

"Oh, do I." Aria chuckles. "One of the tests we perform involves the students reading a short story. They have to answer comprehension questions verbally afterward. One of the stories was about a fish that moved to a new place with his family. The question was, what advice would you give to someone who is moving to a new place? She said, there are many stranger dangers, and be careful if there are robbers and serial killers."

We all burst out laughing. Dad, who had just taken a sip of his lemonade, ran into the kitchen to spit in the sink before he ended up spraying it across the living room rug. I have not heard that story before. Aria laughs too, throwing her head back like a little kid herself.

"I mean, that is some pretty sound advice." Papa Joe laughs, wiping his mouth with a napkin. "What grade?"

"Second," Aria states.

The oven rings, alerting us that the homemade pizzas are ready. We spend the rest of lunch swapping stories and stuffing our bellies until I can hardly move. We tell him about Dianna, who lies on our feet under the table waiting for scraps to fall. Sadie is lying out in the sunroom, basking in the heat.

I miss this. I miss being home with my family, but seeing Aria get along with them is everything I needed to make sure of my coming decisions. Lunch wraps up, and it is time for Papa to return home. We help clean up the kitchen and go to say our goodbyes.

"What's the plan for the rest of the day?" Papa Joe puts his shoes on.

"Ask him. You know he is busy every second he is here." Mom jokes, pointing at me.

"See if some friends want to come for drinks and a fire," I state, wrapping an arm around Aria's shoulders.

"See, I told you." Tiffany rolls her eyes. "Drove all night, got here early this morning, and will somehow be up late tonight."

"I'll sleep when a mission kills me." I shrug casually.

Aria's mouth gaps open, and she slaps me in the chest. Joey just quirks up a side of his lips, throwing his hands in the air, shaking his head. My mom is not a fan of my sarcastic humor when it comes to the dangers of my job. She pushes me on the shoulder, making me pull my arm from around Aria to catch myself against the kitchen counter. Papa Joe laughs and pulls me in for a hug.

"Thanks for having me over. Aria, it was a pleasure." Papa Joe kisses both sides of her cheeks and gives her a hug. "You too, Dianna." He pats Dianna on the head.

We say our goodbyes, waving him off when he steps outside to his car.

"You think you can handle seeing some more people?" I turn towards Aria.

"I can try. I am not going to lie, I am tired, but I will manage. Just give me a few more cups of coffee first." Aria yawns, stretching her arms out wide.

"Whatever you mess up out there, you clean up," Dad says matter-of-factly.

"You don't tell me." I quip back with a grin at our own inside joke.

"I'm tellin' yah," Dad says.

CHAPTER 23

ARIA

While we wait for Antonio's friends to arrive, I go into his room to call Scarlett and Cassidy to check in on my students.

"Can you ever just enjoy a vacation?" Scarlett scolds, picking up the phone. They should have just finished putting the students on the bus home by this time.

"Can you ever answer the phone with a standard greeting?" I quip back.

"It's not within her abilities." Cassidy chimes in.

"I already know what you are going to ask. The usual suspects of your class were the usual suspects. No injuries. Nobody was sent to the office. Your typical student didn't want to do any work and tried convincing the sub that every other hour is recess." Scarlett rambles off.

"I can confirm this is true." Cassidy agrees.

"How is meeting your future in-laws?" Scarlett coos.

"Calm yourself. Ironically enough, Antonio and I did have the whole marriage talk on the way up, but I fell asleep. The conversation never finished. His parents are amazing, though. Feels like a second home already. Met his adorable grandpa. Some friends of his are coming over soon."

"Wait, wait, wait. You will not just skim over the fact that you guys had a marriage convo. What do you mean?" Scarlett screeches.

"He just talked about how basically when you know you know, and that waiting to get married is just waiting on everyone's idea of societal norms to meet their expectations. It hasn't been brought back up."

"Aria! You must bring it back up! Y'all are adorable together." Cassidy chirps.

"I will. We've just been so busy since we arrived, really, there hasn't been much time."

"Yeah. He doesn't let the grass grow under his feet when he is home, that is for sure." Scarlett responds.

"Why do I always forget you know these things?" I laugh.

"You need to get off this phone and talk to your man," Cassidy says.

"She's growing up on us." Scarlett fake cries.

"Ok, Mom, I'm gonna go now." I joke.

We say our goodbyes. I pick out a new outfit for the fire tonight. Turns out, New York is just as cold at night as I thought. I wore an oversized navy-blue sweater with an American flag and a tight pair of black lounge pants. Antonio is outside with his dad, smoking cigars and playing fetch with the dogs. His mom sits in the sunroom answering text messages.

"Any idea who I'm meeting tonight?" I say, sitting next to her on the twin bed turned couch in the sunroom.

"I would say probably Noah and Kelsey."

I don't know why, but hearing a girl's name as a best friend surprises me. Being platonic friends with a boy and a girl is nearly impossible. They must have dated at some point.

"Before you think anything, I know what you are thinking. Kelsey and Ant have been friends since high school. He dated her cousin and best friend, but those two never dated. They have always just been best friends. I think you will really like her."

"That's good to know." I giggle nervously.

"You'll see. She's nice and super mellow. She's just one of the guys. Plus, she has been dating this one guy she's with now for years. You'll like Noah too. They met in elementary school. Noah moved to another school when he went to live with his grandparents, but the two stayed friends. Don't get me wrong, they are nuts together, but a fun pair to be around." Tiffany stares out the window towards Antonio, smiling at a flashback. "Looks like someone is here now."

Antonio motions for me to come outside from the deck. Both dogs take off running towards the black SUV pulling down the driveway. Stepping out of the car is a woman with long black hair and curtain bangs. She is wearing blue jeans and a gray crewneck sweater. She isn't wearing any makeup. I am instantly envious of how she can confidently do that.

I walk out towards Antonio. Antonio grabs my hand, leading me to her car.

"Daughter!" Antonio shouts. She rolls her brown eyes, stepping out to give him a hug.

"Father." She grins. "You're Aria." She extends her hand to shake. "I'm Kelsey."

"The one and only." Antonio beams, coming behind me, wrapping his arms around my waist.

"Nice to meet you," I say, shaking her hand. "Here I thought I was the only one who calls him daddy."

Why do I do this?

Leave it to me to make the moment awkward with one of my jokes. For some reason, my brain immediately finds the worst jokes to say when I am nervous. My sarcastic, dark humor takes the moment by storm yet again.

To my surprise, Antonio and Kelsey are thrown into laughter.

"Yeah. We're going to get along just fine." Kelsey smiles.

"Where's Tim?" Antonio asks, starting to lead us back towards the deck.

"He has physical therapy." She looks at me. "Tim was in a motorcycle crash a while ago. He hit some gravel on a road coming home one day. Pitched him off. He is paralyzed from the waist down. We remain optimistic, though."

Yay me. Another item to add to my bucket list of worries. How endearing! I take a seat on the deck facing the lake. "Oh my gosh. I am so sorry. I'm sure that is extremely difficult to come to terms with."

"It's ok. It's been a little over a year, so we are conditioned to it now." Kelsey shrugs, taking a seat. Joey had already excused himself back inside when he saw Kelsey pull in.

Antonio puts the dogs in the house. Crossing his arms, he leans against the deck railing facing us.

"So where do the nicknames come from?" I ask curiously.

"Oh, you see, you are dating a bossy moron. Everyone has always joked that we argue like a dad and his daughter. He's also older by a year. It just kind of stuck." Kelsey glares at Antonio, who just nods.

"Even pre-Marines, he bossed everyone around." Around the corner walks one of the tallest men I have ever seen. He is a little taller than my dad and has dark chestnut hair. He even has eyes to match. He is wearing a blue NY hat with a red-sleeved dark gray hooded shirt. He paired it with blue jeans. Must be Noah.

Antonio takes off down the deck steps and pulls Noah into one of those handshake guy hugs.

"Hm, I'm still waiting on a run-up greeting." I joke, making Kelsey laugh.

Noah's smile makes his eyes crinkle as he approaches us. Kelsey stands up and gives him a hug. I stand up too.

"Aria, this is Noah. Noah, Aria." Antonio introduces.

"Nice to finally meet you. My ears have been bleeding from the amount of talk he has been calling me about you with." I blush at that.

"I'm just here to collect all of Ant's secrets. You know. Make sure he isn't a serial killer or something." I say sarcastically.

Antonio bumps me with his shoulder. "You wish you could use an excuse to get away that easily."

"Do squirrel murders count? What about deer? Oh, I know, rabbit." Kelsey says.

"Dude! Do you remember?" Noah starts but can't finish. He and Antonio just start laughing, and the rest is inaudible.

"Is this hunting-related or something else?" I say, trying to figure out the joke.

"Antonio's grandpa used to make him drown the squirrels in the lake he found in the barn. The deer and rabbit are just hunting-related. The ones hung in the barn are his kills." Noah says, catching his breath.

My mouth hangs open. "Antonio, drowning squirrels, that's horrible." I scold.

"It's not my fault. They were chewing through the electric lines in the barn and doing all sorts of stuff there. Blame my grandpa, it was his fault. He told me to do it. He would catch them in traps. Then he would have me throw the trap in the lake."

"You guys are sick laughing about that," Kelsey says, unamused. "Plus, how dare you tell Aria to blame it on your dead grandfather?"

"I guess I can't say anything," I say sheepishly. "I accidentally shot a squirrel in the gut in high school with a BB gun sniper rifle."

"Wait, what?" Antonio says, collecting himself. Leave it to the Marines to have the world's darkest humor.

"In high school, I was dating this guy. We were at his house with his friend. They pulled out the BB gun styled like a sniper rifle. They took turns trying to shoot this balloon off a flagpole and couldn't hit it. I asked to try, and the first shot went straight through the balloon and hit a squirrel in a tree." I say, feeling terrible.

"Your girl is a better shot than you, Ranaldi." Noah lightly pushes him on the shoulder.

"Yeah, well, I can still take you on." Antonio takes a running start, and the two fall into a wrestling match, going down the steps, fumbling on the plush grass.

"If you two roll over my garden like last time, you are buying me new seed!" Joey yells, coming outside. He and Tiffany walk out with nuts and a pitcher of spiked lemonade.

"Good to see you guys," Tiffany says, pouring herself a glass. She hugs Kelsey and shakes her head in the boy's direction. Antonio throws Noah onto his back. The move is sexy as hell, considering how large Noah is comparatively. "I swear, boys never fully grow up."

Sadie and Dianna trot out after them, lying on the deck, watching over the chaos.

"Hey, I am just glad to get more insight into Antonio. Is this what he was like pre-Marines?" I ask, laughing as Noah tries to take Antonio down.

"Worse. Much worse." Kelsey laughs along with Antonio's parents. "Still just as funny, caring, and entertaining, just more so. I would say he wasn't as structured, that's the main thing." His parents nod their heads in agreement.

"You are certainly bringing our more carefree, spontaneous, wide-open son back out," Tiffany confirms. She looks over at Antonio as only a mother can. A sudden peace crosses her face.

"Aria! Get over here! Look up." Antonio shouts from the rock wall by the lake, his arms stretched out wide.

I look up in awe. An orange, pink, and yellow sunset spread across the sky. The vastness reflects across the water. Two massive arching rainbows stretch from one side of the lake to the other. I stand up and make my way towards him. Kelsey stays back to talk to his parents.

Noah is busy taking photos of the breathtaking moment. As I get closer, Antonio grabs my hand. He lightly kisses my palm.

"Ok, Sir Bridgerton. Calm down. You are making me swoon over here." I sheepishly say, side-eyeing to see if Noah is watching us.

"Am I supposed to know who that is?" Antonio asks, confused, wrapping his arms around my shoulders, facing me towards the open water.

"Never mind. Didn't you say your unit recently got told they must do book reports?"

"Books on hardcore war, not kissing, and whatever bridge you are discussing."

I bite my lip to keep from laughing. The waves lightly brush against the enormous stones of the rock wall. This place is gorgeous. It is so peaceful. A slice of heaven on Earth. When you think of New York, this isn't typically the first view that would come to mind. Most minds jump to the city. I don't think mine ever will again. Whenever I think of New York, I will think of this property. I will think of Antonio, who has now come to stand behind me, arms wrapped around my shoulders, leaning his chin on the top of my head. My ultimate safe and comfort zone. This is zen.

"Smile, cuties," Kelsey says, coming up next to us, snapping a photo from the side on her phone.

"Alright, enough, enough." Noah groans. "We need alcohol and a fire, people."

"Noah, always bringing us back to the more important items on the itinerary." Antonio's sarcasm rolls off him.

Noah salutes him, then goes to a parade rest.

"At ease, private. Shall we fetch the provisions?" Antonio says with mock authority.

"Sir, yes, sir!" Noah shouts.

"My best friends are weirdos." Kelsey moans, placing her hands on her hips. I could be wrong, but I swear I catch Noah's eyes on her curves.

Antonio quirks his head to the side, giving Noah a devious look.

"Don't you dare, Shorty. I'll beat you there." Noah clearly understands this unspoken language.

"You have almost a whole foot on me. I can't help you; you are bred from giants." Without any further argument, the two take off running towards the garage to raid the fridge of alcohol.

At first, a silence falls over Kelsey and me as the sun rapidly seeps below the horizon line.

"I meant what I said back there. You really are good for him. We talk a lot about his rides to see you. He is happy." Kelsey says, looking out over the lake. "He needs this. He needs someone loyal. Who cares."

"I'm just returning what I am getting." I smile. "I've been through some dark times with relationships myself. I guess you can say I am a serial dater of toxic men."

"Well then, you are a perfect fit because he has picked nothing but women who cheat, it seems like. I think it's safe to call that toxic." A silent rage seeps into her features at a clear memory.

"I would never do that to him. I know what I have in him. I've been out in the world. I know what is out there. I don't want it. I want what he makes me feel. I've been cheated on before, too. Can't really prove it like he can, but a woman always knows."

Kelsey looks at me with sadness in her eyes. "Isn't that the truth?" She mumbles under her breath.

Before I can say anything else, we hear Antonio and Noah's boisterous laughter coming our way. Their arms are full of beer glasses and wine.

"I swear. If I have to help you not catch yourself on fire again, Noah, there will be hell to pay." Kelsey says, eyes glaring.

"Huh?" I question.

"Noah here decided to get blacked out drunk and fell asleep right next to the fire pit, stoking the fire to keep it going," Antonio says, bumping Noah's shoulder. "If it weren't for Kelsey, he would have probably caught fire. They were the only two left up together."

"Whatever amphibian. I'm grown now, ok. I'm a man." Noah responds by referring to the story Joey told me earlier.

If it wasn't so dark, I would hand on a Bible swear that Kelsey is as red as a cardinal. As they start the fire, she rolls her eyes, throwing logs off a stack on the rock wall, and his dad leaves. The boys return to the garage to grab a folding table and plastic cups. I already know where this is heading. Beer pong.

I never had a real party stage in my life yet. After being with an alcoholic, the idea of drinking until you are belligerent is not appealing anymore. To my surprise, they don't even fill the cups with beer. They fill them with just enough lake water to keep them from blowing off the table in the wind.

"What are teams?" Kelsey asks, placing the cups in a perfect triangle.

"Sunflower, get over here," Antonio demands, fixing the cups opposite.

"Oh no. Not pet names. I'm going to throw up." Noah fake heaves.

"Excuse him. He is allergic to happiness and functional relationships." Kelsey crosses her arms over her chest, waiting for Noah to reach his spot.

"Why do you always have to bring my family into things?" Noah mocks offense.

Antonio kisses me on the cheek, and the game begins. First, I miss every shot. Antonio is holding it down for our team. Kelsey and Noah alternate missing a shot, then sinking one, until we are down to only one cup left on our side. Kelsey throws a shot. It spins around the top of the cup. Antonio tries to pick it out with two fingers, but it stops spinning and lands in the cup perfectly.

"Aria, I am so sorry," Noah says.

"Whoa, whoa, calm yourself. She gets a redemption shot." Antonio says, reaching over and massaging my shoulder closest to him.

"I meant, 'sorry you aren't better with those fingers for her.'" Noah balls a hand into a fist, biting it to keep from laughing. Kelsey smacks him with the back of her hand across his arm.

"Aria, you have to make this now." Antonio stares Noah down, flicking him off. Competition is his strong suit.

I look across the table, and the two cups left are split. I ask for them to be placed in a straight line for my rerack. I make a show of rolling my shoulders and pretend to crack my neck. I look Noah dead in the eyes. Without looking at the cup, I throw my pitch. It bounces off the first cup. Noah tries to grab it midair but misses. It banks off the back of the second cup and falls inside. Game over.

"That's my woman." Antonio picks me up, spinning me around. "Say all the jokes you want, Noah. Let me know when you get yourself one of these." Antonio kisses me and sets me back on my feet.

Noah mumbles something under his breath while taking a sip of his beer.

The rest of the night, we play random drinking games. Since I am a lightweight, I am drunk by my third drink. To the embarrassing point, Tiffany comes out to check on us before bed. Evidently, I did not just tell her, but all-out yelled at her that I approve of her. As if she were the one who needed approval in this situation. By the end of the third drink, I have reached nonsense, word vomit, Aria. We sing songs at the top of our lungs and dance around the bonfire.

Kelsey and Noah make the responsible decision not to drive. Noah decides he will sleep on the couch in the living room, and Kelsey will sleep on the makeshift couch bed in the sunroom. We clean up our mess to the best of our drunken abilities and head inside. Antonio has to partially hold me up, so I don't fall over.

"I can't believe you actually got drunk," Antonio says as we settle into his room.

"I blame the chardon- yay." I giggle, plopping down on the bed with my arms and legs sprawling everywhere. "Hey, Ant."

"Yeah?" Antonio says, taking off my shoes since I've lost all my naturally given abilities.

"You asked me what I thought of marriage on the car ride

here." I pause. Antonio suddenly straightens, going rigid, waiting for my following words. "I think being married to you is my destiny. Like you said, we have a mutual destiny, right?"

Before I can catch his response, I pass out. I guess marriage talk can really take the energy right out of you. Twice apparently.

CHAPTER 24

ANTONIO

I wake up with a throbbing headache. I overindulged last night, but not enough to forget what Aria said before she passed out. Call it proper Marine Corps training, being able to drink and remember everything. Even if you don't want to. I have wanted to bring up the conversation about marriage from the car ride, but I didn't know how. Is that what she thinks, or is that a drunken, life-is-not-that-serious moment? Do I bring it up once she wakes up? Will she even remember saying that?

I roll over to play big spoon. When I wrap my arm around Aria, a sound escapes her, and my heart sinks. She's crying.

How long has she been crying?

"Aria? You ok? You feel sick from last night?" I lean on an elbow to get a better look at her.

She further curls into herself like she can disappear inside her own body. Another sob shudders through her body. Worry and anxiety fill me. I want to fix whatever this is. I have to fix it.

Just tell me how.

"I'm… I'm… so sorry." Aria chokes out between sobs.

Ok, now I am panicking. What is she apologizing for? Did she not mean it when she said something about being married to me?

"Aria, please, don't apologize. Come here." I scoop her into me. Her arms come to rest against my chest. Her legs weave between mine. I wrap my arms around her as tightly as possible, as if I were her personal weighted blanket. We stay like that for what feels like an eternity. I know she can probably hear my heart thundering.

"Did I say or do anything dumb?" She looks up at me, and I can see how swollen her eyes are.

Is calling me your destiny dumb?

"Is that what you are worried about?" I chuckle thinking about every idiotic thing I've said or done drunk.

It's as if her whole body crumbles in on itself. Her tears are a steady stream now. I lift her chin so she can see my eyes when I say this.

"Aria, I think I know where this is coming from. Your ex, right?"

She nods. I wipe away her tears.

"He was an alcoholic with a lot of other things going on. *You. Are. Not. Him.* You getting drunk on occasion is not equivalent. You were fun and hilarious. You dominated in beer pong." I laugh and she laughs with me. A bit of relief crept in that she smiled even for a second. "I love you, Aria Jade. Guess what? This is just another petal in the flower that's you. I'm not going to let a single one of your petals fall. I want to see you in full bloom. That means all of you, Aria. Every side you have, let it face the sun because it's my love shining back on you. You can count on that as sure as the sunrise."

Her lips crash into mine. She grips both sides of my face. This has to be the wettest kiss of my life, but I don't care. I need her to understand that I love her beyond anything she considers a flaw. This certainly wasn't one of them. Before things get too heated in my parents' house, I break away, stroking her hair. I cradle her back to my chest.

"I don't understand how anyone can be so perfect. You're always able to calm my nerves. I hope you understand that you can count on me as well."

"I know sunflower." I kiss her forehead. I can hear a few small footsteps in the kitchen. Must be Kelsey or Noah.

"I think I need some water. I am pretty nauseous."

"I'll get it. If you can, try to get ready. I am going to take you on my hangover morning cure."

***

"Greasy food and coffee. I needed this." Noah is practically salivating, staring at the breakfast menu of our local diner. He is still in his clothes from last night. So is Kelsey.

She could take out half the planet with one hungover look. Her face is stuck in the deepest sulk I've ever seen. Part of me knows it has to be because of Noah's presence. When we were in high school, the three of us were inseparable. I always thought they would be endgame, but it never happened. Still, there has always been something there. They try to hide their affection for one another, but I see it in every wisecrack at one another.

We invited my parents along too. They are very accustomed to our late-night drink sessions. Heck, they have joined in quite a few of them. My mom has her tequila; my dad has his beers.

"I will do the 55-plus rise and shine seniors special," Dad says, perusing the menu.

"What's that? The hospice special?" Aria doesn't miss a beat. She is looking at the menu and says it without a second thought.

"I thought I loved drunk Aria, but hangover Aria might be my new favorite." Kelsey burst out laughing, and soon the whole table joined in.

"Sorry. It just came out."

"If you apologize one more time on this trip," I say to her under my breath.

"Sorry." She says sheepishly, then blanches upon realizing she said sorry, again. Before she can apologize for apologizing, I hold a hand up and point to the incoming waiter.

"So, what's the plan for Mother's Day tomorrow?" Noah asks after the waiter takes our orders.

"I didn't know you were going to be here, Ant, so I have no idea," Mom says, drumming her finger on the table, trying to come up with an idea. "I've got it. The zoo."

"The zoo?" I ask, quirking an eyebrow.

"Will there be alpacas or llamas of some sort?" Aria asks, bouncing like a small child.

"Absolutely." Mom replies.

"I'm in." Aria raises her hand with a smile so big you would think it is Christmas.

"Zoo it is then." Dad nods.

We ate the rest of breakfast, detailing the night to my parents. I can tell Aria is embarrassed about getting drunk, but the more my parents laugh, the more weight you can see lifting off Aria's shoulders. By the end, she laughs with them and tells them parts of the night herself. When it is time to leave, we hug Noah and Kelsey goodbye. They both gave me glowing approval for Aria. Not that I need their approval, but it does shift things around in my head. It's further confirmation of everything I am feeling. They have known me the longest. If they think this is a good match, that is saying something. Especially considering I can't remember when they truly enjoyed someone I dated in a serious relationship. Yeah, I dated Kelsey's cousin and one of her best friends, but we all knew it would never be a long-term thing. Her cousin wanted to travel the world, but her best friend couldn't take the long distance. New York to South Carolina is not exactly a short drive away and flights are expensive. We didn't stand a chance.

I am more determined than ever to converse with Aria about our future. I know it is fast, but I understand the stereotype of why military members marry quickly more and more. It is hard to find someone willing and able to understand us. I may not have deployed, but I know plenty who have gone on deployments with the intention of proposing when they got back, only to end up killed in action. It's not the same when their friends have to tell their waiting girlfriend that he was going to propose, but died instead. I've been on pre-deployment trainings where accidents occurred, and everything the Marine wanted to do went with him. I *will* be getting out soon. I've already decided. It's done. This is what I want. Coming on this trip solidified it. However, it doesn't change everything I've learned about time being a thief. I just hope everything she has been through won't scare her off.

***

The rest of the day was nothing but pure relaxation. We played with the dogs outside, watched movies with my parents, and lay around the house. When the sun begins to set, I decide I can't wait any longer. I have to talk to Aria. I asked her to go to a sunset kayaking session on the lake. We grab some life jackets from the garage. Our neighbors who bought my grandparents' house let us use their kayaks, so I grabbed two green ones and loaded them up.

At first, we are quiet. This type of scenery can do that to you. We approach the sunset, heading away from my parents' house. Dianna waits for us on the rock wall. We tied her off to the tree near the water so she could watch us. Ducks with their young pass us swimming by. The sky crashes together in shades of orange, pink, and yellow. We pass house after house and dock after dock. I can't take it; I could hardly see the house anymore. I don't know if it's the soft sun shining on Aria's hair, her cozied up in my old Syracuse sweatshirt under her life jacket, or the look of pure awe on her face, but this moment feels right.

"Aria, I want to talk to you." My voice cracks like I'm some hormonal teenager.

Smooth idiot.

Aria's look of serenity morphs into a stiff panic.

Great, I scared her.

"We keep touching on something. It's nothing bad, I promise." I set my paddle over my lap. I grab her hand as our kayaks drift side by side.

The sunset continues to deepen, and we sit in a small, wooded cove flowing with the current. Aria swallows to calm herself, but needs me to get on with what I am trying to say.

"Last night. Before you passed out. You said you could see marrying me as your destiny." Aria goes to say something, but stops. She bites her lip and puts her head down, staring at our intertwined fingers in her lap. "I need to know if you meant that."

Her eyes shoot up to mine. I smile at her. I want her to know I think of it in a good way. She doesn't need to be embarrassed. When she doesn't answer immediately, I know she must first hear more about how I feel.

"I need to know because, like I said on the ride up here, I don't need years to know if I could marry you. This trip was the last thing I needed to confirm what I have already been feeling. I've seen too many people wait for what they wanted most in life, thinking they had all the time in the world. But time is a thief. They missed their chance, wanting the most perfect scenario. Aria, I want forever with you. However long that forever is."

Aria pinches her lips together, fighting back a smile. "What about your decision to possibly reenlist?"

"It's done. Aria, you have already opened your house and given me a key. I want to come home. I want to finish the rest of my contract, go on this training I must do, and start my civilian life with you." I stroke her cheek with my thumb. I look into her eyes, trying to imagine the war within.

Recently out of a tumultuous engagement, to now a man telling her let's get married several months later. She grabs my hand, rubbing her thumb and closing her eyes. She leans into my hand, taking deep breaths as if grounding herself before answering.

"I am not trying to hold you to anything you said when drunk. I just need to know if you mean it. Can you see a future with me?"

"Yes." She says softly. A smile spreads across her delicate

features.

The ability to use a straightforward word to feel my soul with glee is outstanding.

"Yes? You are saying yes?" I don't know whether I want to jump out of this kayak and pull her into the water with me or if I want to scream in delight.

"So just to be clear, you are proposing?"

"No."

"No?"

I grin mischievously. "This is a pre-proposal. It's a proposal to propose."

My mind is swirling a mile a minute. Now that I know we are on the same page, I have much to do. With merely months left of my contract, I have to get things in motion if I move to a different state when finished. I have to change my address, get new licenses and plates, and ask her father for his blessing to marry his daughter. Call me old-fashioned, but I know Italian dads. My dad would never be ok with my sister going off and getting married without being asked first. I have to come up with an unpredictable proposal that includes Dianna. Thought after thought slams into my brain. So much will need to happen before I go to pre-deployment training.

"I'm lost." In my spiral, I forgot to explain myself to an utterly confused-looking Aria. The sun is practically dipped below the horizon. We need to make our way back before it gets too dark.

"I'm sorry." I lean over and kiss her softly. "Let's start heading back, and I can explain." We turn the kayaks around. We sync our paddles so I can still talk to her about my thoughts. "First, if we are really going to do this, I want to ask your dad's permission to explain why now. I don't need to die at the hands of an angry New York Italian father who thinks some Marine in another state knocked his daughter up to steal her and bring her into base housing." Aria laughs, but her facial features turn serious when it dawns on her that her dad might actually think that.

"Second, when I propose, it will be much better than us in my neighbors' somewhat smelly kayaks. There would be a ring if this were a legit proposal. Lastly, there is something else I need to ask you, or I guess we need to figure out." Nervousness builds inside me.

Would she marry me before I leave for training? Part of it is selfish. Even though it is only a month and a half of training, I will be getting out so soon after. A big part that would ease my anxiety over the separation would be knowing with absolute certainty that after the training, I will be coming back to the rest of my life. That I have a firm foundation. It would only give us about four months to pull off a wedding. There is no way it could be extravagant with that kind of timeframe. I am trading all my plans for this life, I want more than anything, but it still requires security.

"Ok." Aria grunts, fighting the current as we push back down the lake. Dianna lies on the rock wall, slowly coming into view.

"Separating from the Marines and returning to the civilian world will not be easy for me. I must discover a new career in a state I've never lived in. I have to leave for a month and a half-long training. We have both confirmed we know this is it for us." The buildup is killing me. "How would you feel if we married before I left for training?"

Aria's eyes are as big as saucers. "So, in about four months?"

"Yes." I can't even look at her. My nerves are shot.

"Honestly, I would feel more comfortable if we were married when you moved in full-time. I think it would go over better for my family, too. Can I ask *you* something now?"

"Of course."

"Can we just elope somewhere? Maybe a few people, but that's it. I hate to bring up my ex at this time, but it was all about everybody else when we were planning the wedding. I invited hundreds of people I barely talked to or some I never even met, married by a preacher I don't really know, and just did so many things to appease what everyone else thought was supposed to happen. I don't even like being the center of attention. I want our wedding to be just like our marriage. "Ours.""

"Stop it," I say as we return to the house. Dianna runs over on her lead to greet us, wagging her tail.

"Stop what?" Aria asks, not understanding my response.

"Stop proving that we belong together," I smirk. "I would love nothing more than a small elopement with you and the closest people to us." I spin her around in a circle as if we are on the dance floor, tilting her back to give her a kiss she should feel down to her toes.

Dianna jumps on my side, breaking it up. I stumble over the paddles but manage to get us both back upright.

"So, do we talk to your parents then?" Aria asks, rubbing Dianna on the back.

"And give my mom a second heart attack surprise on Mother's Day weekend? No. I will make sure your dad gets the first say. So, let's enjoy this weekend."

"Yeah, could be our last," Aria mumbles as she grabs her kayak to haul back up to the rack.

CHAPTER 25

ARIA

"Llamas!" I embrace my inner child as I sprint for the open llama exhibit.

"Technically, they are alpacas," Antonio calls after me.

"You say potato, I say tomato," I shout back as I reach the fence, rolling my eyes.

"What does that even mean?" Antonio wipes one hand down his face with a groan.

"I think it means you will be a proud llama owner by the end of the day, son." Joey claps Antonio on the shoulder to Tiffany's amusement. "Congratulations. I always wanted a grand...llama."

Antonio and I have been on a high note since his 'pre-proposed' marriage yesterday. Call us crazy, but I don't want to wait either. I have dated enough. In college, I experienced my first real heartbreak and long-term relationship. Then, I dated about every kind of guy you could imagine for fun. My most recent ex showed me *everything* I need to avoid. That relationship showed me what I really need and want in a partner. None has come close to Antonio. Not only that, but I've never experienced a relationship so stable and secure. One where I don't question if I am loved. It took all our self-control not to jump each other's bones last night. I am nervous about what my family and friends will think. It will have to be presented with careful consideration because the immediate conclusion will more than likely be that I am pregnant or have simply lost my mind. Maybe both.

"You ladies check out the llamas. We are going to look at real men's sights." Joey says, puffing out his chest.

"And what are 'real men sights' in a zoo exactly?" Tiffany crosses her arms over her chest, raising an eyebrow at him.

"Lions, tigers, and bears. Whatever causes the most death and despair." Antonio leans an elbow on his dad's shoulder. They nod at each other encouragingly.

"Men." I link my arm through Tiffany's and edge closer to a fluffy brown llama waiting for some feed.

Antonio and Joey head to the next exhibit, but I can't tell what's behind the llama's barn.

"Listen, I'll have to take you to the bigger zoo when you return next year. If you think this is great, you'll love the next one."

Tiffany is already planning on another year of me being around. I love it.

"What makes you so positive that Antonio will keep me around that long?" I try not to let on to anything that Antonio and I have discussed.

"Aria, please. Look at him. I know my son. You're here for the long haul, my dear." Tiffany nods in their direction. I don't see what his dad is looking at, but I can see that Antonio's eyes are locked on me. A smile makes his eyes crinkle in the corner, and his dimples are proudly displayed. I attempt to laugh, but it sounds more like an awkward cackle.

Never let me play poker or tell me any government secrets. I'll crack the first test.

"Guess we'll see. Any tips for the future?"

"Has he told you about his theory on fifty-one, forty-nine?" Tiffany grumbles.

"His what theory?"

"His dad instilled it in him. It's not his fault." Tiffany lets out a breath. We slowly make our way towards our men. "They believe in extreme circumstances where you or he can't agree, the guy holds fifty percent of decision-making. Hence, he is the ultimate deciding vote."

As someone who dislikes making big decisions, this is a relief. I do not like using the word hate, but I *hate* decision-making. As a natural-born people pleaser, my decisions rarely work out to my benefit. I usually end up stressed and regretting my life choices. I'm sure there will be some things I will be adamant about, but I do not despise this idea.

"There could be worse things." I shrug.

"Antonio, geez, go marry the girl already." Tiffany jokes.

"Oh, I plan on it." Antonio pulls me in, whispering and wrapping an arm around my waist.

I kiss him on the cheek, trying not to step on his feet as we take a few steps forward. Now I see that they were looking at a pair of gorillas sitting back and observing the crowd.

"Just look at the judgment of others they display. Isn't it great?" Joey puts both hands on his waist, admiring the lifestyle.

"You have problems, Dad. They are vast and immense." Antonio lays his head on my shoulder, still embracing me from behind.

"You inherited them. Just remember that." He winks.

We spent the rest of the Mother's Day afternoon enjoying the zoo. We feed giraffes carrots, take photos of feeding the birds as they land on us in the aviary, and grab a late lunch at a BBQ shack. As if the day couldn't be any more enjoyable, I discovered that Joey is friends with a local rancher named Buddy. We are going to go help feed and check on his cattle tomorrow. It will be the last thing we do before we drive home.

When we get back to the house, Antonio has determined he can't hold in the secret of us being serious about getting married. He decides we need to call up some friends, so we settle on Chris, Scarlett, and Lee. We will probably tell Kelsey, Cassidy, and Noah on the way home tomorrow, judging by how he is chomping to tell all our closest friends. We desperately want to tell Kelsey and Noah in person while we are here, but we just won't have time to get back up with them before leaving town.

Typically, my brother and sister-in-law are two of my go-to people for advice, comfort, and significant life events. But we decided it's best to keep it just friends until we tell our parents.

First up, Chris and Scarlett.

"Hello," Chris answers the phone. Antonio has it on speaker.

"Hey, man. Scarlett's home?" Antonio and I settle down by the lake. His parents are inside. Dianna is lying on the grass between us, watching the geese on the lake.

"Yeah, why?"

"Put me on speaker and grab wifey. We have something to tell you guys." Antonio looks up at me. His eyes are bright with excitement. He squeezes my hand to the point of nearly no circulation.

"Is everything ok?!" Scarlett's voice fills the air.

"More than ok. Aria and I have discussed the idea of getting married." Antonio kisses the palm of my hand. I smile so wide I feel like my jaw will break in half. Scarlett's reaction is pure screaming. If I were a betting woman, I would say Chris would be rolling his eyes and covering his ears.

"I knew it. I knew it. I knew it!" She screams.

"That's not all." I sing into the phone. "We have also discussed getting married *before* he leaves for pre-deployment training. So, in a few months. We would elope."

"What?!" Chris and Scarlett both say simultaneously. Thankfully, it wasn't harsh; it was more like shocked greatness.

"I have to talk to Aria's dad first." Before Antonio can even finish, Chris is already laughing.

"Good luck, man." Chris continues laughing.

"Parents love me. You know that." Antonio brushes off his shoulder unbothered. "Just thought we would give you a heads up since we will probably need some support next to us that day." He winks at me. It amazes me how his winks melt me to my toes every time.

"I accept. I approve. Oh my gosh! Whatever you guys need." Scarlett's level of happiness is unmatched.

"Thank you both for being so supportive of this. We know it's pretty fast." I say nervously.

"I would have married Scarlett way quicker if I could've. Our families would've killed us if we didn't have a huge wedding. Society just preaches waiting longer, but we knew pretty much instantly." We can hear them kiss.

"Aw, guys. He does have a heart." Scarlett jokes.

We continue to talk to them for a few more minutes. I know I will be asking Scarlett to be my matron of honor. She has been a solid friend. I can tell her anything at any time. The true definition of a best friend. We are on such a high getting off the phone with them. The fact that neither of them questioned us wanting to do this proves their trust in us as individuals and as a couple.

I move to sit on Antonio's lap. After a few steamy minutes of making out as the sun lowers, we call Lee.

"Sup, idiot," Lee answers.

"Shut up, loser. You're on speaker. Aria and I have something to tell you." Antonio is not smiling as much on this call. He seems more nervous. I rub my hand lightly down his arm. My other is wrapped snug around his neck.

"Come on, man. She's pregnant already. Didn't your old man teach you about condoms?" I clasp my hand over my mouth, trying not to laugh but failing miserably.

"He came in and just threw a bag of condoms at me and told me to use them when I was like sixteen. Besides the point."

"No, I'm not pregnant." I state, shifting my position on

Antonio's lap to cuddle more.

"We want to get married." When Lee doesn't respond, he looks at me. I bite my lip and shrug. "We want to get married before I leave for training."

You could cut the tension with a knife. Lee takes a deep breath on the other side.

"Why do you have to do that? Why not wait? Have you even had an argument yet?"

"Why not? We already know we love one another. We have the same views on religion, politics, kids, marriage roles, you name it. We align well. We discussed topics that took me years to get to know people. We haven't argued either, but I don't doubt we could handle it. It's to be expected." Antonio is beginning to get upset. It rolls off him. If he were a bull, this would be the head down, scratching at the dirt, ready to charge moment.

I did not give much thought to the fact that we haven't argued yet. It is a slight concern. Does he fight fair? Does he name-call? Need space? Does he hold things in and bring them up all at once? It is something to consider. I agree with Antonio because we can weather the storm together. Like he said, disagreements are inevitable.

"You two haven't even lived together."

"Plenty of people don't live together before they get married. I practically live with her every weekend."

And the bull is now running full steam at the matador.

"It's ok." I kiss his temple. His whole body is rigid. He shifts in his seat, lifting me slightly, so he is sitting up straighter.

For some reason, the doubt is flying right over my head. A bit of me is sad, especially coming off the phone with two of our closest friends who were so ecstatic for us. I think we will only hear more doubt as more people come to find out. I still cannot even fathom how my family will feel about the news.

"Lee, you know how short life is, man. We know what we want, and it is each other. It doesn't take long to understand who a person is. You know that too. We are going into this well aware of the struggles that could occur along the way." I decide to continue to stay quiet. Reading between the lines, I can tell there are things I may not know about Lee's story. I am going to let Antonio handle this one.

"You don't need my permission. Aria, this is nothing against you. I think you're great. Really. I do. You make him happier than I have ever seen him. You've clearly been doing it for him from the jump. I just think arguments, living together, and time are all things you guys should consider. Like you said, Ant. I would know."

Can steam blow out of someone's ears? I swear it is coming out of Antonio's.

"You know what? We have to be up early to feed some cows. We are going to let you go. Thanks for the support." Antonio doesn't let Lee answer; he just hangs up.

It is silent. The only noises are the lapping of waves against the rock wall, the crackling of wood in the firepit, and crickets.

"Honey, it's ok. We should expect pushback and people not to completely understand. It is bound to happen. If we are nervous about telling our parents because of their reactions, we should expect the same from others. It's not popular to do what we are trying to do." I drape both arms around him, pulling myself into him. I feel him start to relax. His body slumps back into the chair.

"Can we just go to sleep?" I pull back. I wasn't expecting that reaction. I nod and get up. He grabs my hand, leading Dianna and me back towards the house. The night is over.

***

"I am going to name you Tootsie!" I squeal.

We stand in Buddy's cattle field filled with cows and their calves. Buddy's land is massive, with a small pond surrounded by trees to the right. The fields are sectioned off. We will use the truck and feed to get the cows to go from one field to the other so they can eat from a different spot. I have my hand out, feeding a few pellets to a brown, black, and white brindled cow. It is one of the cutest cows I have ever seen.

We never got to discuss the things that Lee said. Antonio is trying to sweep it under the rug for now. He woke me up by kissing nearly every inch of me. The torture of not being able to be intimate with him is the worst type of suffering.

"Aria, you just named a future steak." Buddy and Joey laugh as they continue tossing pellets to get the rest of the cattle around us. "Great, now I have to get her a llama and save a cow from slaughter. Next, she will want a horse." Antonio throws his hands up and places them on his hips. "Before you can ask, no. We do not have the yard for a horse." I see Joey eye Antonio at the mention of the word 'we,' but he chuckles anyway.

I'm checking out Antonio; he makes my cowboy romance dreams come true. The man hunts, fishes, hikes, can ride various forms

164

of transportation, will ride a horse, and looks fine standing in a cattle field. He is wearing a green and blue flannel with Wrangler jeans. He borrowed a pair of his dad's brown boots. He looks *good.*

Meanwhile, I did not expect to come to New York, of all places, and end up on a farm. Hence, the blue jean shorts, lavender V-neck shirt, tennis shoes, and a red Gamecocks hat. I have failed all the ranchers by walking on holy farmland in a pair of gray memory foam sneakers. It might even be a sin.

If my southern grandparents could see me now.
"She is pregnant, so she will be sticking around for a little while," Buddy says, patting Tootsie on the back.

I stick my tongue out at Antonio like the five-year-old heart I really have. "See. Plus, I would ask for a puppy first. Dianna needs a friend." I cross my arms across my chest.

"The only way we have two dogs is if we get a German Shepherd puppy. All black, preferably." Antonio scoffs, throwing pellets out of the bucket.

"Deal! Deal! Deal", I squeal, jumping up and down, making the cows scatter around me.

Antonio wipes a hand down his face.

"You walked into that one, son," Joey says, elbowing Antonio.

"Don't worry, you will walk into plenty more of those compromises. Give it time." Buddy smiles, making his sun-worn face crinkle.

Buddy is the most tried and true cowboy I have ever seen. He is older, probably around sixty. He has on Wranglers, boots caked in mud and manure, a blue jean style button down, and a well-worn tan Stetson hat. Even his skin looks like leather from many hours in the sun on the ranch. Evidently, he was originally from Kentucky with the accent to match.

"How long have you been married, Buddy?" I ask as we load the truck to help push the cattle further into the following field.

"Oh, over thirty years. We will be celebrating our fortieth before you know it." He smiles at a distance as if looking back towards their house, even though we can't see it through the thick set of trees. "Met and married her in two weeks."

My jaw slackens, and Antonio looks at me with a knowing smile.

"That's amazing." Part of me wants to tear up seeing someone successfully married for so long with even less time than Antonio and me.

"Met her at a rodeo. She was a trick rider. I was an announcer about to take over the family ranch. We knew on the first date that this was it. Sure, we had our struggles initially, but those were different times. People fought harder for love. We didn't give up so easily at the first sign of trouble." He takes off his hat and dusts it off on his jeans. He wipes his brow with the back of his shirt sleeve and slams the door back on his head before getting in the small blue truck. Joey climbs in after him in the passenger seat.

Antonio places his hands on my hips to help me climb into the truck bed. He lifts me up, puts me on the tailgate, and jumps after me. We grin at each other.

"What did I tell you? Two weeks or two months. I know what I want. I know we will make it. I want to be with you the rest of my life, sunflower. I'd better die first, though, because I am not going one second without you in this world." Antonio says in my ear. He wraps an arm around me, pulling me next to them on the tailgate. Our legs dangle off the edge, and I lean my head on his shoulder.

I love every piece of this man. I see his value and worth, not just as my boyfriend, but as my best friend. I know his potential to be the husband I've prayed for and the partner I need to raise children with. How quickly he has become the most critical person in my world. I am not saying the road will be easy. I'm sure there are topics we have not yet thought about to discuss or scenarios that will bring out the worst in us. Yet, here I am with hope and another prayer to get us to the metaphorical altar. I'll be here when Antonio is ready to discuss Lee's concerns. I am not going anywhere.

CHAPTER 26

ANTONIO

I have rarely taken a trip that has altered my life's trajectory. In fact, I can only really think of two. When I joined the Marines and went to basic training. Then again upon meeting Aria during my trip to Charlotte. Now, I have a third. This trip to surprise my mom for Mother's Day became a launch point for the rest of my life. After talking to Lee, I was angry. My blood was practically boiling in my veins. I immediately got a tension headache from the sudden spike in my blood pressure. I know there will be doubt around what we want to do, but I was hoping that after he saw me at my lowest point, he would be more on our side after seeing how happy I am now. At the end of the day, that's his opinion and his right to voice it. He is still one of my best friends. Undoubtedly, he will still come when it happens and be planted right by my side in his dress blues.

Watching Aria today felt like I was seeing her in her natural habitat. I've never been with a woman who could embrace the outdoors as much as I. Growing up, I always enjoyed visiting Buddy's ranch. If it wasn't for my desire to serve, I probably would have ended up helping him.

Once we finish at the ranch, we have to get everything ready back at home. Aria is such an organized packer. It took her no time to get packed because she always put whatever she used back as soon as she was done with it daily. On the other hand…if I am not with the Marines, I have no sense of tidiness regarding my luggage. I just throw everything in my bag and call it a win. My motto is: if it fits, let it zip.

We decide on dinner and a movie night before catching an early bedtime, so we can leave at four AM. The truck is packed. We are wearing what we plan to ride in tomorrow. Thankfully, this time, Aria is going for comfort. She wears a cozy white, real tree camo crew neck sweater and baggy sweatpants. With her makeup off and glasses on, she still looks like a goddess in my eyes.

Mom made her pasta with clam sauce, baked a fresh load of rosemary bread, and Dad made his Italian dandelion green salad. Sadie and Dianna lay in wait beneath the table.

"So, what's next when you two love birds get home?" Mom asks, passing the salad around the table.

I see the side of Aria's mouth quirk up. I bow my head to hide my smirk. "Get ready to leave for training in a few months. Guess I need to search some websites for that German Shepherd I promised Aria today." I shoot a glare her way, but she looks up, beaming.

"You what?" Mom swirls a spoonful of pasta onto her plate.

"He walked right into a compromise. It was a dog or save a cow from slaughter." Dad grins, amused at my latest stupidity.

"Yeah, stick with the dog." Mom agrees.

Aria pumps a fist in the air, bringing it back down in victory. I shake my head. Reaching under the table, I give her thigh a light squeeze. That is probably not the best idea since we cannot be intimate here. I can tell how sensitive she is because her legs clench together at the proximity of the contact.

"Aria, what about you?" Dad asks.

"We are getting really close to the end of the school year. We have end-of-year testing and a field day coming up. Antonio said he would volunteer." Aria snickers.

"Wait, what? That's the first I am hearing this." My eyes widen as I grab a piece of bread, almost dropping it to the floor. Dianna sits up quickly, ready for it to no avail.

I love kids, but huh? Did I just get volun-told to do something?

"I'm just kidding. You would have to do a background check anyway to volunteer. It's a form on our website." Aria waves it off, ready to move to the next topic.

"You want kids, Aria?" Mom asks, making me nearly choke. "It's a valid question. I need grandkids at some point in the future."

I let out a slight growl under my breath.

Can't I marry the woman first? Dang mom.

"I do. I would love to if I can. I'm going to be honest, if I had to choose, I would love to have two boys. I grew up a tomboy. I also feel like I wouldn't know what to do with a little girl because of that." Aria lets out a small laugh.

Part of me would love to volunteer for the field day to see her in action with her students. I can see her as a compassionate but fair disciplinarian. When we discussed kids, before we talked about her willingness to do whatever needed to be done. I am all for it if she could still work and balance everything. If she wants to be home to raise the kids and return once they start school. That's great too. I will let her decide what feels right for her and our kids.

"I have to say, Antonio, I approve. Aria, you've been an absolute pleasure. I really can't thank you guys enough for this nice surprise. It has been an amazing long weekend. The best Mother's Day gift a mother can have is seeing her son with a woman she respects and adores. It's like having another daughter." Mom reaches out and gives Aria a warm side hug.

"Well, I approve of you guys," Aria responds absentmindedly. I clench my lips together and close my eyes. I can sense her instant overthinking regret. Her thoughts are practically in my mind, screaming, 'Why did I say that?'

Who tells future potential in-laws that they approve of them? My woman. That's who. My sunflower. Always the fully bloomed, standing ten roots down version of herself. Guess I won't tell her this is actually the second time she has 'approved' of my mother. At least this time she is sober.

"Mutual approval all around. Lucky bunch we are. I, too, approve of you as my parents if you were wondering where I stand in all this." I lift my glass in a cheers motion. I take a swig. Aria's shoulder slowly came down from her ears. Her lips quirk to one side.

"Well, thank God for that." Dad clinks his glass against mine. We all burst into laughter.

We go to bed not too long after dinner since we decided to leave at four AM. My parents wake up when we do to make us last-minute sandwiches for the road. They hug Aria like she wasn't a mere stranger to them a few days ago. I can tell they are just about as invested as I am. I'm pretty sure they would steal Dianna if Aria let them. I'm not telling Aria, but I am anxious to return to North Carolina. When she thought I was sleeping last night, I was making plans with Aria's parents to talk to them. I decided to sit down with them to ask for her hand in marriage. It feels like the most respectful way to put both minds at ease at one time.

On the ride back, we call Kelsey, Noah, and Cassidy with the news about wanting to get married before I leave for training. All three are over the moon excited for us. Cassidy is already talking Aria's ear off about where she could get a dress fast, how she could do her hair, and she is sending photos of both. Kelsey and Noah felt like it was a no-brainer after meeting her. They said if it all works out, they would be more than willing to make the ride down to attend.

We spent nearly twelve hours riding along singing songs. Aria naps or reads a book every couple of hours. Every time I peek over when she is on the phone, I see her poring through Pinterest for wedding inspiration. I try to steer the conversation away from it as much as possible, so I don't tell her my plans to talk to her parents. My insecurity and lack of willpower already had me 'pre- propose', but now I want to make it special. I know many people discussing getting married before the actual proposal, so I don't feel too bad. Since the last time she was proposed to was far from perfect, I know mine needs to be grand. The funny thing is, she isn't a huge gestures kind of girl. It will have to be minimal enough not to cause her to feel uncomfortable or embarrassed. But it must be thoughtful enough, so she feels all the affirmation in the world. First, we have to get home.

***

I stand outside Gigi and Tula's house. My mind is fried from all the driving. I still have hours to go after this conversation…if I make it out alive. Thankfully, Aria gave me some long-overdue physical motivation after I helped bring Dianna and the bags into the house. I tried my best not to seem eager to leave, but I was practically bouncing on my toes to come have this talk. Now that I am here, I am afraid to ring the doorbell.

Come on, Ant. You are a Marine. Pull yourself together. Man up.

Before I can continue egging myself on, the front door flings open. Gigi stands at the door looking massive as ever in his veteran shirt and khaki cargo shorts.

"You going to come in, or do you prefer to continue to speak words of affirmation to yourself on my porch?" He says, pointing to the doorbell camera.

Of course…

I step inside. Tula is sitting on the couch, cross-stitching something on her white shorts. She keeps having to move her pink blouse out of the way. When I come in, her head snaps up and she smiles.

"How was the trip?" She asks, setting down her project.

"It was spectacular. My parents, grandpa, and friends all adored Aria, as you could probably have guessed." I take a seat across from her.

"So, you needed to talk?" Straight to the point, Gigi is back to play.

"Let's sit and relax." I point to the couch. "Wait. Does that give you Air National Guard flashbacks?" Tula giggles, looking over at Gigi, who came to sit down next to her.

"Oh, almost forgot, do I need something to write with? Crayons work for you? You have a preferred flavor? Oops, I meant color." Gigi's mouth quirks into a maniacal grin.

"That was a good one." I nervously chuckle. "I guess I will just jump right in with it. You have a wonderful daughter. Since we are long-distance, we've had the opportunity to talk and discuss topics beyond what I have ever experienced with anyone. Even people I've known my whole life. I've never gotten to know a person so deep, so quickly." Gigi shifts in his spot, crossing his arms over his chest. Tula still smiles kindly in my direction. "I love your daughter." I take a deep breath. "I wanted to come here today to ask for her hand in marriage." Gigi's eyes shoot up to the ceiling. He takes a breath and leans forward with his elbows on his knees. Tula's hand rests on her mouth with her other arm across her chest.

Freaking out.

My heart is beating so hard I can hear it banging in my eardrums. I clear my throat a few times to cover up the fact that it feels as if I am going to hyperventilate. I would rather do the rappelling wall without proper equipment than wait for this response.

"I know it seems sudden. I can assure you that she is not pregnant, and this isn't some benefits scam. Her ex asked for permission before, so this probably comes as a bitter reminder. I wouldn't have come here today if..." I don't get to finish. Gigi holds up his hand to stop me.

"You're wrong." I gulp as he stares me down intently.

Here it comes. The rejection.

"Her ex never asked me permission to marry her. I never heard that he loved her, would take care of her, any of it." He looks me in the eye. Tula rubs his back as he sits back up. "I respect you coming and asking us. Many men don't do that anymore. It means a lot to us. I would be remiss if I didn't ask and tell you a few things." I nod, remaining silent. "Let me start by saying I knew this was coming. I didn't know it would be coming so soon." He tilts his head and shrugs.

"But I knew you were it when you told me your intentions and why you named her sunflower. You and she are adults. It's your decision to do this. I would hope for at least a lengthy engagement?" Tula looks to me on this and nods in agreement.

Oh boy.

"Actually, sir. We want to get married before I leave for training in October." You would think I punched him in the gut. He leans back on the seat, wiping his mouth with his hand.

"Ok, so you two have already talked about this?" He replies.

"Yes, sir." Gigi looks at Tula. She gives a weak smile.

"Right. So let me ask you this then. Why? How do you two know this is it?"

"We don't want to wait to be married just to make everyone around us feel comfortable with the timing. You don't have to date someone for years to know if you are perfectly fit. Marriage isn't easy. We are going to have hard days. We might have a hard season, but that's when we will return to who we are at our core. At your daughter's core is a loyal, God fearing, compassionate, intelligent old soul. She is so wise, furiously independent, and stubborn. We are both stubborn. That's another reason I know we won't let this ever end. Once we love someone, we love them hard. Nothing or nobody will get in the way of that." Tula's smile makes a grand return on her features. Even Gigi can't help but smile.

"Listen, we like you. As her father, I will tell you that if you two ever can't do it anymore, you bring her home to us." A wave of emotion takes over him, and his shoulders shudder. Tula's eyes grow glossy. "I wish I had gotten to say these things before. As her parents, I need you to promise that no harm will ever come to her. I would lay down my life for her soul. I would do it for anyone in my family, including you. If I am going to say yes to you, I need you to promise me those two things. That if things go bad, just bring her back to us, and that you will sacrifice whatever it takes to ensure her safety." Tears stream down their faces now. I can't help it; I tear up too. I think about everything she went through in her prior engagement.

I stand up and walk forward to them with an outstretched hand. "Sir, as soon as my contract is up, I am coming home to her. I take my signature on documents seriously. If I signed up to fight for a whole country of people I don't even know, imagine the fight I would put up after signing a marriage license for the most important person in my world. Your daughter will be loved to the depth of my soul and protected with every fiber of my being." Gigi stands up.

For a brief second, I doubt that he will shake my hand. He shakes his head, and my heart drops into my stomach. It is a shock when he grabs my hand with force, bringing me into a tight hug. Tula's hand comes up to her mouth as tears stream down. She gives me a hug, too, before we all sit back down.

"So," Tula says, wiping her eyes with a tissue from the side table. "How do you plan to propose?"

A slow smile creeps across my face. "Now that is where I will need some help from you two.

***

"I'm going to give you one opportunity to explain why you are being such an unsupportive jerk." Lee sits in my barracks room. I bite out each word. I may still be flying high from getting Aria's parents' blessing, but the rage I feel about my best friend not being all for this is eating me alive.

Lee rocks forward. He rests his arms on his legs, hanging his head. His massive hands rub the back of his neck, where post-workout sweat still beads. "There are things you don't understand about me. You don't know everything about my last deployment. I have good reason for my reaction beyond just wanting to protect you after your post cheating spiral."

I thought I knew everything about his last deployment.

"What does that mean?" I plop on the bed facing him.

Lee pauses, and then the most unexpected thing happens. His shoulders quiver, and he begins to sob. "I killed them. I made the call. They all died because of me." He chokes out.

"Whoa, whoa, what are you talking about?" My brain scrambles in a million directions.

Is he talking about his squad? I know one guy who died by suicide, but he wouldn't tell me what happened.

"We were doing routine checks of cars at a checkpoint. It was monotonous. We did it practically every day. Everyone always stopped. We would check their identification, check the car for weaponry, and let them on their way." Lee sits back in the chair, looking out the window. "We had a car coming. Private Erikson and I were waving the car down to stop, but they kept coming. We radioed back the situation. They told us to make the call on what to do next. We shot in the air, trying to prompt them to stop, but they wouldn't. They kept coming." Tears stream down his face the longer he explains. "I was the higher rank. I had to call it, so I did. We shot the car as it came closer. When we checked the car, we realized it was a family. They were all dead. The dad. The mom. The...the." Lee can't contain it anymore; his sobs overtake his whole being.

No, no, no. Don't say it.

"The baby. A bullet had somehow hit the baby in the seat behind the driver." Lee folds over himself, burying his head in his arms against his legs.

"Lee, I am so sorry, I didn't know. But more importantly, you didn't know. You were just doing what you thought you needed to do to keep the base and others safe. You didn't mean to do it." I hop off the bed, laying a hand on his back.

"Private Erikson couldn't handle it when we got back to base. He ended up shooting himself. Everything. It was my call. My decision. It's my fault. I couldn't deal with it all once I returned home. My girlfriend didn't understand at the time. She couldn't handle the PTSD or my inability to discuss it. She left. That's what I am trying to protect you from. Falling for someone who may not stay. You two haven't even really disagreed on anything. I can't have another friend die."

I've never felt worse in my entire life. It all makes sense now why he can't stay in a relationship, why my darkest moment affects him so much, and why this wedding idea is astronomical to him. "Lee, I am never going to do something like that. Can't you see that Aria gives me a reason to want to live even more than I already realized before meeting her? She isn't going to leave at the first sign of trouble. If things get terrible, we have her therapist to whom we can always talk." I pause, not wanting to make him shut down. "Lee, I think you should talk to him. He has really helped Aria. He could help you, too."

"There are so many layers to that day. So much happened. I can't even get into it all right now, and I just don't want you to think I am a jerk for no reason. I am truly sorry. I want to support you. I will. Maybe I should talk to someone." Lee wipes his tears with the sleeve of his gym shirt.

"First things first, can you please apologize to Aria? Then, we can find out if you can talk to her therapist." Lee stands up, and I pull him in for a hug. "Let me support you now, man. It's time for me to step up for you. Thank you for telling me. I know that wasn't easy."

Lee steps back. "Thanks for listening. If you tell anyone I cried, I'll assign you extra PT for at least two weeks. Now, give me your phone so I can call Aria." He holds out his hand.

And he's back, ladies.

CHAPTER 27

ARIA

JUNE

"Antonio, it is your birthday, how is it that you are the one bringing me a surprise?" Here we are again, the three of us driving down the road. Me, Antonio, and Dianna. Our own little family unit.

"It really is something for both of us, I would say. Trust me, I will get as much out of this as you are."

School just let out for the summer, and Antonio wants to take me out to celebrate that I am officially off probationary teaching license. I am fully certified. The last few weeks have been a whirlwind. We hung out with my family, and not mentioning to them what we discussed in New York is eating me alive. I want to tell them so bad. Thankfully, talking about it with Scarlett and Cassidy has helped tremendously.

I don't know how we didn't get in trouble the last two weeks of school. Testing was over, so we spent every second getting our classes together to pull dress, ring, and decoration inspiration together. We used the excuse that my second graders needed exposure to what third grade would be like before they went for summer break. Whenever I found a ring I liked, Scarlett would screenshot it and send it to Antonio. Poor guy had his phone blown up for days on end. I don't even know if he could afford to buy a ring immediately if he does propose soon. Military members don't exactly get paid their worth either.

When Antonio returned to base, he and Lee talked long about us wanting to get married. It turns out his grumpy disposition on the whole thing is just being protective, and there are other aspects he said he couldn't describe to me yet. He even called to let me know he was available, not if, but *when* I decided to leave Antonio 'on the curb.' Thankfully, I can take a joke, and he can take a long walk off an extremely short pier. Lee apologized at least three times and said over time he would tell me everything so I could understand him better, but for now, all I needed to know was that it was mission-related on a deployment. I know when to take the hint and not ask questions. I accepted the apology, and we have moved on.

I have no idea where he is taking me; by the sounds, he seems confused, too. He mutters a string of curse words under his breath, holding his phone up to his face that keeps recalculating.

After about three hours, I realized where we were going. We are heading towards Myrtle Beach. Now this is the way to start a summer vacation season.

"The beach?!" I squeal excitedly.

"Bingo." He pats my thigh, keeping his eyes on the road ahead.

He drives us directly to a small parking lot between two hotels. You can see the sand and glistening waves crash against the shoreline. I used to go to the beach all the time growing up. My Grannie Annie had a beach house here in North Myrtle.

"Oh my gosh. I didn't bring a bathing suit." I huff at people walking onto the hot sand carrying towels with wagons of gear.

"Hold on." Antonio gets out of the truck. I feel the truck shake as he grabs a bag from the truck bed. I see him holding up one of my Lily Pulitzer bags in the rearview mirror.

This man thinks of everything.

"Let's go check it out first before you change. We should see where we want to set up for the day." Antonio throws the bag over his shoulder. He opens the door to the backseat, and Dianna hops down, sniffing her surroundings.

He opens my door, helping me down. We walk onto the sand. Dianna's leash is strapped around my wrist. I carry my brown flip flops in one hand and hold Antonio's with the other. As the ocean wind picks up, my curled hair blows around my face. I didn't know where we were going, so I wore a white tank top tucked into a pair of blue jean shorts. At least I brought sunglasses.

We make our way down to the water. The beach is packed

with people and umbrellas. School is officially out, so everyone is already flocking here. Dianna acts scared at first as the waves quickly approach. Every time one comes near her, she jumps back, pawing at it. Before long, she throws herself fully into them, chomping her massive jaw. Antonio keeps looking around up and down the beach. His protective instincts never take a day off.

"Ready for your surprise?" He asks, stepping before me with his back to the waves. He holds my hips in place so I face him and the endless waves ahead.

"I thought this was the surprise." I pull him towards me as a wave comes crashing behind him.

"Turn around."

I turn around and at first, I see absolutely nothing but massive amounts of sunburnt beachgoers and children playing in the sand. Then, I see them. Scarlett, Chris, and Cassidy walk through the sand straight for us. It's not just them. Scarlett is snuggling what appears to be a small, black pom-pom. That can't be right.

Oh my gosh.

"You didn't!" I scream. It is an all-black German Shepherd puppy. "Shut up! No way!"

Scarlett and Cassidy look at one another and take off running. Scarlett's hair streams behind her in flowing waves. She wears a royal blue two-piece bathing suit with a white crocheted cover-up dress. Cassidy's blonde hair is bouncing, tied up in a high ponytail. She has a neon pink one-piece with a white buttoned collared dress shirt open and blowing out behind her. Their grins are huge. Chris rolls his eyes, shaking his head. He throws his hands up in the air. He walks behind them carrying all their supplies.

"Say hello to Dianna's new best friend." Scarlett squeals, holding out the pup.

The puppy uncurls from the ball she was in with a big yawn. She has a thick coat with plush black fur. One ear pointed straight up; the other was bent, not yet fully erect. She let out a small pink tongue and began excitedly panting. She is pawing in my direction.

"Oh, my goodness. She is so cute. Dianna, look! You have a sister!" I kneel to her level, letting them sniff each other. Dianna pounces on her front paws, bending down with her rear in the air, ready to play. "They like each other."

Chris catches up, laying chairs, towels, and bags onto the sand a few feet from us before heading over.

"Thank you, guys, for picking her up." Antonio bro hugs it

out, then hugs Scarlett and Cassidy.

"Of course, dude. It was no problem." Chris says, wiping his sweaty hands off on his navy-blue swim shorts.

"I can't believe you did this. What are we going to name her?" I tuck into Antonio's side. He is wearing khaki cargo pants and a gray striped collared shirt. Not your usual beach attire, but I suppose he was just trying to throw me off.

"Guess we will have to figure that out. Cassidy, do you mind holding her for a minute?" Antonio says, taking the pup into his arms and handing her off.

"Is that even a question?! Give her here!" Cassidy wastes no time. She grabs the pup and heads towards the beach chairs to set one up. She sits down with our new puppy.

"There is one more surprise", Antonio says, grabbing my hand. Chris slaps Antonio with a light pat on his shoulder. He throws an arm around Scarlett's. They go join Cassidy, swooning over the puppy.

Antonio turns me back to the waves. The breeze blows against my face.

"Do you mind holding this?" Antonio says to someone behind me, handing off Dianna's leash. I turn my head to see which of our friends it is.

"Lee?"

"For one night only." He winks, taking Dianna's leash and slapping Antonio a low high five. He backs away towards the rest of our friends. I suddenly realize they are not alone.

Gio, Carly, and Cam all stand behind them. Cam is playing with the sand at Gio and Carly's feet. They wave enthusiastically.

"What is going on?" I turn to ask Antonio, but I don't see him.
My heart!

Antonio is kneeling on one knee in the sand. "Hey, Gigi. You have it?"

Stop! Let the ugly cry commence.

Dad walks over with a small black box. Mom has her arm through his. When they reach us, they pull me into a hug. They swipe away a few tears. Dad hands Antonio the box. Looking into his eyes, I can see how big this moment is for him. His eyes show the emotion of a father who watched his daughter go through hell. They show the handing over of trust, protection, and love to another man. He knows the value of handing over this box. A literal circle of trust enclosed inside. He clasps Antonio with a squeeze on the shoulder. Dad and

Mom join the others.

"Aria, I wanted as many of the most important people to us to be here as possible." I look at him through blurred vision since I can't stop the waterworks now. "You've become the most important person in my life. You're my best friend. I love your soul and your spirit. You take care of the people you love. I know that quality will one day make you a phenomenal mother. I want to show you my devotion to you every day for the rest of my life. I want to be your protector and provider. I'm not saying every day will be a cake walk. We will disagree on things. It will happen, but won't change how you live in my heart. You are it for me and always will be. Aria Jade Pecorelli." My chest heaves knowing what is coming next. Small sobs escape me. "Will you please do me my life's greatest honor and be my wife? Will you marry me?"

"Are you kidding me?!" I yell, tossing my head into my hands. "Of course I will!" Antonio punches the air in victory. He opens the box, and a silver ring with a perfect diamond sits in the middle. It's precisely what I would have picked for myself: simple, elegant, timeless. He jumps up, pulling me in for a kiss. He lifts me up. I swing my legs around him. Everyone on the beach is cheering. Dianna is barking as Antonio spins us in circles. I've never cried out of happiness, but there is a first time for everything.

"Dog pile!" Chris and Lee yell in unison.

Gio, Carly, Chris, Scarlett, Cassidy, and Lee run at us. They tackle us into the waves, clothes and all. Gigi and Tula embrace each other and hold onto Dianna's lead. Cam plays with our nameless pup, who jumps around him in circles.

Antonio helps me get back to my feet in the water. None of us can stop our laughter. I hang onto Antonio, wrapping my arms around his neck.

"So, future Mrs. Ranaldi, were you surprised?" He asks, placing his forehead against mine as a chaos of splashing ensues around us from all our friends.

"I don't know how you pulled this off. I am beyond surprised."

"Everyone got here last night and stayed at that hotel." He points to one of the hotels behind us, right on the beach. "When I went to the truck bed to get the bag of clothes I snuck out of the house last night, I also texted to let them know we were here. I told you. This is just as much a birthday gift for me as a surprise for you."

"You're incredible." I kiss him deeply.

"Don't forget, we need to name our newest addition." He swipes my hair back. I am sure it is a hot mess now.

"It's your birthday weekend. You should pick."

"You saying yes was my gift."

I splash him playfully. "Aw, come on. Please." Antonio ponders for a moment. He watches as Lee picks Cassidy up over his shoulder, running deeper into the water. "How about Nala? Like the lioness from The Lion King. It was my favorite childhood movie."

"I love it." I hug him as tight as I possibly can.

CHAPTER 28

ANTONIO

"Thank you, guys, so much for your support. I appreciate you watching the dogs and Cam for us all tonight." Gigi and Tula are loading up their truck to head back home. They agreed to watch Cam, Nala, and Dianna for the night back home so we could all go out and celebrate around Myrtle Beach tonight.

"You two deserve to be celebrated." Tula pulls us in for a hug.

"Bye, Zia!" Cam yells at Aria when Gigi goes to close his door.

"Bye, Cam!" Aria is bent down, one arm wrapped around Dianna and the other clutching Nala to her chest. "Ugh, it feels wrong to let them go and not celebrate with them tonight, too. I just got you." Aria nuzzles against Nala's back, who nips at her hair.

"Don't worry, you'll have lots of fun potty training her when you get home." Gigi reaches out to grab Nala.

"Yeah, sorry about that one. You will be alone, dealing with that until I am officially home." I give a weary grin.

"How convenient. She should be fully potty trained by then." Aria puts her hands on her hips.

"I'll make it up to you." I wink suggestively. I kiss her temple as I wrap an arm around her shoulders.

"And that's our cue! Alright, have fun, be safe. Congratulations again." Gigi pulls us into hugs. He heads to his side of the truck, putting Nala in the back with Cam.

"When you return, we have a quick little wedding to plan." Tula quips with excitement. She gives us another hug, taking Dianna's leash.

Once they pull away, we turn around to look at our friends and family. Gio and Carly are getting their clothes back on over their swim attire. Scarlett and Chris sit in their beach chairs, looking at something on Chris's phone. Cassidy is talking Lee's ear off. Dare I say, he looks like he enjoys whatever she is discussing.

"Alright fiancés. What's the plan?" Lee crosses his arms over his chest as we walk over, trying to figure out a game plan for the evening.

"First, Aria and I need to get changed. We also need to make a few calls. Let my parents know she said yes. Let's take about two hours or so, then we can meet in the lobby for some drinks, dancing, and food. Sound good?" I look around at all of them and Aria to check the reaction.

"Oh my gosh! Yes, we need to call them, let's go!" Aria grabs my hand, jumping in the sand.

Gio hands me our room key. He went ahead and checked in for us earlier today. I am ecstatic to tell my parents about the proposal. After Aria's parents said yes, we formulated this proposal together. I called my parents when I got back to Beauford Air Station to explain my proposed plans. There were a few questions, like, why not live together first, etc. But they concluded that it was much better than when I surprised them by joining the Marines. They also know my stubbornness and that I would do this no matter what. I FaceTimed them when I picked out the ring at the on-base general store called the PDX. I have never contemplated ring shopping, so they were a big help. So was Scarlett's harassing bombardment of photos she sent.

We make our way up to our room. I insert the key, opening the door. Before Aria can enter the room, I sweep her off her feet into a cradle hold to go over the threshold. The room is flawless. The walls are light blue. The decorating is all nautical theme. A small kitchen, couch, dining room set, and TV exist. Our room is to the left. A giant king bed with two nightstands and lamps are in the center of the room. I sprint to the bed, throwing Aria on top of the sheets. She giggles, sprawling out across the comforter. She pats next to her for me to join.

"I just can't get over it. You thought of everything. You really did." Gigi and Tula had brought up our bags for us when we were still in the water, so they sat in the corner of the room.

"I want to know your thoughts about the ring." I pick up her left hand, twirling it around her finger. "Your mom and I took a guess at the size."

"I adore it. It fits great. This is exactly what I would have chosen for myself." Aria looks at it affectionately, but her features quickly shift.

"What's wrong?" I am concerned that there is something wrong with the ring.

"I don't have anything to wear tonight," She pouts.

"Aria, honestly, I'm offended. Of course, I grabbed you something. Something new. Go look in your bag." I lay back on the pillows, propping myself up with my arms behind my head.

Aria giddily jumps off the bed. She grabs her bag and pulls out a gray shopping bag. She opens it up and instantly covers her mouth. She pulls out a pearly white mini dress covered in lace. The neckline is a deep V with a ruffle along each side. The bottom of the dress also has a ruffle around the edge.

"As much as I would love the credit for this one, Carly helped me pick it out."

"It's gorgeous. Thank you so much. Your planning of all of this has been impeccable!" She continues to hold up the dress, perusing it with her eyes.

"I'm a marine on a mission, what can I say?" I shrug.

"Oh, really?" Aria places the dress back in the bag. She puts it on the ground and slowly crawls on all fours up the bed. It is the sexiest thing I have ever seen. She kisses all the way up to my mouth. "Interestingly enough. I have a mission."

"What mission would that be?" I ask breathlessly, grabbing her hair in one hand, leaving the other behind my head.

"My mission is to show you what you just asked for, for the rest of your life."

"By all means, show me what I should be expecting." She grins mischievously. Aria makes her way up, so she is straddling me. We transcend into full-blown ecstasy together.

***

"Hey, Mom, Dad, have you met my fiancé?" I flash my camera phone toward Aria, who has taken a shower, glammed up, and straightened her hair with the white dress on. She waves, smiling from ear to ear.

"Aria! I knew he needed to go to Charlotte. I called it. I told you, you weren't going anywhere!" Mom shouts into the screen, clapping.

"Congratulations, you two! Sorry, we couldn't be there for the proposal, but you had better believe we will be at the wedding. We will bring along Papa Joe with us." Dad places an arm around Mom. They are sitting at the dining room table in their house.

"My heart is branded as hers now. My body is just the temple that protects it at this point." I lean my head against her while she straightens each chunk of hair.

"This man." Aria eyes me. "Thank you for raising the kind of man women pray to find."

"You are going to make me cry." Mom swipes a tear away. Dad caresses her arm soothingly.

"We will celebrate, but I just wanted to call and show you my future wifey. She is over here looking hot in some wedding white. You know what I mean." I show her again. Her face is now bright red as she swats at the camera teasingly.

"Have so much fun! We will help you two with planning, however we can. We love you both! Talk to you, love birds, later." Dad leans towards the camera.

"We love you too. Bye!" Aria and I wave, hanging up the phone.

On the way down to the lobby, we had already thrown ourselves into the thick of wedding talks. Almost everyone we would want in our wedding party, besides Noah and Kelsey, is already here. Once we get to them, we will ask them to be by our side on the big day. Scarlett will be the matron of honor, and Chris will be the best man.

When we arrive downstairs, everyone is already waiting for us. Cassidy is in a pastel purple mini dress, Scarlett is in an olive-green skirt with a cropped top combo, and Carly is in a mustard yellow body-con dress. The guys all wear blue jeans with casual collared shirts halfway buttoned up. I dressed the same but ensured my collared shirt matched Aria's white shirt.

When they spot us, the girls take off towards Aria, throwing on a Bride To Be sash, a silver tiara, and a light-up ring. They are giggling so much, all I picture is how little girls talk about their first crushes on the playground.

The guys are gathering around me, watching the women. I can't help but notice Lee's eyes drifting over Cassidy's frame in the room. I don't know what could develop there, but I don't want to know. Lee isn't the relationship type.

"Everyone, gather around, please! We have something we need to ask you all." Aria walks over to me, intertwining her hands with mine. I nod to her. We say at the same time, "We want you to be our bridesmaids and groomsmen!"

"You know what? I did ask for a bridesmaid for Christmas this year. I accept." Lee glances in Cassidy's direction. She gasps and covers her mouth. Her entire face is about as red as a tomato. Aria stares him down. It's like a big sister watching a man flirt with her little sister for the first time. Cassidy is too enamored to notice.

"We do too!" Scarlett raises her hand, doing a mini dance next to Chris.

"Although it's still weird to think of you getting married and not my kid sister anymore, we accept." Gio wraps his arms around Carly.

We will ask Scarlett and Chris to be our matron of honor and best man while we celebrate tonight. Now, it's time to party!

"Now that, that's out of the way. Let's go celebrate!

We spend the night hopping from bar to bar. We eat at Joe's Crab Shack because Aria swears it's necessary for a beach trip. By the end of the night, we ended up at a nightclub. As much as I want Aria pressed as close to me as humanly possible, we must talk to Scarlett and Chris first. While everyone else is dancing, we pull them to the bar.

Aria's eyes remain laser-focused on Lee and Cassidy. Cassidy laughs and twirls. Lee spins her around the dance floor as if they are the only two.

"Aria, she will be fine. Tonight is our night. It's ok to think about yourself for one night." I muse into her ear. Chris and Scarlett are ordering a round of lemon drop shots.

"She is my mentee. I feel responsible for her well-being. Lee doesn't exactly fit the, I'll take care of her, ideology." She huffs.

Oh, he will take care of her, all right. If it is anything like I've seen him do with any other woman. Maybe just not the way one would prefer.

"You aren't at school; she is an adult who can make her own decisions, Mom." I tease.

"Fine. But I will have a firm conversation with her when we get home." She finally looks away when Scarlett hands her a shot.

"Who, Cassidy? Let the girl have fun. See, they are already gone somewhere." We look back out to the dance floor, but Scarlett is right. Only Gio and Carly remain from our group.

"Oh heck no." Aria starts to walk away, but I grab her arms.

"We have something we need to ask them, remember?" I tilt my head, lifting my eyebrows. She nods and slams her shot.

"Ok, on that note, we have something to ask you both", I say, signaling the bartender for another shot for Aria.

"You two are the reason we were able to meet. I know, Chris, you have been my best friend forever. I want you to be my best man.

"And I want you to be my matron of honor!" Aria yells, fist-bumping the air.

"I thought I already was, but sure, let's give it a title." Chris high-fives me and pulls me in for a hug. Scarlett is tearing up and giving Aria a hug.

"Cheers to destiny and a great night. We love you guys. Time to get planning. We have much to plan and a short time to do it." I raise my shot. Shots for the shotgun wedding.

CHAPTER 29

ARIA

SEPTEMBER

Time flies when you are planning a wedding. We shocked both sides of our Italian families when we told them we kept the wedding intimate. Getting almost three hundred people to come on such short notice would have been too hectic. I hate being the center of attention, and we would not have been able to plan the wedding exactly how we wanted. We are having our bridal party, parents, and Papa Joe attend.

Cassidy, Scarlett, Carly, and my mom helped me pick a gorgeous dress last week. That was the one thing I had to have. They also took me to a fancy Italian dinner for my bachelorette party, complete with a lingerie shower. Antonio and his groomsmen went camping one weekend for his bachelor party. Though Noah, Kelsey, and Antonio's parents could not do too much, being so far away, they still helped set up catering and find decorations.

The plan is to get married on a mountain overlook in Pisgah National Forest. That's where our first real date was and where he asked me to be his girlfriend. It just feels right to go back where it all truly began. After much consideration, we decided to tell Noah to be the officiant. Originally, Antonio wanted him to be in the wedding party, but he wanted to ensure Noah had a special role. Noah had to officiate a friend's wedding before, so it only made sense. Cam is going to be our ring bearer. Nala and Dianna are going to be our 'flower girls.'

They will walk down the makeshift aisle with floral collars on.

Once we are married, we will return to the house for a small reception. Kelsey said she would DJ for us. We wanted to respect having the traditional father-daughter, mother-son, and couple's first dances. When we told him our song would be *You Make Me Feel So Young* by Frank Sinatra, Gio relentlessly made fun of us. He thought it was ridiculous because we are already young. Antonio shut the jokes down when he explained he wanted us to have a song that we can dance to in the living room when we are in our eighties, looking back on the life we forged together.

The only things left at this point are applying for a marriage license, finding which overlook we want to perform the ceremony on, and all the last-minute things we can't do until the day of. I already purchased Antonio's wedding band. I am going to surprise him with a silver and copper wedding ring. Across the band is an intricate engraving of a mountain range.

This weekend we are going to relax. We have been non-stop since the beach trip. We decided we needed one weekend just to connect and be present with each other since he will be leaving for training soon.

Currently, Antonio is inside one of my favorite burger joints picking up an order for us. I'm scrolling on my phone, looking up updates on my Refit workout app. I've taken up Zumba-style workouts to keep myself from gaining weight. My dress is snug as it is.

I hear a car drive by with a loud bass, and my heart drops when I listen to what song is playing, *D3mons* by Machine Gun Kelly featuring DMX…

Adonis.

My body goes into a panic overdrive. I am torn between wanting to crawl into the next seat to drive away and to melt into the car seat. My arms are board stiff at my sides. I feel like I am hyperventilating. My back is pushed as far as I can into the seat. My eyes are going wild staring at the door where Antonio should be coming out any minute now.

What should I do?
Do I run in? Tell him to leave the food, and let's go.
Then, Adonis will see me. Would he hurt me? Would he hurt Antonio?
Run, hide, fight.
DO SOMETHING, ARIA! NOW!

Turns out the only thing my body could do was remain petrified as his car pulled in right next to mine. I don't even have to look to confirm. I only know one man who would play that song with his windows down, at full blast. My entire body is already sore with tension. I feel like he won't see me if I keep from looking at him somehow. It's completely illogical, but my brain is unwilling to try now. Never has a song made me feel so nauseated, pissed, and fearful all at once.

I see movement out of the corner of my eye. Antonio is coming out of the door with our food bag in hand. I steal a glance to see where Adonis is. My heart stops.

He is looking at me with a sneer. My eyes jump to Antonio in complete panic mode. We have to get out of here, now. I look back at Adonis. He eyes me and then, as if in slow motion, his head turns to lock on Antonio. This just became his favorite game. Adonis looks back at me. One side of his mouth quirks up. He opens his car door and steps out.

"Adonis, no," I say sternly, stepping out of the car to stand directly before him. He always wears his standard black muscle tank with baggy, ripped jeans. He doesn't even look at me. His eyes are on his target.

I hear Antonio come up behind me. "Do we have a problem here?"

Antonio places the food on the hood of my car. He pushes the sleeves up on his long-sleeved Columbia shirt. He steps slightly before me, almost chest to chest with Adonis. Adonis is cracking his neck from side to side.

"Honey, please let's just get in the car. Please, let's just go." I plead.

You will not cry here. You will not let Adonis earn one more tear from you.

Antonio kisses my forehead, handing me the bag of food. Military mode is activated. Both look ready to kill.

"Yeah, just go. You couldn't handle what I would do to you anyway." Adonis grins.

"Aria, get in the car." His eyes lock on mine. I can tell it is not a suggestion. "Please." He opens the door. I slide in but keep the window rolled down slightly to hear. His back is to my car door.

"I don't need to do anything to you, Barbie GI Joe. From what I know of you, you already made the worst mistake of your life. I'm not talking about your choice of military branch either. Although that's a close second." Antonio sneers, making Adonis bristle. He is fuming. "You lost when you wronged her." He points to me over his shoulder. "Let me show you how a real man handles this situation."

I am astonished when Antonio steps away from the door,

knocking into Adonis's shoulder, and comes around to the car's driver's side. Adonis follows behind him. I don't know what to expect.

Is he going to grab him from behind and slam him in the car?

Why would Antonio turn his back on him?

Sensing Adonis, Antonio whips around. The two are face-to-face. Chest touching chest.

"You see that woman in the passenger seat?" Antonio points to me. Adonis looks at me. He stands taller, puffing out his chest even more. His mouth quirks up on one side. "We are getting married." Antonio didn't have to do anything physically. Those four words alone caused Adonis to deflate. It made him stumble back as if it were a sucker punch.

Adonis's mouth is clasped tight in a thin line. He won't look at me now. Antonio opens the car door. "I've got to let you know. I wouldn't expect an invitation to the wedding. Unless it is the Devil sending you a one-way ticket to hell. Semper Fi, brother." Antonio mock-salutes and gets into the car.

Antonio doesn't bother putting on the seatbelt. He starts the engine and backs up. Adonis watches us. When Antonio puts the car in drive and begins to drive away, I watch Adonis punch the hood of his car with a loud grunt. His fist comes back up, and I can see blood across his knuckles.

The car descends into silence. My mind is freaking out.

Is Antonio mad at me?

"Are you ok? Are you mad?" I ask with my head down.

"Yeah, Aria. Why would you get out of the damn car?" Antonio raises his voice.

That's the last thing my brain could handle. I went into a complete shutdown. He isn't one to curse, especially with me.

I caused this.

I'm the problem.

Involuntarily, my body cocoons in on itself. My knees turn towards the furthest point outside as they can, which is flush against the car door. My head leans against the window. My arms come to wrap around my middle. All thinking ceases. I am paralyzed.

"Aria? Aria, talk to me, please." He is also starting to panic, but I can't help him. I can't help myself. It feels like my jaw is locked. I feel trapped in myself.

Antonio pulls the car to a stop in an empty parking lot. He reaches out to touch my leg, making me recoil more.

"Aria, I am so sorry. I shouldn't have raised my voice. I walked out and immediately could tell who it was based on what you told me. I saw you put yourself in harm's way to try to stop him from getting to me. Something just snapped." He drops his head into his hands. A soft sob escapes him.

Hearing him get emotional makes me snap out of my paralysis. I can unlock my body to sit up straighter.

"I am so sorry. I just made everything about that worse. I know you had to be petrified. I would have loved to punch him square in the jaw, but I know he wanted that. I can't lose you, Aria." His shoulders shake with his cries. "I'm so sorry I scared you."

"Antonio?" My voice is quiet, but at least I can talk now.

He looks up. His eyes are crystal blue with tears.

"Thank you for standing up for us like a gentleman. But don't you ever raise your voice like that at me again." Antonio reaches across and, in one smooth motion, pulls me onto his lap. He pulls me in, so my head is resting on his shoulder. He holds me like that for a long time. He takes deep breaths. I try to match the rhythm so we can both calm down. Our adrenaline is spiked.

I lean back to look him in the eye. Looking into his eyes, a realization dawns on me. This is the last thing I needed to happen. I am sitting in the lap of a man who will fight for me. Not *against* me. A man who can take responsibility and feel bad for his words or actions. I didn't know I needed to see Adonis again for some type of closure. It's like this happened, so I can look at Antonio without a shadow of a doubt that I made the right decision. We were made to take care of each other. We aren't two halves coming together to create a whole. We are two full hearts freely giving ourselves to one another for safekeeping.

We sit kissing in the car for an unknown amount of time. Enough time passes that the windows are fogging up.

Antonio pulls away, kissing my neck. "I have somewhere I want to take you."

"Now?" I straighten my oversized pastel green sweater and jeans.

"Now. Can you call your mom or brother to let Dianna and Nala out at some point? We are going to be gone for a bit."

***

"Welcome to our altar."

It took about a two-hour drive, but Antonio stands on a mountain overlook off the road of the Blue Ridge Parkway. The sign says,

Hominy Valley Overlook. His arms are extended to both sides as if trying to absorb the view into his body.

This overlook is part of Pisgah National Forest. It is also along the route you would take to get to the hike we did on our first date. Lush green mountains roll as far as I can see. The view is symmetrically framed by trees. It is a photographer's dream. By the time of the wedding, the leaves should start to change colors, too, adding bright red, orange, and yellow to the background.

"I've been investigating the lookouts. I think this is the best one. I am happy to continue looking, though, if you want. This is our wedding. I want it to be somewhere we can return to for the rest of our lives. I want to bring our kids here one day and show them this is where their lives truly started." Antonio grabs my hands, pulling me up on the small sidewalk. "We would stand just like this right here."

I look around again. My eyes shift back to Antonio, taking in the view. Hominy Valley. It makes me think of harmony. When I think of that, I think of something pleasing and consistent. Comforting. Just like us. It reminds me of the word homily, too. What is a marriage without God? He brought us together after all. God saved me that night with Adonis so I could be here today. In this spot. With this man.

"Antonio?"

"Yeah, sunflower."

"Let's get married right here," I say, looking onwards.

CHAPTER 30

ANTONIO

OCTOBER 7

Today, I will make Aria Jade Pecorelli my wife.

Waking up, I am blown away by my fierce, protective, overpowering, ingrained love for her. I slept at Chris's house with him, Lee, and Noah. I did not sleep at all. Last night we had an engagement party mixed with a semi-rehearsal dinner. We held it all at Gigi and Tula's house. My sister, Kate, shocked me by flying all the way from Argentina on her world travels to be here to support me on our special day. She and Aria hit it off so quickly. We spent the night eating cake, stuffing our faces with quality barbecue, and jumping into their pool. Watching Aria and my sister, Kate, laugh the night away warmed my heart. I have always valued her opinions and life experiences because she is ten years older than I am. By the end of the night, my sister came up to me with tears in her eyes, telling me she could see precisely why we were able to develop so quickly. She thinks Aria is the coolest, sweetest, and most sincere woman I have ever dated. I couldn't agree more.

Aria spent last night at our house getting it decorated and set up for the reception after the night ended. Scarlett, Kelsey, and Cassidy all helped. Gio stayed home to keep Cam, so Carly could help. She is the creative one after all. They spent the night with her. I wonder if she was able to sleep.

My parents, Papa, and sister stayed together at a local hotel. They are going to be here soon. We are going to drive two cars up to the mountains. Lee and I will be in our blue dresses. Noah and Chris are wearing suits.

The past month with Aria has been daily proof of why we are getting married. This wedding came together quickly, but Aria epitomizes patience, calm, and soothing energy. She had to plan so much of this without me because my time has been consumed with my leaving for a month-and-a-half-long training tomorrow. I am trying hard not to think about that today. Today, it's all about us. This will forever be our day. The day we chose each other. The day my life finally makes sense.

In a classic guy move, I still need to write my vows. It's not that I have nothing to say; it's the opposite. I have too much to say. I want to get across every emotion she makes me feel. She must feel her importance to me. To know that I will sacrifice life and limb to protect her at all costs. I need to ensure that she understands I see every part of her.

Since everyone is still sleeping, I use this time to write. Right now, I assume Aria is getting her hair done. I have no idea what her dress looks like. I don't want to know. I want to be fully surprised when I see her. She could wear a paper bag and still be gorgeous.

They say a little rain on your wedding day is a sign of good luck. As it stands, it is supposed to rain in Charlotte while we are in the mountains. When we are back in Charlotte, it is supposed to stop and start raining in the mountains. Timing is everything.

Now, it's time to write these vows.

***

"You ready, son?" Dad asks. We stand at the mountain overlooking the vast landscape.

I turn around to look at those who love me most. Today I get to add another. Papa Joe is talking to Mom and Kate. Lee, Noah, and Chris laugh at something on Lee's phone. I smile to myself. The midday sun shimmers through the trees. A vision of yellow, orange, and red spreads as far as you can see. The peaks and valleys glisten with the dew of early morning fog.

"I was ready the day I met her." My dad pats me on the back. He gives me a hug and steps down from the sidewalk.

Lee steps up next to me. Just two Marines supporting each

other. As it should be. A proper brotherhood. "You made the right decision."

I look at him with a smirk. "I know."

"It was her beauty that did you in, wasn't it?" Lee bumps into me, making the ribbons on my uniform fling to the side.

"Don't get me wrong, she is the most gorgeous soul I've ever seen. It's not her piercing eyes. Her body to die for. Or the lushness of her hair. It's the fact that every moment we are apart, we long for each other. It's the way she loves me. It's everything that makes her, her."

A sadness crosses over Lee's features. He looks out towards the road as if looking for someone. "I hope I get to experience something like that one day." I'm shocked to hear him say that, but I can tell he is serious for once.

"You will. If you let it." I reach over and give him a hug.

Noah and Chris rush over to hug me right when everyone else parks at the overlook. Mom, Papa Joe, and Kate look at the cars pulling in. They turn to me with apparent enthusiasm pouring from their features. They walk over to my side. Aria must be in her parents' truck because the back windows are covered, so nobody can see inside.

"And now my son becomes a husband." Mom tries to hold in tears, but is doing a poor job.

"You guys really aren't upset over the quickness of it all?" I ask.

"Ant, have you ever done anything as expected?" Mom laughs. She kisses me on the cheek.

"What if I'm not good at being a husband?" I say; my biggest fear.

"Just like there is no manual for being a proper parent, there isn't one for marriage either. We all do the best we can by the ones we love. One thing I always admired about you is your stubbornness." I don't know whether to be offended or proud, but I let her continue without interruption. "Stubbornness in love can take you a long way in a marriage. It makes you hold on and endure when things get tough. I think she is stubborn in love, too. It's a quality you both share. You both love a God you can pray to when you don't have the answers. You also have all of us." She gestures to the small gathering around us and beyond the cars, where Aria's family begins to get out of the vehicles. "Just love each other. The rest will find a way."

"Great. Now I am crying." Kate wipes her face.

"I couldn't have said it better myself." Papa Joe says. They give me a hug.

Car doors close. I look up to see Gigi climb down from his truck. He looks in my direction. Our eyes find each other. He waves and gives me a thumbs-up.

"Alright, bro. Let's get in position." Chris puts an arm over my shoulders, leading me to my spot on the sidewalk. I face the cars, trying to glimpse Aria as more car doors open and close. I will give it to them. I haven't even seen the bridesmaids. They planned this entrance without flaw.

"Oh no, you don't." Noah turns me around to face the mountains. "I will tell you when to turn around." He gets into the position to my left with a paper in hand to lead the ceremony.

My parents, sister, and grandpa sit in some camping chairs we brought up. To my right stand Chris and Lee. Noah nods to Mom. I look over my shoulder at her. She picks up her phone from her lap. A song starts to play through a speaker we brought, *A Thousand Years* by Christina Perri.

I shift my gaze over to my left shoulder. Around the string of cars walk Kelsey, Cassidy, and Scarlett in a straight line. Their hair is all half up and half down. Their dresses are varying shades of pink with nude-colored heels. My breath catches when I see Aria's bouquet choice: sunflowers. They are all smiling ear to ear. They walk down, standing to Noah's left.

"You are going to die when you see her." Scarlett mouths to me. The other girls nod in agreement.

Next, Gio walks out holding hands with Cam. Tula walks with them, holding Cam's other hand in a deep red laced dress. Everyone is immediately goo-goo eyed. Gio is in a black suit, but Cam is stealing the show. He is wearing gray dress pants with matching shoes and a vest. He has a white dress shirt underneath and a blue tie. If cuteness could kill, we would all be dead. When they reach us, Tula picks Cam up and takes him to a seat. Gio gives me a fist bump and joins my side next to Lee.

A giggle breaks out. Carly steps out from behind the cars with Dianna and Nala. They both wear collars made of sunflowers. Nala playfully pulls at her leash, trying to walk down our makeshift aisle. Carly's pink dress flows as she approaches us.

"If you can all please stand." She says to my family, Tula, and Cam.

She sits next to Cassidy, making the dogs sit by her side. My heart rate picks up. I look up towards the sky. I can't cry before I even get to see her. I know when I turn around, that's it. I am a goner for this woman.

Everyone lets out a collective sigh and 'wow.' My head snaps up to Noah's grinning face. He puts a hand on my shoulder. Time to turn around. When I turn, I keep my head down for an extra second.

Time to watch my future walk towards me. My wife. My life.

I look up and everything stops. I've heard of the moment when time seems to stand still, but this is unimaginable. Gigi is arm in arm with Aria in his suit, holding a Bible. I barely notice him because my eyes are locked on hers. She smiles so wide and so bright it's dazzling. Her hair is curled and partially held up with diamond hair pieces. Her makeup is classic and elegant. It doesn't overpower the fact that she is a natural beauty. The dress. My gracious, the dress. It is a strapless, brilliantly white mermaid-style dress with horizontally spaced lace stripes all the way down. It fits her chest, torso, and hips seamlessly. She is timeless. Everyone else disappears. It's me and her 'til the end of time. I don't even know where I am anymore.

Gigi and Aria stop in front of us. I'm pretty sure everyone is crying because all I hear in the background is sniffles. I must be leaking tears, too, because Chris gently elbows me and hands me a hanky.

"And who gives Aria away to be wed today?" Noah asks, bringing me back to the present.

"Her mother and I do." Gigi kisses Aria's hand as he unwinds himself from her. She smiles, giving him a hug.

Without hesitation, I grab her hand, helping her onto the sidewalk. She hands her bouquet to Scarlett. I shake Gigi's hand. He reads 1 Corinthians 13:4-8. "Love is patient, love is kind. It does not envy, it does not boast, it is not proud. It does not dishonor others, is not self-seeking, is not easily angered, and keeps no record of wrongs. Love does not delight in evil but rejoices with the truth. It always protects, always trusts, always hopes, always perseveres. Love never fails."

After that, I couldn't tell anyone what happened. Aria and I stared at each other. The world faded away. We had our own unspoken conversation. She lifts her dress enough for me to tell that she is wearing cowboy boots. She lifts it a bit more, and I can see they have sunflowers on them, too. I shake my head, smiling ear to ear.

"Antonio." I look at Noah, confused as to why he is here. "Antonio, your vows, man." He whispers.

"Oh, right." I turn to Chris, who hands me my vows. Aria giggles at me.

I clear my throat, feeling everyone's eyes on me. I look into Aria's eyes, full of light and love.

It's just me and you.

"Aria, you are the happiest, kindest, warm-hearted woman I have ever met. You are caring and honest. A smile from you brightens my day. Every day we've spent together, you have always been filled with surprises, and there has never been a dull moment. I love you and am so lucky to have found you. So, in front of our friends and family, I promise to stand by you and stand up for you. I promise to support your goals and dreams. I will be your partner through all of life's adventures. When you are sad, I will soak up your tears. When you are happy, I'll share your joy. Even to this day, you make me stumble over my words. But I wouldn't want it any other way. Thank you for being my sunflower." Pure everlasting, unfiltered love fills the wind that billows around us. Aria is the one needing a hanky now. I give her mine. She dabs her eyes.

"Aria, it's your turn." Noah smiles.

"I have to go after that." Everyone laughs. "Oh gosh. Ok."

I squeeze her hands and give her a wink. She reaches into the top of her dress.

What the…

Out comes a folded piece of paper, making everyone laugh more.

"Antonio, my once-in-a-lifetime true love and best friend. Before I met you, I did not believe in love at first sight. With all the odds against us, God's plan brought us together, and you are living proof that such love does exist. Though we met with distance, I have never had my heart so full of trust and happiness that it makes being with you easy. For me, home went from places and family to wherever you are, and we are together. For the rest of our lives, I vow that when we go through difficult times, I will always do my best to listen, understand, remain patient, and reassure you of my devotion to you. I promise to remember your sacrifices and compromises. I will do the same for you and help you love life daily. I promise to keep you laughing with my horrible puns and be goofy with you, even if we weird people out with our sarcasm." We all burst out laughing. Aria stifles some tears. "I promise to never stop being your girlfriend, best friend, and loyal wife. When the time comes, I promise to be a nurturing mother to our children and the loudest one at their games or shows. You have given me immeasurable courage, confidence, and inspiration. In return, you will always have my respect and support. Take these vows as an ever-growing list of promises as we grow together. I loved you the moment we met, I love you now, and I will love you more every day into our eternal lives."

I've never wanted to kiss her more. Blast this waiting to the end, insanity. We lean our foreheads together.

"Whoa, whoa, not yet, you crazy kids," Noah says, breaking us apart to everyone's amusement. "The rings."

Tula brings Cam up, who hands Noah two small brown ring boxes.

We both kept our rings a secret from each other. Aria doesn't know that her wedding band is the one my dad gave to my mom on their twenty-fifth anniversary. With the engagement ring being a little simpler, I wanted the band to be elaborate and sentimental. The band is silver with tiny diamonds on the edges and a flower pattern in the center made of more diamonds. When Noah opens the box for her, Aria's eyes turn as wide as saucers. She looks from me to the band in disbelief.

"With this ring, I thee wed." I bring her hand up to my mouth, giving her a light kiss over the set of rings.

Noah opens the following box. My jaw slackens. I've never seen a ring that looks more tailor-made for me, especially with the silver mountains and copper-colored sky. I didn't even know there was a possibility for a ring like this. Aria grins proudly at what she accomplished with the purchase.

"With this ring, I thee wed." Aria slides the ring on my finger.

"By the power vested in me by the state of North Carolina, I now pronounce you Mr. and Mrs. Ranaldi!" Noah yells, and everyone starts hollering.

Aria and I crash into each other. I kiss her like it is our last few seconds on Earth. I raise my hand, punching the air. She smiles against my mouth.

We did it!

CHAPTER 31

ARIA

"Oh, I got something made that I wanted to show you!" Antonio and I just got done taking our wedding photos with everyone. We must return to the house for the reception before it rains here.

I couldn't have asked for a better wedding ceremony. It went off without a hitch. Antonio, in his dress blues, was outstanding. The perfect combo of sexy and handsome. I'm trying my best to stay present all day today, even though he leaves to return to base for his extended training starting tomorrow. I race back to the car, grabbing my newest Etsy purchase and hiding it behind my back.

"Ta-da!" I rush back to Anthonio, drawing the deep red pullover sweater behind me. On the back, it says Ranaldi with an extra-large Marine Corps symbol in glittering gold. "Remember that one time the guy in the club said he didn't see your name on me? Well, now everyone will."

"Yeah, you can't miss those sparkles." Antonio laughs, kissing me sweetly.

"Guys, if you want to beat this rain, we must go now." Chris waves us on from the cars.

Antonio sweeps me into a cradle, running me to the truck. Everyone else piles into the rest of the cars.

***

"Introducing Mr. and Mrs. Antonio and Aria Ranaldi!" Kelsey

bellows as we walk out of the French doors of the living room and out into the backyard.

We walk outside, raising our hands with everyone clapping and cheering. Everything turned out beautifully. We stayed up late last night, but it was all worth it. Lights stream across the backyard. The house is filled with sunflowers and pink roses. The catered food is neatly organized in the kitchen. The empty extra living room in the front of the house came in handy because we could fit all the seating to eat inside. We all decided to stay in our outfits until after the cake and all the typical festivities are done.

"You ready to dance?" Antonio says in my ear, pulling me into him under the twinkling lights.

"With you? Always." He kisses my forehead. Kelsey begins to play Frank Sinatra's *You Make Me Feel So Young*.

The dance is slow and sweet. We rock back and forth, going in a circle. I lean my head on his chest.

"Is this everything you wanted?" Antonio asks quietly.

"No," I say straight-faced. Antonio pulls back, giving me a bewildered glance. "It's so much more than I thought I would ever get to have."

He kisses me to everyone's delight. "Same here."

We do all our dances. I dance with my dad to Tim McGraw's *My Little Girl*. Antonio dances with his mom to *Simple Man* by Lynyrd Skynyrd. Afterwards, Kelsey announces it is time to eat and do the toast. The food is delicious. Endless amounts of bread, pasta, salad, and Italian sausages. Scarlett and Chris do a shared toast. They make everyone laugh, recounting our first meeting and how we ended the night playing the world's most unsexy game. We cut the cake. We wouldn't be us if we didn't smear a little on each other's faces, so we did. It allowed us to excuse ourselves to get changed. I change into the white dress Antonio gave me when we got engaged, while he changes into khaki pants with a blue button-down shirt. We dance for hours. I am exhausted when it is time for the garter and bouquet toss.

Kelsey and Cassidy are the only single ladies. I toss the bouquet backwards, firmly in Cassidy's outstretched arms. She blushes on impact. For the men, it is only Noah and Lee. Lee rolls up his sleeves, as does Noah. Those two could turn anything into a competition. It doesn't escape me that Lee also spent all night dancing with Cassidy, occasionally letting Noah cut in. Antonio flicks the garter back. Noah and Lee push and shove as it flies through the air. In one solid motion, Lee jumps on Noah's back piggyback style and snatches it from the air.

"You know what that means?" Kelsey says slyly into the mic. "Bring out the chair!"

I look around, confused. Gio's mouth quirks to one side. He hands Cam to Carly, runs inside, and returns with a kitchen chair. Scarlett grabs Cassidy, placing her on it. Gio grabs the garter from Lee, handing it to Scarlett.

"Put it on, dear," Scarlett says, handing it to Cassidy. Cassidy's entire face is red now.

"What?" Cassidy shrieks.

"Do it!" Everyone cheers.

Cassidy hoists the garter onto her leg. She clearly has never worn one before because she puts it as high as her mid- thigh before cutting off circulation. I cover my mouth, trying not to burst out laughing. Before I could correct her, Kelsey was talking again.

"Alright, Lee. It's time to claim your prize." Kelsey muses. Lee places a hand on his chest, trying to act humble. Cassidy covers her face with her hands. The song *Earned It* by The Weekend begins to blast through the speakers.

Lee puts on a show. I am glad he changed out of his uniform because he is on the ground, crawling towards Cassidy, the next thing we know. She shrieks and giggles, crossing her legs under her pink dress, which she decided to keep on. Lee stands up and rips off his T-shirt over his head, swinging it around in circles. He throws it over her shoulders, dropping to his knees. Cassidy's hands cover her face, but he grabs her arms, holding them down. He looks at her in the eyes and then bends his head, grabbing the garter with his teeth. We are all screaming, cheering, and shouting now, egging the whole thing on. Lee rips it down her leg slowly. Once he gets it over her foot, he stands up, grabs it out of his mouth, and spins it around his finger in the air. If Cassidy had been red in the face before, now her whole body is red. She stands up and gives him a hug.

I don't even care to put any energy into what is happening between them. I still don't know where they went when they disappeared while celebrating at the beach. I never asked. Cassidy has always been private. I don't even know if Kelsey is in a relationship either anymore. I still haven't met her boyfriend. When she showed up with Noah, she had no explanation for why he didn't come with her. Right now, none of that matters but my husband and me. Cassidy was a grown woman at the beach, and she is a grown woman now. She can figure it out.

We all dance to a few more songs before calling it a night. Everyone was a big help after the cleanup. They fill trash bags, box food up, and tidy the house. Dianna and Nala are already passed out on their beds in our room.

Once everyone leaves, Antonio and I sink down onto the couch. We are beat.

"I don't think I can move." I groan, lying across his lap.

"Hate to tell you, but we still have one more thing to do." Antonio shrugs.

"Oh my gosh. What is it?"

"Well, the way I see it. I leave tomorrow for training. That's a long time away from my wife. Looks like we have some consummating to do. You know, for legalities, of course."

"Wouldn't want to mess up the law."

"No. Never. Let's go, wife!" Antonio stands up, putting me on his back, rushing to the bedroom.

****

It is safe to say this marriage is fully intact. We spent the rest of the night making sure it is entirely consummated. We even had to stop at points to warm up leftovers to re-energize. The moment we have been dreading for months has come. It's not that he is going away to some dangerous area or for an excessive amount of time. Antonio is dreading the monotony and loneliness you feel at this training location. We both dread not seeing each other weekly for the first time since we met.

We spend our morning looking at photos and videos from yesterday. We don't even leave the bed. We lay in bed, barely clothed, in a heap of cuddles. When we finally get up, it's to read the notes left behind in our guest book. Our guest book isn't a book. It is a framed map of the hike we went on in Pisgah National Forest during our first date. Everyone signed it.

We make breakfast together. We sit at the bistro table with the dogs happily lying on the ground beneath us.

"Very soon this will be us all the time." Antonio takes a big bite of bacon.

"Not soon enough." I swirl my coffee, feeling the weight of the impending departure looming near.

"I know. Yesterday's greatness will carry us through this next month and a half. I'm already looking forward to the homecoming."

Antonio wiggles his eyebrows.

"Ok, husband."

"Best nickname I've ever had."

We finish eating breakfast. Antonio gets everything packed up and ready to go. I walk him to the front door. I don't even bother getting dressed. I just threw on pajamas, prepared for my pity party when he is gone. Antonio fiddles with my rings, spinning them around my finger.

"Yesterday was truly the greatest day of my existence. Watching you walk towards me in that dress will forever be etched in my mind." He places his bag down by the door.

"It was for me too. Trust me. I will have plenty of dreams of you in those dress blues." I wave my face like I am hot.

"Thank you for my ring too. It's better than anything I would have imagined for myself."

"Thank you for mine. I love the sentiment behind it. It is stunning." I say, admiring it. Antonio told me about the meaning and origin of the ring last night. I may have cried a little.

"Like someone else I know." He kisses my cheek. "As much as I hate this, I must get going, sunflower."

"I know." I bite my lip, fighting back tears.

We stand in the doorway kissing and embracing one another. He pulls away, leaning down to snuggle the dogs.

"Be good for momma while daddy is gone, girls. Dianna, kill anything that comes near your mother. Nala, try not to pee on everything."

Antonio stands up, giving me one more kiss and hug. He walks to the truck, climbs in, and kisses me, pulling out of the driveway.

Just like that, my husband is gone.

EPILOGUE

ANTONIO

FEBRUARY

"I'm free!" I yell out my truck window to Lee, about to leave the base for the last time.

"Yeah, yeah, just remember I know where you live. I don't mind dropping in for a visit if I have to." Lee crosses his arms across his chest. Twenty-Nine Palms did nothing but make him more massive and tanner. The few months following didn't cause it to fade either.

"If that's the excuse you are going with." I shrug. "Wouldn't happen to be because of a certain blonde friend of Aria's?" I raise an eyebrow.

You would have to be blind and have low mental intelligence to not see the clear attraction between the two.

"We haven't talked since your wedding." Lee looks down at the ground, kicking a rock with his boots. I've never seen him like this about women before. Then again, he has been acting differently since telling me about his deployment. Maybe he is softening.

"Doesn't mean you don't want to. Anyway, I have to go. I have that appointment to get to."

"Ok. I'm going to miss you around here, man."

"Don't be getting soft on me now. It will ruin your image." I joke. He waves me off. I slapped him on the back and gave him a high five.

Pulling away, I am a ball of nerves and adrenaline. Nothing

makes me happier than the idea of being home with Aria. Noah called his connections in the world of land surveying. Turns out his office in New York also has locations in Charlotte. I was able to interview. I start in about two weeks. My first post-military civilian job.

I told Aria I wouldn't be at the house until closer to six. I didn't tell her I won't be home until that late because I am getting my first tattoo. It will be in her honor. I am getting a set of mountains with waves rolling across the front. Behind the mountains is going to be a sunflower that takes the place of the rising sun.

"You ready?" The tattoo artist asks when I walk in.

"Ready."

***

I pull into our driveway. My chest is throbbing from the tattoo. The seat belt rubbing against it the whole ride didn't help matters. When I pull in, I notice the house is dark. Aria's car is in the driveway, so I know she is here. I don't bother getting anything out of the truck. I am too excited to see my wife.

"Aria? Wifey? I'm home." I yell out as I walk into the front door. It is so unlike her to not meet me at the door.

Why is it so dark in here?

I walk past the kitchen, turning on the living room light. "SURPRISE!" I nearly had a heart attack.

From behind the couch, Gio, Carly, Cam, Gigi, Tula, Scarlett, Chris, Cassidy, and Aria pop up screaming. Aria is wearing one of the Raiders jerseys I left behind. It swallowed her, but she made it dress-like by putting a thick black belt around the middle. Talk about a turn on. I'm surprised the Raiders fabric on her Carolina Panthers soul doesn't burn at contact.

Aria runs over to me, jumping into my arms, wrapping her legs around my waist. I kiss her like it has been years. Dianna and Nala jump up on either side of us.

"Hubby." She flashes me her rings.

"Wifey." I flash mine back. "How did you all pull this off? I didn't see any of your cars." I set Aria back down on her feet. I give both dogs a good pet behind the ears. I can't get over how much Nala has grown. She grows more every week.

"We parked down the street," Gio says.

"Good to have you home for good, man!" Chris says Coming over to give me a hug.

"Good to be home."

Everyone comes over one at a time, giving me hugs and congratulations. I never let go of Aria's hand.

"It's permanent! You're home!" Scarlett squeals.

"That's not all that is permanent." I pull my shirt collar down, showing the tattoos splayed over my heart.

Aria's hands cup her mouth.

"I wanted to have a physical representation of the mark you have on my heart and soul. Something more than the ring."

"That's the sweetest thing I have ever heard." Tula has her hand on her heart.

Aria places her hand over the tattoo gently. "I love it."

"Good because I can't really return it too easily."

"So, what's next for you two?" Gigi says, putting an arm around Tula's shoulders.

"Well, we never got to go on that honeymoon." I wink at Aria.

"Honeymoon here we come!" Aria shouts victoriously.

I never have to leave home again. If I do, home is coming with me. Amazing what can happen in a year.

ABOUT THE AUTHOR

Anna Renne lives with her husband and two sons in Catawba, North Carolina. She went to college at the University of North Carolina at Charlotte. She graduated with a degree in elementary education. Her concentration was in English and communications. After nearly eight and a half years in the education field, she temporarily became a stay-at-home mom. Upon her career change, Anna wrote a book about her love story with her husband, Anthony. They met when he was in the Marine Corps stationed in Beaufort, South Carolina. They married one another within six months. Anna is an advocate for mental health as well as domestic violence survivors due to a prior abusive relationship. She spends her quality time with her family, dog, and church. Anna enjoys reading, cooking, and watching shows or movies.

Instagram- @rennereads

ACKNOWLEDGEMENTS

I would like to first take the time to acknowledge my husband, Anthony. Meeting you and becoming your wife has been my destiny and an absolute blessing. You have shown me how to confidently embrace every part of me, being unapologetically myself. Without you, this story would not be possible. Being able to capture so many aspects of our grand story to share with the world has been a beautiful walk down memory lane. Thank you for your unwavering support for me. I love you forever.

I want to thank my beta readers: Lauren Benjamin, Sierra Zinke, and Stefanie Steck. Lauren, thank you for being the best wing woman I could have ever asked for. It was a joy to include our powerful friendship and how you helped me find my husband. Your friendship means the world to me. I am so lucky to have met you when I did. We have been through many of my life's biggest and best moments together. You are a huge reason why any of it was possible, so thank you. Sierra, thank you for your feedback and for helping me understand the process of writing this first book. I am thankful for your encouragement and willingness to help me succeed. Stefanie, you have been the ultimate source of inspiration and confidence-building. This book could not have happened without you. Your feedback is something I hold in the utmost esteem. I am thankful for our friendship, which we found through the love of stories.

To our families, I cannot thank you enough for all you have done for me. For my parents, who instilled a love of reading and writing. I am thankful for your support and encouragement in writing this story. Sal, you have always been my role model and best friend. The person who gives tremendous advice while providing the relief of a good laugh. Thank you for helping me edit this book and giving me the confidence to move forward. The motivation you all provide to go for my goals is extraordinary.

I have many friends and family members who are represented in this story. Each of you has been a huge reason this story is possible. You are part of the building blocks that helped Anthony and me build a successful marriage. You are the reason we can have our own beautiful family. Your love and support of us is a guiding light.

To the readers, thank you. Thank you for taking a chance on me and for the time you took to read about my love story. I hope this story shows you that there is light in darkness. Sometimes the best days of your life are after some of the worst. Do not give up on your life story. In my darkest times, I didn't think I would get a happy ending. But this story is to help others see that it can happen. It will happen. Whatever happiness means to you. You will find it.

Thank you to Erika Plum for the beautiful masterpiece you made for the cover. You captured my ideas with precision. It is eye-catching. Thank you for helping me understand the process and being there to answer questions.

To all service members and their families. Thank you for your service. Your bravery, courage, and sacrifice are etched in history.

Lastly, but most importantly, I am thankful to my Lord and Savior, Jesus Christ. I am grateful for his protection, guidance, and unfailing love. I am thankful for the many blessings, lessons, and talents he has bestowed upon me. You were beside me even when I couldn't understand or hear you. I pray this book shows your ability to drive evil from our lives. If we put our trust in you, we can do all things. I pray that if anyone has experienced any of the topics mentioned in this book, they will turn to you, feel your presence, and find ways to discover you. Amen.

Stay tuned. There are more stories to come!